REBEL WITHOUT A BRA

Planet Hy Man Book Two

KERRIE A NOOR

CONTENTS

REBEL WITHOUT A BRA

Planet Hy Man Book Two

By
Kerrie Noor

MEET THE GANG

Legless: a man from Planet Hy Man who is past his prime. No one knows why he is called Legless, but he is a man elusive as a shadow, as well as the reason for the whole saga that you are about to read.

Beryl: a woman way past her prime. She is the leader of Planet Hy Man and has been since this whole saga began—and intends to remain so.

Mex: a woman from Planet Hy Man who is angry as she is courageous. She is of the age where a pension is within her grasp and smart enough to be planning for it.

Woody: a dwarf from Earth, unemployed but young enough to still have hope.

Vegas: a young ambitious woman from Planet Hy Man. She believes in many things but is logical enough to know when to ditch said beliefs.

Hilda: a woman from Planet Hy Man who has more ambition in her little finger than an American running for president. She is in her prime and will step on anyone who dares argue.

Pete: Mex's robot—or android, as he likes to call it. Pete has plans and is smart enough to keep them well hidden.

Don: a cabbie from Glasgow with a soft spot for the character below . . .

Bunnie: a round woman who puts one in mind of Dawn French. She has a way with men, dogs, and lonely women. Except in times of stress, when she throws such "ways" to the wind for a more dominating/shouting approach.

DJ: a young DJ born in Glasgow. He is the same age as Woody and as tall as Woody is short. He is a man frustrated with his mentor, who is also the character below . . .

Archie: an Earthly pensioner who is old enough to know better and old enough not to care. His advice is ignored by many.

DBO: a teenager from Planet Hy Man. She is ignored by many, and she would like to change the status quo but is not sure how.

H2: a twenty-year-old woman from Planet Hy Man. She looks and acts much older than her years, which is probably the reason no one hangs around her.

New additions

Baby: one of the youngest of the Voted In who was actually voted in by the Voted In. It was either that or put up with her constant complaints on the radio where she worked before becoming a Voted in.

Senator: a rare Voted In with a conscious, she had the same privileged background as Beryl. She was one of the first to have no father; her mother did have some feeling for those lower than her and was often seen buying things in the market to boost the economy.

Pot, Prudence and Pope: the other three Robot 33. Like Pete they are smart but unlike Pete not smart enough to hide it.

Verruca: Is H2's gran a savvy woman who deserves a better name.

Eunice and Patsy: Bunnies' neighbours. A couple who firmly believes that a couple who argue together stay together, their making up is legendary.

PLANET HY MAN—GLOSSARY

Voted Ins: Planet Hy Man's politicians. A contradiction in terms as they were never voted in. In the past, they were also known as the "Blue-Rinse Brigade," when they were young enough for hair dye to make a difference.

Whip: also known as a flesh-cracker. In the past used by Man Spies to round up men like cattle during the great coup 1958, now worn like a peacock parading its virility.

Man Spy: women bred to act like men, who captured any free men to be "cared for" and/or "appropriately employed" for the greater benefit of the planet.

Manifesto the Great: the last man to rule Planet Hy Man, he wrote his memoirs while still ruling. In fact, he was so busy writing that he didn't notice the great coup of 1958 until it was too late. His last few years were spent in exile, editing the *Hy Man's Geographic*, a magazine no one had read for years, which is now mainly used for lighting fires when the price of energy goes up. It was also he who developed the early stances of the *incognito pose*.

Incognito Pose: a pose adopted by robots and the masses, helping them to blend into the background, or at least let those of great importance know that they are not worth noticing.

Teflon: a by-product of egg popping, and a material like no other. It is so flexible that a robot made of it will never age and finds yoga as easy as the mere blink of an eye.

Telespray/Telespraying: inspired by Planet Hy Man's first truly scientific woman who had a crush on *Star Trek*'s Captain Kirk. She was an enthusiastic shower-maker who designed a power shower so strong it moved women from inside the shower to outside—she saw the potential.

For a while it was all the rage for the Voted In as they telesprayed from one shop to the next, frightening shop assistants until the shop assistants rebelled and started charging *startle* charges.

Cheese Pizza: a secret passion for many on Planet Hy Man. Once someone discovered how to make hemp pulp *sort of* taste like cheese, the pizza was revived, celebrated, and eaten whenever possible. Hemp pulp never, however, managed to work in cheese sauce.

Caffeine Blast: coffee on Planet Hy Man is for the elite and was introduced mainly to keep the Voted In awake during meetings.

Illegal Beverage: caffeine for the masses is as illegal as bootlegging was on Earth. Keeping the masses alert is greatly discouraged by those in charge; weak decaffeinated tea is all they are allowed.

Egg Popping: a recently accepted profession established by the first retired man spy. Eggs (also known as valuable real-estate) from a successful woman can earn her a tidy commission—which Mex was banking on to provide her with a better robot than the damnable Pete.

Contemplation of the Navel: a practice recognized by the robot-training board as an adequate way of make the passing of time productive, as well as cutting down on minding others' business.

Arts and Stuff: anything gift-wrapped.

Limo Drivers: the last driver retired years ago and now mans the footman's residents' reception. He never remembers any names but he does a good toasted hemp pulp.

The Scent of an Identity: women who have a "longing" or a "something is missing" feeling are more susceptible to the scent than contented women. Men are completely immune.

ESP-ing: the ability to communicate without speaking aloud; a form of mind reading. Outlawed on Planet Hy Man as it made bugging —a truly profitable pastime—pointless.

Messenger: an envelope-like device that usually contained orders of an unpopular nature.

H-Pad: looks like an iPad but has the ability to answer back and is not nearly as much fun.

Sparkly: sparkling water that tastes like champagne, costs a bomb, and can cause great clarity of thought or at least the illusion of it.

Strengtheners: like straighteners, but also work as a bugging device. For years, much was collected from what women said while straightening their hair, until it was discovered that what they talked about while grooming was pretty much the said grooming. Scientists are currently working on a handless set.

New additions

The earphone: when Manifesto the Great saw these on a Star Trek repeats he was entranced, "at last a way to block out the chatter from the other half," he exclaimed.

Mind fudging: is the only defense for mind reading. It involves not thinking about what you want to think about but rather creating a thought decoy.

Blow up & blow out: a term used for H-Pads and the like, nobody is sure of the difference except a blow-out is preferable to a blow-up.

Tablet: a homemade sweet Scots claim as their own, sort of in between fudge, and toffee but carries greater mystical qualities.

Last hoorah home: bit like a rest home but with better sandwiches.

The C-Pad, H-pad, H-pad 11 and other pad malarkey: all fore-runners of the iPad, which evolved with the *I know better than you* app some would call virus. The iPad metamorphizes from the C-Pad thanks to a liaison with Legless and very smart IT student during Legless's lost in San Francisco years.

A Scrapper: a forgotten element from a forgotten time on planet Hy Man when real animals roamed. A scrapper fed animals scraps from the food chain, it was a dirty job. Now the term is only used when pickle swearing will not do.

Hilda's energy plan: similar to Beryl's but with more options.

Balancing platform: Hilda dreamed of a balancing platform from the day she was first ask to go out and pick herbs in the compound. She looked at the muddy field and thought there must be a better way.

Jock strap: one of man's best kept secrets on Planet Hy Man. All men on Planet Hy Man looked well-endowed and woman never knew why.

Alice: similar to Amazon's Alexa's with many of *the I know better than you* bugs still intact. No metamorphizes or IT students involved.

PREVIOUSLY ON PLANET HY-MAN

Beryl, leader for more years than anyone could remember, has been outsmarted by her arch-rival Hilda—a younger upstart who thinks she can run Planet Hy Man way better than Beryl.

Planet Hy Man's energy is running out, and the only hope is Legless, a man Beryl double-crossed and sent to Earth fifty years ago. Beryl sends Mex, the greatest hero of all time, to Earth along with her *I know better than you* PA/personnel android. They meet up with Woody, Bunnie, and a few others, and they suspect that Legless or someone who can lead to Legless is performing at the Edinburgh festival, Free Fringe.

A place which Woody explains has nothing to do with a haircut.

Beryl had kept the whole energy issue under wraps, even spinning a yarn to all about Earth planning to invade Planet Hy Man *as laughable as Pete trying to ride a bike.*

Hilda finds out.

She double-crosses Beryl and sends her to Earth along with H2—a *know-it-all* who frequently reminds Beryl how on Earth they are equals. They have to find Mex, to find Legless, and it is Archie, a taxi driver, who offers to help.

Meanwhile, on Planet Hy Man, Vegas has to enter into uncharted territories to find the library, which may or may not have the energy spark plug Hilda and Beryl are looking for.

While DBO has taken over the shed, the connection to both Earth and Planet Hy Man, and proceeds to defend her planet from the doubles-crossing of both Hilda and Beryl.

As you can see, there is a lot of double-crossing going on.

PROLOGUE

The footman slid his hand around DBO's ankle and admired her toes. There was not a bunion in sight. Her nails were a perfect line of tiny white soldiers and her heels were smooth—not a crack to be found.

He wrapped his forefinger around her big toe and began.

"That feels funny," said DBO.

"Bear with me, ma'am."

"I mean really funny."

The footman continued.

DBO pulled a face.

"Now the second toe," he muttered.

"Must you?" said DBO.

"Yes, but you get use to it."

"Hmmm. Oh; I see what you mean. It's starting to hurt less."

"Yes. Then it hits somewhere higher," whispered the footman.

"Oh my pickled egg," whispered DBO.

The footman worked through her toes, moved to her heel, and then worked up to her ankle joint.

DBO began to sigh.

"And the other foot?" she muttered.

Chapter One

THE SECOND MASSAGE

"The rubbing of a toe is greatly undervalued."–An elderly footman

Hilda stared out of the window. It was dark, with no outlook but the wall of the building beside it—hardly a penthouse view.

It wasn't her choice; it wasn't anyone's choice. Even an Operator's grannie would have turned down Hilda's so-called penthouse suite. Beryl claimed it was "temporary."

That will soon change, thought Hilda. *But first things first: overthrow, divide and conquer, overthrow some more, and*—she smiled—*the trappings will soon follow.*

Hilda had watched Beryl's landing on the streets of Dunoon. She also watched as Beryl and H2 left the Argyll. The H-Pad [1] was able to tap into CCTV and gave Hilda a clear picture of Beryl and H2 taking shelter in a doorway. Hilda found great pleasure in watching them huddle together for warmth.

Only the masses huddled.

Beryl rarely shook hands, let alone touched, and there she was closer than a set of glasses on a nose to an Operator of the lowest order—H2, a woman who was lucky to get a nod from a kitchen porter let alone a shoulder from the leader.

Hilda let out a loud, maniac laugh that jolted her snoring footman awake. Beryl's days of leading were numbered.

"Switched the H-Pad on replay. Back to the first arrival," she shouted, then eyed the footman. "How about a massage?"

She wanted to bask in her brilliance, enjoy her triumph and perhaps . . . relax . . . just a little. Soon she was so relaxed she fell asleep and woke to the H-Pad replaying Beryl's time in Sheila's diner, and her footman doing something painful with her small toe.

The footman was staring at a clear picture of Beryl, H2, and Archie looking dry and warm in Sheila's diner with Archie tucking into a plate of meaty food glistening with fat. The footman mesmerised by the eggs, bacon and extra-large Cumbria sausage; had stopped mid manipulation. As he watched a large forkful of sausage enter Archie's mouth he squeezed and forgot to stop he could just about taste the gristle . . .

Hilda's mouth almost watered until she pulled herself together.

"Get me more bubbly," she shouted.

"But . . . your bunions, ma'am, I haven't touched them."

"Bunions? The leader has no bunions." She paused for a minute. "This is an earphone moment."

The footman's face filled with dread. "Ma'am?"

"Yes, I think earphones are called for."

The footman gulped.

Earphones were one of the few things never modernised on Planet Hy Man, and were, according to all footmen, a "bastard" to set up.

He gestured about the empty room. "But who is here to hear . . ."

Hilda glared at him; he stopped mid-"ma'am?"

"These are dark times; no one is to be trusted, not even those dozy footmen out there," she said, gesturing to the corridor. "Who knows if they are really dozing?"

He looked at her. Was she mad? The footmen were so old even if they did hear— *which they couldn't*—they wouldn't know what to do or even care if they did. They had, like their out-of-date hearing aids, given up, packed it all in, and were waiting for the day of "shuffling off." The day a letter arrived at the footman's bunkhouse stating . . .

"Service no longer required, pack your things"—which was a mere backpack or two—"the resting home awaits."

The resting home was a place where, rumor had it, old men could finally stop standing and had a view worth staring at.

Hilda motioned a "what are you waiting for?" wave.

The footman, wiping his hands, went to the "only open when absolutely necessary" drawer and pulled out a bowling-ball bundle of ancient earphones glued together.

Resignedly he began to untangle.

"Hurry up," she snapped.

He fumbled as nerves got the better of him.

She grabbed the ball and began to jiggle, pull, and shake while swearing the standard selection of salad vegetables.

"Beetroot and pickled egg, who was the last to use these?"

"You were, ma'am."

She glared at him.

He tried to help, pulling and tugging, then after some undignified slapping from Herself, a set fell to the floor. The footman bent to pick it up with a groan.

"Hurry up," she snapped. "We may be missing something, some thoughts even."

"Ma'am, it is but a mere rumor that earphones pick up thoughts."

"We'll see about that, bring them here."

"But you don't know where they have been," said the footman pulling a face.

"Just hand them over."

The footman, after a ceremonial flick/wipe of his lace handkerchief, suspended them in front of her with a look of distaste.

Hilda snatched them from him, eased the tiny piece into her ear, and stared at the H-Pad . . . she had a perfect view of Sheila's diner.

The waitress handed Archie a brown bag of something, and thanks to the footman, she had no idea what. She threw him a "now look what you made me miss" look.

"Tablet,[2] ma'am, don't you remember?"

"Ah yes," she smiled. "Mex's downfall."

Hilda stretched out her other foot. "What about the other small toe?"

The footman left Hilda's room, pulling faces at the other footman in the corridor.

"Earphones, now," he tutted.

A few tutted, except for one footman—the footman who had just spent his "sleep" night massaging DBO's feet. Without a word or a gesture, he waited for his shift to end and made for the shed.

He coughed at the door as instructed by DBO and waited for her answer.

Earphones, he thought. *I wonder what her in the shed will think of that?*

---

1. *The C-Pad, H-pad, H-pad 11 and other pad malarkey: all forerunners of the ipad, which evolved with the I know better than you app some would call virus. The iPad metamorphizes from the C-Pad thanks to a liaison with Legless and very smart IT student during Legless's lost in San Francisco years.*
2. *A homemade sweet Scots claim as their own, sort of in between fudge, and toffee but carries greater mystical qualities.*

Chapter Two

THE MANUAL

"A man and his manual shall never be parted."–The writer of said manual

Hilda had picked the wrong footman to bribe, but Hilda was not a good judge of men. She assumed they were all the same and the only thing a footman wanted was to be was off his feet with a decent sandwich, along, of course, with the chance to do a foot massage.

So, when she called the youngest footman (who was at least seventy) to spy for her, she thought a few pseudo egg sandwiches, some decent shoes, and he was hers.

She had no idea that a foot massage could arouse feelings, or to be honest that a footman had any, apart from a desire to retire.

"Give me a footman any day," she used to say. "So easy to bribe. Not like those smart-arse robots."

It was Hilda who pushed for the "shuffling-off day." And it was she who insisted on a limo to take them to the "Last Hoorah" home.

For once, Beryl agreed.

Some were suspicious of the so-called "Last Hoorah" home. But when the first batch of footmen sent back an "It's true!" mandatory survey, the footmen were convinced.

They took one look at the survey stuck on the men's john and sighed . . .

How clean was your room? Ten out of ten.

How warm is the sun? Almost a ten.

How is your view? Ten and more!

How often do you put your feet up? Impossible to count!

And the sandwiches? Need you ask?

Hilda's plan had worked. The footmen, it seemed, had a future—a future worth obeying for.

DBO pulled a set of earphones meticulously wrapped in individual bundles from a box. Effortlessly she unwrapped one pair and slipped the earphones [1]into her ear.

The footman watched. Was there no end to this woman's talents?

When he first walked into the shed, DBO was sitting comfortably on a pile of cushions looking far from stupid. He was taken by surprise; he had been told she had as much intelligence as a cooker. And there she was, legs crossed, working on an H-Pad like she knew what she was doing. Then, when she asked him his name, he was swept off his feet. No one had asked him that before. Now all he had to do (apart from what she asked) was try and remember it.

DBO fingered the dashboard searching for the socket—the shed was in darkness so as not to attract attention. She plugged in her set and another for the footman.

The footman shook his head with a surprised "me?"

"Watch," said DBO.

The footman looked at the earpiece with suspicion.

"It's clean," muttered DBO.

The footman, unconvinced, pulled a lace handkerchief from his pocket.

They waited for a picture to appear on the H-Pad. They could hear Hilda tucking into hemp biscuits as boredom raced through her mind, followed by frustration.

DBO smiled. "Let her try the manual."

The footman looked at her. "I thought they were burned—tossed —forbidden?"

"Not all," said DBO, "the secretary is a great collector of all things technical."

She nodded to a dark corner. The footman, after several fumbles, pulled a slim book from the corner.

Manuals were slim books that expanded open into unrecognizable diagrams and maps. Some expanded so large they could only be viewed on the floor. Reading them required window- and door-shutting to prevent any "catching of the wind," pressing the corners with something heavy to prevent any "rolling up," and a dictionary (yes, another manual) to understand the wording.

Manuals were designed by men for men who told women that technical stuff required big words that took training to understand.

However, once the C-Pad had developed its "ask me anything" applicator the manual and its man-made language was obsolete. Soon mountains of space were cleared, painted, and filled with other things where manuals used to gather.

For a moment he looked at it with a fondness for the good old days. He fingered the cover and then slid his finger under a corner.

DBO threw him a glare. "Not on my watch."

He snapped it shut. "Yes, ma'am."

---

1. *When Manifesto the Great saw these on a Star Trek repeats he was entranced, "at last a way to block out the chatter from the other half," he exclaimed.*

Chapter Three

THE FLABBERGASTING OF ARCHIE

"When in Rome, eat pizza."–Archie

Archie stood at the front of Bunnie's house, wondering what he had got himself into.

He liked women, and when he first caught sight of Beryl he thought he'd like her, despite her purple beehive. In fact, it was her rigid beehive he spotted first, like a beacon high above a sea of blonde heads. She seemed so vulnerable and out of place, despite the leather . . .

What a fool.

He arranged to pick up Beryl and H2 from the bus shelter, and he arrived early in the morning to find Beryl like a wet kitten shivering by a young woman in a soaking jumpsuit clinging to her skin. They were real damsels in distress . . .

As if!

Archie took one look and headed to DJ's, helped himself to a few decent jackets, left a "I'll explain" note (which DJ had seen many times), and took the said damsels for a right good slap-up breakfast at Sheila's Diner. A Sheila fry-up, washed down with stain-your-teeth tea or coffee that gave you heart palpitations, was what they needed.

Soon he was staring at his plate, full of regret and wishing the Earth would swallow up the not-so-vulnerable Beryl. Helping a damsel in distress was supposed to be received with gratitude, smiles, and a promise of something more—not disdain, disappointment, and a volley of insults.

His choice of jackets was greeted with a disappointed "Me in that tent?" And as for Sheila's Diner? Beryl sniffed at it with a "Must we?" followed by a "Shut it" shove from H2.

The diner was empty apart from a waitress, a cook, and a trucker, all mesmerized by the woman wrapped in a camouflage jacket with a beehive as high as her six-inch boots. A woman old enough to remember the fifties, dressed like she had been out on the town all night, *in Dunoon.*

The waitress couldn't even remember the last time she'd been at an all-nighter. Dunoon was as dead as Woolworths; you were lucky if you got a takeaway after nine, let alone a decent night out in Dunoon.

"Two breakfasts—the works," she said to the cook and sighed. When had she worn leather?

The round waitress slapped the plate in front of Archie. Beryl stared at the grease around the bacon. When the waitress slapped another in front of Beryl, she glared with disapproval.

"What is this?" said Beryl, gesturing to her plate.

"A full Scottish breakfast," said the waitress with pride.

Beryl sniffed. "Do you know what this does to your tubes?"

Archie looked up mid chomp of a mushroom. "What's tubes got to do with things?"

"My gran says sausages are made with innards," said H2, who had insisted on "just toast."

"And what's your gran, a butcher?" said the waitress.

"Butcher?" H2 pulled a face. "She's an expert on many things, but a butcher? Never."

"An expert called Verruca," muttered Beryl.

"Verruca? What sort of name is that?" said the trucker on the next table.

Archie, speechless, sliced his bacon into bite-size portions, pressed a snippet of potato against it, dipped it into brown sauce then placed it in his mouth.

Beryl watched.

Archie, a little unnerved, swallowed.

"Do you know what a pig went through for that?" Beryl continued.

"No, I just eat it."

"Try it with that red stuff," said the trucker, thrusting a sauce-covered sausage in his mouth.

"And these things," Beryl said, pointing at an egg. "These are for baby-making."

Archie spluttered, "Must you?"

The trucker stopped mid sausage-dipping. "Babies from a free range—you on something?"

Archie was beginning to think of escape. *I could down my breakfast,* he thought, *make a dive for the gents and escape out the fire exit.*

Archie was a slim man with clean fingernails and a fondness for large rings and bonnets. In fact, he had a whole collection of both at home, and at the moment he wished he was back there rearranging them. He was a man of habit, from the way he folded his underwear to the way he told stories to woo women. Which in the good old days before Germaine Greer and bra-burning had worked; now his standard wooing practice was as out-of-date as brill cream, and, it seemed, his choice of women.

He pushed a coffee towards Beryl.

"What is this?" said Beryl.

"Coffee," said H2. She nudged Beryl and whispered, "My gran says when in Rome . . ."

"Rome?" said Beryl. "What has Rome got to do with . . . it?"

"It's a figure of speech," snapped Archie. He pushed the cup toward Beryl. *Anything to shut her up.*

"Sugar?" he said, and when she didn't answer he placed a couple of cubes into her coffee.

Beryl sipped. The caffeine was rich and strong, better than any on Planet Hy Man, the sugar hit sending her taste buds into a frenzy. She let out a long, slow sigh and slid another sugar into her coffee.

"My gran says sugar is a mother's ruin," said H2.

"Some cream?" said Archie.

"And cream is the route of all indigestion," said H2.

Beryl nodded. The taste slid down her throat like silk, dairy, sugar, and caffeine. She drained her cup and looked about for more. She even felt like smiling.

"Try the brown," said the truck driver, now curious.

Beryl lifted a brown sugar cube into her coffee and stirred in more cream; she was in mouth heaven.

The trucker watched, mesmerized. *If that is what coffee did to her, what about a dram?*

"You'll pay for that," said H2. "All that animal stuff, my gran says . . ."

"What would Verruca know," said Beryl with a lick of her lips. "She said Legless was a victim . . . of circumstance."

Archie looked up from his egg. "Legless? You know of a Legless?"

Neither answered.

Archie stood to pay.

It was obvious that Beryl's whole BBC fancy-dress story was a load of bollocks, just like her *I knew Bunnie from school* story. But Legless? Was it true; was he the same Legless?

Thirty years ago, Archie was the mentor of all mentors. Every morning, surrounded by a circle of Identities hanging on his every word, Archie told stories of their forefather: the great Legless. Now he had only one—DJ. The rest laughed at his stories. The young generation had no time for Legless, called him a myth, but Archie, despite never meeting Legless, knew they were wrong.

Had he stumbled onto more than damsels in distress? Was (fingers crossed) their so-called Legless his hero?

Beside the till were bags of Sheila's homemade tablets, two for the price of one. He picked up one, then looked at Beryl merrily dumping sugar cubes into her third coffee.

"I'll take the lot," he said. "This stuff is loaded with sugar."

Chapter Four

NOTHING TERMINAL

"Even Lycra has its limits."–Legless

Hilda pushed an empty glass under the dispenser, allowed two chunks of ice to plop along with the bubbly, then waved away the simulated lemon slice.

Unlike Beryl, Hilda enjoyed the sense of panic and was wondering how or even if she should explain the energy crisis to the masses. Thanks to her, the energy crisis was no longer so immediate. She would soon have the Voted In installed in the gym, and once they were riding the stationary bikes, it would be like old times . . . well, except for Lycra shorts. No Voted In would be seen dead in one of them—and she did have some heart.

The ol' fella appeared on the screen.

Hilda slid her earphones in and watched as he negotiated his motorbike with as much panache as a footman on a pushbike. He fumbled, wobbled, skidded, and then headed into a garage.

For a moment the screen went blank.

Hilda downed her bubbly, then stood up for another as the garage door flashed back on the screen.

Hilda sat down; a van was parked in front, covered in dents and scratches.

"What the beetroot happened to the ol' fella?" muttered Hilda, as an old lady strutted by with a jaunty swing of her cane.

Hilda, after a string of curses, tossed the earphones aside, jiggled the connector on her H-Pad and cursed again.

She had lost him . . . so soon.

The H-Pad spluttered and blacked out. Hilda paced the floor. How could she keep an eye on things?

She thumped the H-Pad, ignoring its *"Earth's fault, blame it on British Telecom"* moan, and thumped it again.

Dunoon's ferry car park flashed onto the screen; it was empty.

Hilda sipped her fizzy (forgetting it was empty) and stared.

Why here?

She flicked pause, then the 36 degree surround button. There was nothing . . . anywhere. Just a couple of sorry-looking shoppers huddled in the bus shelter clutching their coats against the wind.

Hilda was about to thump the H-Pad again when Don pulled up.

He's catching a ferry?

Hilda zoomed in on Don's car. She watched as he tucked into his roll and sausage when a large white van entered the car park.

Hilda glanced at the deep scratches on both sides of the van.

The same van?

The van circled the car park several times as the wind turned into a gale.

Pete and Mex were in the back arguing over the point of Mex's log. Bunnie and DJ were arguing over the leaflet and its cryptic Edinburgh address, while Don was tucking into his roll and sausage with relish. Only Woody and Hilda saw the van circle like a shark fin in the ocean.

The van pulled up inches from the car. A gust of wind blew a seagull across the windscreen; it screeched as the old lady moved to open the van door.

"Mind . . ." shouted Woody.

The wind caught the van's door.

Thump—jolt—crash . . .

"Jesus," spluttered Don.

Hilda watched the old lady land with a thud onto the tarmac and tug her walking stick from her seat. A couple of lager cans cluttered to the ground as the old lady, with great strength, pulled the van door now wedged against Don's car free.

She examined the van door for scratches.

"What about my car?" shouted Don.

The old lady waved her stick at Don; the wind slammed it into the side of Don's car. "My door's fine, thanks," she said.

"Not your door, my friggin' car," shouted Don.

The old lady, with an "I'm a sweet old lady" look, tapped Bunnie's window with her cane.

"The toilets near here?" she shouted over the wind.

Bunnie wound down her window. "You'll need to wait for the ferry."

Don stretched across Bunnie and shouted at the old lady, "What about my car?"

The old lady gave him a wave, muttered "right enough," opened her door—allowing it to hit Don's car yet again—and climbed in.

Don jumped out of the car and raced to the van as she started the engine.

"What about my car?" He tapped on her window.

"Don't worry, the van is old."

"No, my car?"

"Not a scratch, don't worry," she mouthed through the window.

Don began to shout as the sound on the H-Pad died.

Hilda watched Don mouth "For fuck's sake . . ." then the screen went blank.

"For beetroot's sake," snapped Hilda.

She jumped up and began to pace, twirling her earphones with frustration.

"Let me think," she muttered.

"I can help," said the H-Pad.

"You?" snapped Hilda.

"It is part of the prototype type," muttered the footman. "To have up-to-the-minute updates every . . . er . . . minute."

"Thank you," purred the H-Pad.

"You can thank Beryl for that, she likes to know what's going on," muttered the footman.

"Going on," said Hilda, "she only wants to know what's happening so she could make cuts."

"The woman's a barber," said the footman.

"Butcher," said the H-Pad.

Hilda glared with a "I make the comments" look, then continued on with her pacing. The footman watched as the earphone twirling became more frantic.

She needed something better, way better, something befitting of the superhero, the leader that she was destined to be . . .

Silently, a manual slid from beneath her door.

Pete had been taking in the air, as Bunnie liked to put it. He had spent the ferry journey in search of a view and was not prepared for the rain in all its glory. He took one look at the grey waters in the biting wind and headed to the lounge area.

A funny sensation hit his stomach, a sort of squeezing, knotting, *something bad is going to happen* feeling.

Bunnie called it intuition; Don called it indigestion. Either way, it played havoc with the roll and sausage he had just demolished.

He had an urge to do the plough, to clear things. He looked about for a quiet spot and found the "john," as it was known in some circles on Planet Hy Man. It was too small for the plough, so he went for an *arm above the head on your toes* stretch, accompanied with an *om*, until someone knocked on the door.

"That you, Pete?"

"Om." The last person he wanted to hear was *Herself.*

"I know you're in there squeezing in a stretch," said Mex with a strained voice.

"Five minutes, ma'am . . . om."

"I need you," she muttered in a voice Pete had not heard before. He pushed open the door halfway to see Mex breathing like a rabbit caught in a spotlight. Her sugar high had dipped like a ship in the high seas, leaving her feeling sick, guilty, and panicky—feelings unknown to her.

The ferry jostled with the waves, bumping Mex into the wall.

"Ma'am, it is merely a sugar dip. I did warn you about the tablet."

Mex put her hand to her mouth. "Don't mention that stuff." She pushed Pete out of the way and made for the toilet.

Pete closed the door on her retching. "And possibly seasickness."

Chapter Five

THE MOANING OF DON

"Never toss a roll at a seagull."—Archie after cleaning his windscreen

unnie and Don remained in the car for the ferry journey. Thanks to the old lady, Don was in a foul mood. The ferry had no sooner left Dunoon, and the old lady was out of her van hobbling with her stick uselessly swinging in front to her. Even AC DC classic hits couldn't shift his mood.

"Of all the friggin' car spaces she had to park next to me?" muttered Don.

The old lady caught sight of Don and mouthed a "hello" with a *poor little me* stance that would annoy even a comatose footman. Don gave up on his roll and sausage.

Bunnie waved back.

"Don't encourage her," he snapped.

Bunnie tried to calm Don.

Don huffed. In the dark morning it was hard to see the damage. But by the time they were on the ferry and sun was up the damage scrapped across several panels of Don pristinely polished car could not be missed.

Don was anything but calm. In fact, he was as scratchy and unbearable "as sand in your knickers," according to Bunnie, a turn of phrase that had Pete, Mex, and DJ leaving the car for a "wander."

"Cheer up," said Bunnie with a paternal pat on his knee. "You've got her details."

Don, with a dramatic sigh, took aim at a seagull with his half-eaten roll; the seagull dodged with a screech.

"Well there was no need for that," muttered Bunnie, and turned up AC/DC.

DJ's mind was full of Beryl; she had captivated him. He could not get her face out of his head. There was more to her than a one-night laugh and an all-night romp.

Where did she come from? And why? He wanted to meet her—but how?

The ferry arrived with a bump at the other side of the Clyde.

Hilda watched as *Mex's gang* (which she now called them as opposed to *Beryl's entourage*) drove off the ferry.

Hilda pressed the *36 degrees and more* button. The view panned out, catching sight of the old woman's van at the back of the queue.

"I wanted a close-up, not a panoramic view."

The H-Pad zoomed in on the old lady's van backfiring into action.

"Not her—Mex's gang."

The van, under a cloud of black smoke, drove off the ferry and followed Mex's gang.

Hilda watched the two vehicles continue down the same road. "Follow that van," she shouted.

The van turned off a side road.

"No, now the taxi."

The footman spied the manual on the floor. His fingers itched to hold it—open it. He went for a foot around the book followed by a pull towards him; no one noticed, as the taxi had sped out of sight.

Hilda watched as the van headed down a side street and then another.

"You've got the wrong car," she shouted.

The van finally jutted into a pile of empty boxes behind a chip shop and stalled. The old woman jumped out, skidded on several chip wrappers, and righted herself. Hilda watched as the old lady slipped off her jacket.

"I want the taxi," she shouted.

The old lady thrust the jacket in the van along with a javelin toss of her cane.

"The taxi, not this old lady," shouted Hilda.

"Old Lady does not compute," said the H-Pad.

The old lady tugged off her bonnet and shook her head; thick luxurious grey hair cascaded down like a shampoo add.

"Compute?" said Hilda.

The old lady pulled her hair into a ponytail, dismissed her comfy shoes with a karate kick, and pulled her bra from underneath her clothes. Mountains of tissues tumbled to the ground as she, with the swing of a striptease, tossed it into the van.

"I knew it," muttered the H-Pad.

The old lady jumped into the van and minutes later appeared dressed in bike leathers wheeling a small 50cc motorbike. She was no longer a she but a he.

Hilda stared closer; it was the ol' fella.

She slid on her earphones and listened. The ol' fella was thinking; a few disjointed words crackled . . .

Feeling . . . his prostate . . .

"Prostrate?" muttered Hilda. "What the pickle?"

"He said his prostate never lies," said the H-Pad.

The ol' fella jumped on his bike and motored off as Hilda wondered what a prostate had to do with things, or for that matter what it was.

The footman watching Hilda took a chance.

He slid the manual under one foot, then the other, and stood on it.

"What are you up to?" snapped Hilda.

The footman coughed, stuttered, and began to embark on a lecture about the prostate when disjointed thoughts racing through the ol' fella's mind began to blare from her earphones.

"The *Herald*."

"Malarkey."

"That'll tackle it."

"Oh bugger."

"And prostate . . . yet again."

Hilda began to grimace, pushing her half-finished breakfast to the side, she cursed. It seemed following the ol' fella was not the breeze she thought it was.

Was he deliberately revving his engine, blocking her?

Hilda, exasperated, tuned into the shed, remembered it was empty, flicked to the room with a view. Then remembering it was full of the Operators who were still waiting for their induction, shouted, "Oh for pickle's sake," jolting awake a few of the footman in the corridor.

"Ask me anything," purred the H-Pad.

She glared at the H-Pad with an "I was just about to" look, and shouted, "Look up 'prostate'!" which echoed through the corridor.

A few of the footman winced.

"And while you're at it, 'malarkey'!"

One footman peered from under his white fringe. "Malarkey," he muttered, "that's a good old-fashioned word that!" and fell back to sleep.

The H-Pad began to talk about prostate until Hilda told her to stop—she had just had her breakfast.

The H-Pad, moving on to the meaning of "malarkey," captured Hilda's attention for a second. "That's enough, I get the picture," she shouted as the footman caught her eye . . . he looked taller.

"What have you been eating?" said Hilda.

"Ma'am?"

"It's just that you look . . ." Her eyes ran down to his feet, where she spied the manual, "The Job of Mind-Reading for Men."

Oh, bugger, thought the footman.

Chapter Six

THE SCRAPPER

"Never laugh with a full bladder."—Bunnie

Archie stared at Bunnie's run-down porch as H2 glared at the back of his head; he turned and caught her glare. For a moment their eyes locked, and then she felt a tugging at her thoughts, a switching around in her head . . . she looked away.

Recovering from Sheila's Diner hadn't been easy for Archie; it was one of his favorite places. He was, however, hopeful that Beryl knew more of his Legless.

Archie had spent the morning driving with his eyes flitting from the road ahead to Beryl's beehive bouncing in the rear-view mirror, trying to make eye contact. Occasionally their eyes met, and each time she took his breath away. He had never before met such a complex, hard-to-fathom, pain-in-the-arse woman. Her mind was like a fortress which no amount of ESP-ing could crack.

And H2 wasn't any easier with her annoying "know it all" talk. She contradicted Archie like Jeremy Paxman on *Newsnight*; he was only trying to lighten things, add a little humor . . .

"It's just a bit of banter," Archie muttered after one of H2's "I hardly think so" comments.

"Yes, well," said H2. "The Big Yin did not invent the tattie and a wee man's ferret does not swing between his legs . . . like part of the furniture."

"It was a figure of speech," said Archie, negotiating a roundabout. "A joke. Do you not have any sense of fun?"

Archie let out a long sigh. *The ferret joke always worked.*

"Where I come from, a sense of humor is not the be-all," said H2.

"But we're not there now so shut it," muttered Beryl.

"You can't tell me to shut it *here*, you're nothing *here*, you're the same as me *here*—no one gives a toss for you, you're a minion, not a ruler."

"Yes, all right, there's no need to be so blunt . . ." snapped Beryl.

Archie's bunion pulsated like a lighthouse in a storm. *Ruler?* There was definitely something afoot, his bunions never pulsated for nothing. He thought about the tablet in his pocket. Several bags should be enough to work a little magic—soften the tongue, if not the mind.

"So, this is Bunnie's house," said H2.

"Looks like it."

"What do we do now?" said H2.

Beryl, consumed with feelings unknown to her, was looking a little shaky. Her body was under the influence of coffee, sugar, and dairy—the last two of which her body had no idea of. Her head was fuzzy, her hands trembling, and her stomach felt empty. In fact, all she could think about was something sweet.

"I'm starving," said Beryl.

"Well, if you had eaten some of that toast, instead of . . ." H2 stopped as Archie pulled out a brown bag and gestured to the both of them.

H2 smelt sugar and resisted.

Beryl smelt sugar and her mouth watered.

"My gran says sugar is what killed the nation," said H2.

"That and a whole bunch of men," muttered Beryl.

"Men?" said Archie.

"She says it corrupts the mind, inflates things."

"Inflates?" said Archie.

"Your gran ain't the be-all and end-all," muttered Beryl.

"Have some tablet," Archie said with a shake of the bag.

"My gran knows heaps about that sort of thing," said H2, waving the tablet away.

"She lives in a shack and does her own cooking," muttered Beryl she looked inside the bag.

"My point," says H2.

"Mine too," said Beryl, who had confused herself. She dipped her finger into the bag and licked it. Sugar hit Beryl's tongue with an explosion of taste and tingling; her face beamed with pleasure.

Archie watched with anticipation, H2 with trepidation.

"Oh, my beetroot," sighed Beryl.

Sugar and dairy raced through Beryl's virgin bloodstream like a ton of dope, a bottle of bubbly (the real thing), and a couple of magic mushrooms.

"When in Rome . . ." She smiled.

"Rome?" said H2. "They tossed women aside like used tissues, they treated them like objects to battered, sold, used, and abused. Did you know in Rome a woman could not even vote, let alone own land? She had nothing without a decent set of . . ."

Beryl glared at her.

"Well, that's what my gran says."

"Verruca," said Beryl, "is not here." She took another piece and waved it under H2's nose.

"Legless wrote about sugar in his *Sugar Is the Noose Around the Universe* book," said H2. "And look what happened to him."

"Legless?" said Archie.

"Who reads Legless books?" said Beryl.

"You're talking about Legless the Great?"

"Did I say Legless?" said Beryl.

"What happened to Legless?" said Archie.

"She meant sugar makes, you . . . err . . . legless," muttered H2.

"Did I?" said Beryl. She turned to H2 and waved the tablet under her nose. "Have some."

H2 shook her head.

Beryl was soon knocking back the tablet like Mex at the ol' fella's. For the first time in a long time, she felt positive; suddenly this pickled egg of a mission seemed as easy as buttering toast.

H2 watched in silent panic. Her leader was starting to look weird—animated. Beryl's once frosty face was now alive with emotion and bulging eyes. And, even scarier, her once immaculately rigid beehive was now tilting to one side with a few wisps of hair straying.

Beryl poked the plugulator. "Who needs a scrapper[1]?"

"Scrapper?" said both H2 and Archie.

Beryl tutted. "Yes, this burnt-out thing. There is as much life in that scrapper as Hilda's wig."

"Hilda has a wig?"

"Who's Hilda?" said Archie.

"She's a fruit loop," muttered Beryl, "and a fruit loop to be watched."

"With a wig?"

"And capes," Beryl chuckled. "Looking stupid for her is as easy as sucking on a tablet while putting another in your mouth." Which she did with a satisfied grin.

Beryl picked up the plugulator; it fell apart in her hand. "My life self-destructed the day I meant her . . . and him," Beryl mumbled through a full mouth. "And there is no way back, only forward . . ."

"Ma'am," said H2, "perhaps we should think of . . . moving on?"

"But do I look worried?" said Beryl wiping her mouth.

"Worried is the last thing you look like," said Archie, taking the plugulator from her.

"That pickled egg of a woman has no idea who she is dealing with," said Beryl with a large swallow.

"You talking about Hilda?" said Archie.

"Who needs a scrapper?" said Beryl.

"It's a plugulator, ma'am, and perhaps you should stop talking and wipe your mouth again."

". . . when there are three of us and my brain?"

Beryl, refusing H2's offer of a tissue, grabbed the plugulator from Archie and tossed it at Bunnie's roof. It hit the chimney, clattered down the tiles, and fell with a crash onto the dustbin. For a moment it stopped, they watched . . . then it began to roll, picking up speed . . .

"It's like it's got a life of its own," muttered Archie. As it finally landed onto the bin toppling it to the ground. They watched as a few cans cluttered out . . .

"As I said, a life of its own," muttered Archie.

Izzie, who had fallen asleep pining for Mex, looked up.

"There are other ways," said Beryl.

"Ma'am, let's take a moment to perhaps make a plan?"

Beryl, with a dismissive wave at H2, straightened her beehive, marched to the front door, and rattled it. "Anyone there?"

Izzie began a volley of barking.

Beryl looked about with confusion.

"It's a dog," shouted Archie.

"My gran says never trust an animal that barks."

"Why don't we get back into the car," said Archie, hiding the rest of the tablet.

"You standing on something?" said Hilda to the footman.

"Ma'am, it is but a mere . . ."

"Reception excellent at Bunnie's," interrupted the H-Pad with an elevator voice.

Hilda looked up. "What?"

"Beryl is high on sugar, ma'am."

"Sugar?"

"Like Mex—the ol' fella's tablet."

"Argh, yes. Maybe now I can read her mind."

"Infiltrate," said the H-Pad.

She threw a look at the H-Pad. "Well, yes . . ."

A perfect picture of Bunnie's house came into view, which as the H-Pad explained was all thanks to several robust arguments with BT. Bunnie, a first-class complainer, got the best superfast Wi-Fi, which now made watching Beryl's tossing burnt-out "scrappers" onto roofs a doddle.

"BP?" said Hilda, watching the plugulator clatter to the ground.

"No, BT," said the H-Pad.

"I see," said Hilda with a confused look.

"Installation of the internet," muttered the footman. "There are many to choose from."

Hilda shot a look at him. A footman talking about installations like a sandwich filling?

She wondered. When she was a nobody, people talked like she wasn't there, and Hilda soaked it all in, learned many things—surprised them all in the end. *Had he soaked things in? Was he a soaker of sorts?*

She studied his wrinkly neck, the papery skin. If she knew how old he was, it would help. She could trace his past, where he came from . . .

Ageing, however, was a long drawn-out affair on Planet Hy Man. There had been great strides, with sun filters, water filters, DNA, and vegan eating all prolonging the onset of many things, including wrinkles and stooped walking. And as for gnarled joints and wobbly chins, they appeared way after ninety. Plastic surgery on Earth was seen as a complete joke by many, way off the mark; good air, plant food, and a few facial-stretching sessions was the answer.

Hilda's eyes trailed down to his sunken stomach, the loose trouser legs indicating muscle-less thighs, and mentally counted the decades until she spied the manual again.

"What's this?" she said, snatching the manual from under the footman's feet. The footman stumbled, staggered, fell, then pulled himself up.

Without a glance at the footman, the length of the stagger was noted.

Totally ancient.

Hilda fingered the manual.

"Is there anything about a prostate in here?" she said.

The footman coughed. "Ma'am, I have only but stood on it."

---

1. *A forgotten element from a forgotten time on planet Hy Man when real animals roamed. A scrapper fed animals scraps from the food chain, it was a dirty job. Now the term is only used when pickle swearing will not do.*

Chapter Seven

IZZIE

"Never sneeze with a full bladder."—Pete

"Your gran is an inspiration," muttered Beryl. And before H2 could work out the sprit in which such a comment was meant, Beryl was around the back of the house, shouting, "Anyone who can face the world with a name like Verruca has to be."

Archie followed, while H2 grabbed the plugulator, slid it into her knapsack, and followed.

Soon they were staring at a run-down back porch and a tiny white dog bouncing up behind a window with demented determination.

Archie, who was still coming to terms with the name Verruca, stared at the wiry frame as it appeared in front of the window mid snarl. "Verruca?" he muttered with a glared look, as the wiry frame disappeared into a crash of geraniums and bric-a-brac.

Izzie had been locked in Bunnie's porch until the neighbor was free to pick her up. Things were moving in the bladder area, which, now awake, she was painfully aware of.

"Funny looking rat," muttered Beryl.

"It's a dog," said Archie.

"Never seen a rat jump like that."

"It's a dog," said H2.

"He'll do his joints."

Thud, crash, yelp!

"We could climb through that window," said Beryl. "Easy done."

"What about the dog?" said H2.

"Rats are nothing to fear," said Beryl. Who, having spent time in the stationary gym back in the Legless cycling days, knew a thing or two about them.

"Small dogs are the worst," said Archie.

"I'm sure it'll just scuttle away, rats always scuttle, they're famous for it," said Beryl. She made the famous bit up, but who was to know? She had a mission to accomplish: spark plugs to source, energy crisis to solve. She couldn't let a rat-scuttling issue stand in her way.

Izzie continued to bark . . .

The three stared at Izzie, who finally managed to clutch the ledge with her paws just long enough to hold a snarling glare at Beryl, accompanied by a dribble.

"I think scuttling is the last thing it's thinking about," muttered H2.

Archie, for the first time, agreed with her.

Izzie's right paw lost its grip, intensifying her snarl to a growl. She tried to grab on again, scrabbling her lower legs on the wall, her dark eyes fixated on Beryl.

Grrrrrr . . .

Finally, she clattered to the ground, which was now a sea of broken crockery.

Yelp!

"A dog like that doesn't scuttle, it sinks its teeth in, holding on for an eternity." Archie's mind flashed back to an incident that still caused him to clench his buttocks.

Beryl looked at the single glazed sash window as Izzie flashed up behind the window mid dribble, then disappeared.

Feeling and memories came back of the time when Beryl steeled about her planet unnoticed. *It's been a long time,* thought Beryl, *but I can still steel . . . about.*

"I used to jump like that," said Beryl, "higher than Mex."

"Mex?" said Archie. "Who is Mex?"

"All's I need is a diversion—breaking in would be a piece of beetroot."

Archie looked at H2.

H2 thought on her feet, something her gran advised against.

"Let's try the front," she said.

"Yes, good idea, perhaps we can sneak in there," muttered Beryl.

Hilda watched. She had seen rats too; there were many mechanical rats at the compound, and they never looked anything like that wiry thing. And they didn't dribble.

"This tablet," muttered Hilda, "do we have any?"

"Tablet requires dairy," said H-Pad. "But I do believe there may be some ideas for reconstruction in the manual."

Hilda turned to the manual sitting like a solid brick by her feet as the parcel-bearing footman knocked and waited for the order to enter.

"My cape," Hilda said with a gleeful clap of her hands as the footman entered.

Chapter Eight

THE BREAK-IN

"A massage by any other name still requires oil."—A very old footman.

As Beryl, Archie, and H2 walked back to the front of the house, Izzie went mad.

She circled the back porch in a crazed barking fashion until her feet caught the curtain. Archie, H2, and Beryl heard the clatter of a fallen curtain pole, a yelp, then silence.

"One scuttle too many," muttered Beryl.

No one answered.

H2 tried to manoeuvre Beryl into the car. But Beryl, filled with the "I can do anything" side effect of sugar and burning with memories of a time when she could *beat the pants* off Mex, was immovable.

She stared at the run-down porch at the front of Bunnie's house. It was even older than the back porch, with a half-opened single glazed window that refused to budge. In Beryl's eyes it was begging to be broken.

"It's hardly the Kremlin," she grunted with a feeble shove at the window.

"Yes, but it is someone else's porch."

"I could easily squeeze in."

"Look," said Archie, "I don't know where you come from, but here squeezing into other folks' porches is not done."

"Why don't we go back to the car, have a little think?" muttered H2 with a tentative push at her leader's shoulder.

"Legless squeezed into things all the time."

Archie stopped in his tracks. "Legless?"

"Ma'am, it is probably wise to stop reminiscing under the influence of tablet."

"Legless—what do you know about a Legless?" said Archie.

Beryl picked up a rock.

"Don't think you should do that, my gran says that rocks are best left on the ground . . ."

"Legless was a man of action," said Beryl with a crazed look.

"Action?" said Archie. He had never heard it called that before.

"And this is what Legless would have done."

Smash . . . crash . . .

Izzie let out a strangulated yelp.

H2 stared at the broken glass. She had a sneaking feeling that breaking windows was frowned upon on Earth, let alone climbing into someone's porch.

Archie, spying a neighbor looking from her window, began to panic. Police and Identities didn't mix well.

Beryl, with a flamboyant toss of her camouflage jacket, shouted, "I'm going in."

A few schoolchildren stopped to stare; Archie tried to usher them on.

Beryl, a slim and supple woman, had no problem "sneaking" through the battered glass of a porch window, just as she had no problem battering it with a rock. She pushed the broken glass in with her elbow, looking scarily like an expert, then with eel-like fashion slid one leg in. Her foot crunched on the glass.

The neighbor began to film the lady with the beehive on her phone. Archie waved at her using his old-fashioned Identities eye-contact charm, which she ignored.

Beryl slid her other leg in, staggered, and righted herself along with her beehive as the burnt-out H-Pad fell from her pocket and rolled across the room. She didn't notice as she took in the cluttered surroundings; there was nothing but potted plants. Suddenly she real-ized she had no idea what she was looking for.

Izzie began to bark again, this time jumping at the door into the house.

"Come on in," shouted Beryl to H2. *Maybe she would know what they were looking for.*

Izzie swung on the door handle, and the door opened. She burst through and raced from one room to the next . . .

Archie smiled at the neighbor with a wave.

Beryl picked up a plant in a pot and turned it about. *What the pickle?* "Honestly, there is nothing to be afraid of," she shouted.

Izzie burst into the porch, looking nothing like a rat.

Beryl dropped the plant, it crashed to the floor.

Izzie tripped over the H-Pad, skidded, turned, looked at it, and then bit into it.

Beryl watched the "rat" begin to shake the H-Pad like a rag doll. The H-Pad went into flexible, made-of-rag-doll mode and went (as programmed) with the flow. Beryl (thinking on her feet) grabbed the other end. There was a tussle, growling from Izzie and pickle-swearing from Beryl.

"Give me that," snapped Beryl.

Saliva oozed from Izzie's mouth and trickled into the H-Pad. Beryl heard a sizzling noise and a muffled growl, followed by a silence.

DBO was in the shed with her new best friend the footman. They were both watching Beryl on DBO's recently charged, wireless-yet-connected-to-everything-including-Hilda's-H-Pad screen. A screen that still had the footman speechless with admiration for DBO's tech-nical abilities. Just as they were now speechless at the antics of their high-on-sugar leader.

The manual would hopefully give DBO time to divert Hilda, but she had to act fast or soon Planet Hy Man's only hope would be crushed under the jaws of a tiny white dog called Izzie, or "Bichon Frise" as the footman called it.

As the saliva hit the H-Pad, the shed dashboard lit up. In a second DBO wondered . . .

She had heard about rat's saliva; it had properties, and there had been experiments, reports and rumors . . .

Saliva, a richer component than water, had the sort of glopping in-one-place consistency (unlike water) along with enzymes that, in theory, should connect in an electrical current–type way . . .

Would it work with a Bichon Frise? thought DBO.

She stared at her dashboard—gambled, flicked a few switches, turned a knob, and prayed.

Izzie's eyes glazed over; she flopped to her side and farted.

Beryl stared at the tiny furry face with the buzzing H-Pad still clutched between its teeth.

Up close, Beryl could see Izzie was nothing like a rat. She tentatively tugged the H-Pad.

"Leave it, ma'am."

"Who is that?" said Beryl.

"Your fairy godmother," said DBO.

Archie and H2 watched Beryl's beehive disappear from view. They heard the clatter of potted plants, barking, growling, then silence; neither wanted to investigate and neither noticed as the neighbor joined them.

"That dog may be small," said the neighbor, "but it eats postmen for breakfast."

"So does she," muttered H2.

"None gets the better of that dog," said the neighbor.

"I wouldn't count on it," said Archie.

"Not when you break in. I mean how do you think Bunnie gets away with leaving that window like that"—the neighbour gestured around her—"in a street like this? That dog is like a . . ."

The neighbor stopped.

Archie muttered an "I told you" as Beryl walked out of the porch like a fireman saving a kitten. She had the H-Pad rebuilding itself in her pocket, a dog in her arms licking her face, and her "fairy godmother" telling her what to do.

"Just pick up the dog and walk, ma'am . . ."

Chapter Nine

THE DASHBOARD AND THE H-PAD

"Even the footmen laughed at Legless's books. Some even used them as footstools."—A footman's diary

The last half an hour of barking had been erased from Izzie's mind, along with any reason why she was barking. Instead she woke to find a funny-looking woman playing "give it to me"—her favorite game—as something in her mouth was giving her a warm tingling.

"It's in the H-Pad," muttered DBO.

"Is that so?" muttered the footman.

"Yes, you see, I flicked the head-buzzing switch here and turned the connector knob beside it."

"Impressive." The footman pulled some oil from the shelf with a *massage, ma'am?* look.

"The head buzzing has the effect of electroconvulsive therapy, but without the seizures." She paused with pride. "We are civilized—unlike Earth."

The footman asked DBO how she knew about such knobs.

"It was Hilda's favorite," said DBO. "She used it on all the new Operators who hadn't learned to wait until she was out of the shed to ask questions—it stuns and erases."

DBO, pleased with herself, gestured to her feet. The footman, impressed, threw himself into the task with a vigor he had not experienced in a long time.

DBO's feet were like her: fresh, young, and clean.

He had a feeling that DBO was destined for something greater and his massaging was all part of it.

Perhaps he wasn't "past it" after all.

Chapter Ten

THE GARAGE

"'What tickles your fancy is similar to 'slap and tickle' but not quite the same."–Archie

M ex, along with the rest of the gang, had spent the morning in a garage for, as Don called it, "a quote." Which led to the car staying in the garage and Don getting the use of a people carrier, once sorted.

Don did explain what a quote was, but Mex didn't listen. She was too busy looking about the garage, a perplexing place full old equipment, noise, and strutting men—a sight she had not seen in a long time.

Mex wanted to inspect, pull apart, and explore. She wanted to stand underneath a car high up on a ramp and see what archaic instruments they used, then shout over the radio, the blasting machines, and the yelling men how there was an easier way of doing things and, of course, put the men back in their proper place.

Pete managed to stop her; he grabbed her arm and shouted, "Health and safety, ma'am."

She stopped and looked at him. Had he caught a glimpse of what was running through her mind? "What do you know about health and whatever?" she shouted; a drill-like noise drowned out her voice.

"What?"

"I said when did you become such an expert?"

"It's a people carrier," shouted Pete.

"That's not what I said," shouted Mex as Pete, not hearing, gestured to Don standing by a large van with windows and a mechanic under the bonnet.

"He's just sorting the engine," shouted Woody.

"And they're experts?" said Pete.

"That's not what I said," shouted Mex.

Woody and Pete stared ahead.

"Ten minutes and she'll be ready for anything," shouted the mechanic from the bonnet.

"Whose ten minutes will that be then?" shouted Don.

"Aye, very funny."

"What?"

"I said *very funny*!"

"I wasn't trying to be funny."

The mechanic stood up, wiping his hands on his greasy overalls. "What?"

"I said cheers."

Mex nudged Pete. "Why don't they turn down the music, switch things off? Save all this shouting?" she shouted.

"All part of the rich tapestry of a mechanic," shouted Pete.

Woody laughed; Mex didn't. She looked at Pete with a *what the pickle has happened to you* look. She could no longer fathom her faithful servant. He had changed. Not that he was particularly faithful on Planet Hy Man, but at least he knew his place. Here he was starting to strut, walk with purpose. He seemed to embrace this place and its sarcasm.

"When did you become such an expert?" she asked again.

Pete threw her a look. "Ma'am, it is but mere observation," he said, then guided her to the reception area, suggesting she "join Bunnie."

Bunnie was sitting on a couch that had seen better days, clutching a paper cup of undrinkable tea. She had spent a lifetime in garages. Memories came back of her first job making tea in a poky reception. Dino, the owner, had a way of "trying it on" that put her off tea, overalls, and the smell of grease. Dino was not the first man to try it on, and Bunnie soon learned that playing "hard to get" got her nowhere, and neither did "giving in," except for a dose of crabs.

"Men," said Bunnie, handing Mex a suspicious-looking coffee.

"Men?" said Mex.

"Aye, men," said Beryl with a distracted toss of her cup.

Mex watched the cup land with precision into the bin—not a drop spilt. She tossed her undrinkable coffee. It missed and splattered onto the floor with a plop.

Beryl looked at her. "That was 50p."

Mex said nothing. Instead, with a sigh, she looked at her reflection in the cracked window. What the pickle had happened to her?

She used to be a superhero—the good old-fashioned kind. Strong legs that could crush a man, along with the ability to read a man's mind and not be sick . . .

Now she couldn't even hit a bin two feet away.

Not that she was ruthless, more a black-and-white sort of woman doing her job—hero and villains. Men were the dark villains trying to take back what they had lost, and it had been her job to stop them.

"I used to slay things," muttered Mex.

Bunnie looked at her. "Slay? You can't even hit a bin."

Mex said nothing as Don entered with a "come on let's go" grunt.

The people carrier was high, but no one was aware of how high until Woody tried to climb in.

DJ wrenched the stiff sliding door open and with his long legs climbed in. Don handed him his AC/DC CDs and picnic bags and with several grunts followed. While Bunnie, surveying her passenger's seat with a *how high can a van be* look, hitched up her jacket and with the aid of Pete climbed in as well.

"It's the best I can do at such short notice," shouted the mechanic, wiping his hands on a greasy cloth. He slammed the boot shut. Mex watched, making a comment about spare spark plugs.

"Spark plugs?" laughed the mechanic. He shouted to the others, "She's asking about spare spark plugs."

The other mechanics laughed. "What century you in, love?"

"What the hell is a spark plug?" joked another.

Mex stared at the pair of feet poking from under a car. There was plenty she could say and some was on the tip of her tongue. Woody, however, stopped her. "Get me a stool or something," he said, "so I can get in the van."

Hilda opened her package and looked at her new outfit. She couldn't wait to try it on and see the Voted In's faces.

It was a long pseudo-leather cap designed by Kismet and made by grannies. It had a bright blue mask designed in the spirit of Batgirl—*which didn't do her any favors*—and could be attached to anything, including Hilda's onesie. And it would fit perfectly with her newly acquired hoverboard, or "flying platform[1]" as some liked to call it. A device so expensive only two had been made.

She held the cap up into the light; this was going to push her command to a new level.

Hilda had already laid the foundations of her energy plan[2]. She had handed around leaflets to the workers at ground level and memos to the Voted In, preparing for the new stationary initiative.

When the sparkplug first came out, it was a whole new concept. Spark plugs not only stored energy like microchips stored information but sourced it—a huge leap from relying on men riding stationaries.

Solar power on Planet Hy Man had been around in the days when men were young and trying to clear up the mess made from years of industry. But the smog-infested atmosphere made it unreliable and inefficient. Even now after all this time, the pollutions from past decades were still present. A clear day on Planet Hy Man was a miracle, a sunrise a past memory.

Soon gyms began to be seen as a new, innovative way of making energy. At first it was the poor people looking for credits that rode the bikes, until women took over and sent the men. No one thought about ageing. And as the men aged, stationary energy became as unreliable as solar power, due to speed dips and bouts of coughing, and "catching one's breath" led to blackouts.

The spark plug saved the day.

Now it was up to the stationary again.

Hilda looked at herself in the mirror. *This will give body to my memos.* She threw a girlish twirl and attempted a grin. *Yes, this will confuse and control, at least until Vegas finds the library.*

Now all's she had to do was unpack the flying platform, charge her up, and practice.

A few rounds around the kitchen should do the trick, thought Hilda, who had never even balanced on a stationary before.

---

1. *Hilda dreamed of a flying platform from the day she was first ask to go out and pick herbs in the compound. She looked at the muddy field and thought there must be a better way.*
2. Similar to Beryl's but with more options.

Chapter Eleven

THE LICKING OF IZZIE

"A dog's bark does not always precede a bite."–Beryl

Archie had been all for dumping Beryl and H2 at the nearest bus station until he heard the word "Legless." He stared at a remorseful-looking Beryl and an agitated-looking H2; he was a lucky man.

Beryl sat in the car with an empty feeling, made worse by her now-dropping sugar level. Never had anyone played with her, let alone licked her face. The only touch she had experienced was a "rubbing" from the dry, cold hands of a half-asleep footman—nothing like the experience of warm dribbling, wet paws, and snuggling, as Archie called it.

She thought it meant something. Now Beryl was disorientated, confused, and desperate for a wet wipe.

When Izzie woke up and saw the nice lady, she jumped into Beryl's arms and licked her face.

"Pat," said the fairy godmother.

"I beg your pardon?"

"You know how to pat, don't you?"

Beryl felt Izzie's warm tongue on her cheek.

"Just make like a hairbrush and brush."

Beryl soon got the hang of *patting* and within seconds Izzie was on her back revealing a complicated-looking round tummy. Beryl had never seen a tummy like that before; she stared at all the lumps and bumps until Izzie barked and she was told to "take her outside."

As Beryl carried Izzie, she nuzzled Beryl's neck and licked her ears. Her soft tongue sent shivers to places Beryl never knew had feelings. She thought about turning back until the fairy godmother intervened and told her to focus.

Beryl, clutching Izzie, made for Archie and H2. Izzie took one look at the neighbor and without a backward glance jumped into her arms. Beryl, adopting a *that's got rid of him* stance, watched as Izzie licked and nuzzled the matronly looking woman.

"Let's get on with things," Beryl muttered and headed for the car.

As Archie drove off, Beryl, clutching the rebooted, refurbished H-Pad, stared ahead as Izzie's wagging tail disappeared into the distance. Izzie didn't even look up, she was too engrossed in licking the neighbor. Beryl felt a stabbing feeling in her heart.

"She just jumped ship," muttered Beryl, "no last lick, nothing; just like that flat-faced, double-crossing Legless."

Legless, a mere man on Planet Hy Man, came into his own on Earth; a place where women were as eager to procreate as a man. Although they didn't call it that. They had assorted names for that sort of thing, and Legless embraced them all just as he embraced the very act of making love itself.

Instead of conserving his seed, as advised, he spent his seed like a gambler in a casino; threw it about like fertilizer on a farm. And now years later he was paying the price with Earth ageing and poor intellectual reason.

He'd lost the ability to tell a story no matter how hard he tried, and the only way to keep his legend alive was to become invisible.

Of course, Beryl had no idea of Legless's ability to tell stories. He had wanted Beryl to listen, read his contemplations, "take him seriously." But the only thing she was interested in was watching him in Lycra riding a stationary. Preferably, *when extra energy was required* standing up. His butt always looked best in the upright position. It reminded her of the time she first saw him, egging the men to all stand up and peddle like champions . . .

"Come on lads, the energy's dipping."

In fact, sometime after a particularly tiring day, so desperate was she for a view of such a butt upright, Beryl would run all the hot taps, leave her straighteners on and turn up the heating.

Beryl sighed at the memory. His butt always made her sigh. She called it charismatic presence—lost as soon as he opened his mouth.

Legless wanted to write, Beryl couldn't care less.

"Tell me what tickles your fancy and I'll write it," he'd say.

"You in Lycra, parading and posing for me to enjoy and shout *more*," she'd shout.

Beryl sighed in boredom at a man who intellectualized when unasked.

He should have stuck to Lycra he was never boring in Lycra.

"There's more to a man than two tight cheeks," said Archie. "We weren't made just to be looked at."

"In your case that is probably a bonus," said Beryl.

H2 nudged Beryl and gestured to Archie. "He's EPS-ing while driving," she mouthed, "multitasking."

"What man multitasked?" Beryl mouthed back.

"That whole multitasking thing is a myth," snapped Archie

That's what Legless used to say, thought Beryl.

"And he wrote about it too," said Archie.

Chapter Twelve

THE VOTED IN

"To wear a suit takes more than a good fit."–A Voted In

At four in the morning, Hilda, wearing her favorite onesie, entered the Voted In's apartment floor. Attached to her onesie was her new cape, and as she marched down the corridor it flowed behind her like Darth Vader.

She was up before anyone had thought of coffee—before the footman had taken up their posts. She had planned it that way, she was a woman on a mission and surprise was the key to her plan.

She marched into the beverage area, did a secret twirl with her cape and her illegal beverage heated up.

She took a sip . . .

Arrrrh!

She loved to surprise, put women off guard, and she was an expert at it. Even as a child she dreamt of "surprise plans," which was a complete waste of time; back then no one noticed her. No one noticed anybody living in "the complex"; "the complex" was where those from the "wrong side of the track" were brought up, and "the complex" seemed intent on keeping it that way.

"You are nothing special" was plastered on the walls, along with "keep it zipped," "don't ask questions," "selfishness never fed no one," and "what have you done today to make Planet Hy Man a better place?"

Hilda always wondered about the last two. Porridge was rationed to a spoonful covered in hemp milk, and she had no idea what Planet Hy Man was like outside the complex.

Those from the wrong side of the track were brought up in out-of-the-way complexes on a diet of "serving the planet is its own reward" drivel, as digestible as the morning porridge.

She drained her illegal beverage, and pulled yellow "do not enter" tape from a pocket in her cap.

"Times are a changing," she muttered to herself as she stretched the tape across the entrance of the beverage room and sealed it in place . . .

Later that morning, Voted In Two sauntered from her room to the beverage room. She walked past the footmen now lining the corridor and straight into the rigid yellow tape blocking the doorway.

"What the beetroot . . . ?"

A footman smirked.

Voted In Three arrived bleary-eyed, her hair like a bird's nest; she stared at the yellow tape scratching her behind.

"What the gherkin?"

Voted In Five peered from her room down the corridor. Voted In Two and Three looked at her. "Coffee machine on the blink?" said Voted In Five.

Others began to peek from their doorways.

"What, no coffee?" shouted one.

"Did someone drink it all?" shouted another.

"Brazilian, hardly think so," muttered Voted In Two.

Due to budget cuts they were forced to accept the undrinkable.

The Voted In were mature women in their sixties and beyond, and they all lived on the same floor. They found comfort in routine and followed the same procedure every day, which involved peeking from their rooms and shouting from doorways.

"Which blend today, girls?"

"Black or white?"

"Hemp milk or dairy free?"

"To froth or not?"

Followed by a saunter to the beverage room, lots of sipping, sighing, and gossiping. It was, as any footman would say, a long-drawn affair.

The footmen were so used to the morning ritual they barely fluttered their closed eyes—until this morning.

This morning, the footmen had arrived at their appointed "standing to attention" spot, saw the yellow tape, and silently looked at each other. They watched as one by one the Voted In appeared in their regulation black silk PJs clutching empty mugs. Soon they were huddled in a confused group, scratching their heads and butts while muttering to each other.

"What does this mean?"

"What'll we do?"

"How can I think without my coffee," screamed Voted In Three.

The footmen pretended not to listen. One coughed and, with a tentative finger pointing, gestured to Hilda's signature.

Panic set in as the footman retreated back to his position.

"What does this mean?"

"What'll we do?"

"I need coffee," screamed Voted In Three.

"Shhh," muttered a few.

Another footman coughed as a unfamiliar mechanical humming sound filled the hallway.

"The beverage room is off-limits," shouted Hilda.

The Voted In turned to see Hilda, posed at the other end of the corridor on her "flying platform" a foot from the ground. The flying platform shifted from side to side.

The Voted In watched. Nothing about Hilda surprised them anymore.

"Not until you have proved yourselves," said Hilda.

The flying platform began to move higher up one side of the wall and then the other. Hilda, struggling with her balance, ordered the platform to move forward with a "Now!" It spluttered, then stopped.

"It's water and weak tea for you all," she shouted.

"What?" shouted Voted In Three.

"I said it's weak tea and—" The flying platform shot forward like a bullet and stopped just shy of Voted In Three's face. Voted In Three stared at Hilda's groin inches from her nose and held her breath.

"Water," snapped Hilda.

"I see," muttered Voted In Three.

Hilda readjusted her pose. "You're moving."

There was a sharp intake of breath.

"And where you are going there will be no coffee."

"What?"

"Why?"

"Some would say readjustment," said Hilda.

"When?"

"Where?"

She smiled. "Near the seaside."

"Never heard of it."

"Not many have," said Hilda.

"Isn't it for healing?" muttered Voted In Four.

"Some would say," said Hilda.

"But out of action?"

"Well, yes, that too."

Hilda began to reverse with speed down the corridor, her cape flapping in front of her; she pushed it back with a small skid.

"Pack your things," she shouted.

The flying platform jolted to a halt at the entrance; Hilda clutched at the doorframe for balance. "Apart from your suits you won't be needing them."

"Suits—how can we be without suits?"

"We make decisions in suits."

"We are suits."

"I said you won't be needing them," shouted Hilda.

The Voted In looked at each other.

"Why, is it warm there?"

"Is it a holiday?"

Hilda let out a cackle, slapped her thigh with her whip, and turned to the footmen. "What you think, boys? A holiday?"

The footmen said nothing. They had been there, and it was nothing like the seaside.

Hilda reversed out the door. Once out of sight, she jumped off the flying platform, slid it under her arm, and took the stairs two at a time to her room. *So much quicker than any lift.*

Her *H-Pad has spotted something* wristwatch was beeping.

She raced into her room, tossed the flying platform to the side, and commanded, "View now."

Chapter Thirteen

CONNECTIONS

"Everyone knew that solar panels had had their day, but no one said anything. Instead, gyms were sprouting up everywhere."– Verruca's diary

While Beryl, Archie, and H2 were driving under the influence of a rebooted, refurbished H-Pad, the ol' fella was making plans. He had spent years incognito and now Mex was here; he had to act.

He knew Beryl like the inside of his wig, and she wouldn't be far behind.

The ol' fella revved up his moped and let his thoughts flow, hoping the loud hum of a 49cc moped would drown out his thoughts. He suspected he was being watched and his thoughts possibly read. Nothing surprised him with those women.

Halfway to Edinburgh, he stopped; the vibration of the moped were playing havoc with his arms. He pulled into a McDonald's, ordered a "flat white," and took a seat by the John. He took a sip, it was a gamble he knew, but McDonald's was noisy enough, especially during the cleaning time.

Hilda watched the ol' fella turn into a McDonald's, the H-Pad struggling to catch any thoughts. She slipped on the earphones as the ol' fella headed up to the counter; she had heard the Wi-Fi was strong at McDonald's. But so was the noise of the children, the hoover going full pelt, and the constant noise of the hand dryer each time someone left the john.

"Of all the seats," muttered Hilda.

She paraded about in her caped crusader outfit. *It was like he knew she was trying to read his mind. Was he that smart?*

She looked at herself in the mirror and flattened down her short hair. Light beamed onto her just-sixty face, highlighting what many would say was "great skin for her age." The only wrinkles she had were lines between her eyebrows, which at the moment were working overtime as she pondered.

"Why can I only hear useless noises?" she snapped. "As if I am interested in the parading from the john."

"Ma'am?"

"Alls I want to know is if he has the blasted spark plug."

"Ma'am, I am only as good as the connection," said the H-Pad.

"You said the Wi-Fi was strong?"

"That was the footman."

The footman coughed. "The Wi-Fi, ma'am, is only as good as the H-Pad's filters."

"Filters—what next? How can I run things if you keep interjecting?"

The H-Pad tried to explain about the ozone, the smog, the millions of mobiles, and satellites.

"Filtering is not an easy task for a lone H-Pad," said the H-Pad in a flat tone.

The footman stared ahead.

Hilda, exasperated, took in a deep breath, then spied the manual. "We'll see about that," she muttered.

She slid the earphones off, tossed them at the footman, and picked up the manual. The pages multiplied as she opened it; it got so heavy she had to lay it on the ground.

The footman, lifting the earphones from the floor, looked up. "Perhaps ma'am could give the ol' fella a rest."

"Wait until the McDonald's event is over," said the H-Pad.

"Maybe I'll try Archie," said Hilda, ignoring the sharp intake of breath from the footman.

DBO and the footman were listening in.

DBO looked at the footman. The footman looked back. "Would ma'am like to celebrate with a foot massage?"

Archie was pleased with himself. He had saved the day with his thinking on his feet. Not that either of the women from *who knows where* appreciated it.

Patsy, the neighbor, wanted to know why a gran dressed as a porn star was "burglarizing" (as she put it) her "best pal's house and traumatizing Izzie in the bargain."

Beryl was speechless; she was more interested in keeping the dog than saving her skin. And it was he who came up with the "school friend from the past playing a prank" story.

Even H2 looked convinced.

Archie was a first-generation Identity who told stories like no other. In the old days, finding an audience was never a problem; the audience found the storyteller. People were hungry for stories, easily captivated, and could concentrate for at least half an hour. But now, thanks to iPads, satellite TV, Kindles, mobile phones, and all the other boredom-soakers, finding an audience was like finding a worm in a henhouse, and captivating them was like trying to hold the said worm.

Luckily, Patsy was a mature woman with a vivid imagination and a fondness for listening.

Archie was an Identity of the old school. He, thanks to noisy nightly visits and a decent amount of birthday cards, fervently believed in Legless. He, like most first-generation Identities, was brought up by a single mother regularly visited by Legless at night. His childhood memories were a mixed bag.

His early years saw a happy mother. At night he would wake to hear footsteps on the stairs, laughter, followed by "Oh, Legless" sighing. Then, in the morning, his mother with a glow would make her wonderful son a "full English" along with an extra pound for school dinner and a Snickers bar. Every birthday came a card signed Legless, always with a piece of cryptic reading. As he grew older, the advice developed into ramblings which both he and his mother read over several times in search of *the point*.

Archie, like many Identities, had never met Legless but understood the power of this faceless man. His mother had told him not only the "hanging out the washing" story but also stories of another planet run by women.

"Not like me of course," she said, "but more a Maggie Thatcher type. Women to be feared, who doubled-crossed as quickly as changing their knickers. The worst being some *Beryl lady* with a beehive who had no idea what "slap and tickle" meant, let alone "a little of what you fancy does you good.""

At the time, Archie thought his mother had been heavy-handed with the Prozac.

Over the years, Legless visits dwindled until finally one day they stopped. Archie by then was a man of eighteen, with a good understanding of his Legless legacy. He could not only cheer his mother up but read her thoughts. Unlike his mother, who couldn't read body language, let alone moods. She took to Prosecco and shouting "That bastard" down the phone to other women who Legless had also stopped seeing.

They became the Legless widows, or *victims*.

Archie from an early age could read the thoughts of unhappy women. It seemed to him that there was a mountain of women like his mother. And he had a burning desire to help.

And it wasn't long before Archie along with other Identities began to organise "dos" for unhappy women. Finally, after one too many, "that bastard" phone calls from his mother Archie brought a fellow Identity to his mother's home on the pretext of fixing the telly.

Not only was the telly fixed, but Archie's mother was given a good eye-contact connection.

"Fancy a bit of slap and tickle?" said the telly man. And soon she was attending "dos" and learning to enjoy the memory of Legless like many other women.

However, reading an Identity's mind when you are not an Identity is like trying to read underwater. Identities were not only excellent mind blockers, but fantastic at mind fudging[1]—the ability to multitask thoughts. And it was Archie who developed the said talent.

He developed, mastered, and taught mind fudging. Which meant reading his mind was like trying to read a map of the London Underground while listening to the ramblings of Beryl high on tablet and several espressos.

And Hilda had never seen an Underground map in her life.

------

1. *Is the only defense for mind reading. It involves not thinking about what you want to think about but rather creating a thought decoy.*

Chapter Fourteen

MISCONNECTIONS

"A blow-up is not the same as a blow-down but still makes the same mess."–H-Pad

It was not long before Hilda was swearing every pickle under the sun and repeating them. It seemed that reading a manual was not as easy as she thought and reading a mind was not as easy as the manual stated, let alone someone like Archie.

"This instruction manual is a load of old gherkin," said Hilda. "It talks of connecting like it is as easy as slipping on an earpiece."

"Ma'am, it also says in the manual—depending on the weather, hills, and clarity of thought," said the H-Pad. "And clarity is the last thing you are going to get with an Identity, you may as well zone in on a gaggle of geese."

"Geese?" said Hilda and the footman together.

"Trying to connect with an Identity will cause a blow-up."

"What the pickled egg is that?"

"Similar to a blow-out but less messy," said the H-Pad.

Hilda tossed the instruction manual at the footman, which was not an easy feat, considering how heavy it was.

"Tossing, ma'am, is not recommended for equipment . . ."

"Tossing? This thing should be torpedoed out the window, which is what I intend to do right now."

A threat Hilda immediately regretted, but with a footman watching and the H-Pad answering back an "If one must," she had to carry on.

Hilda grimaced; now she had to open that pickle-forsaken window, which required the strength of an elephant while tossing against a tornado of a wind.

After the third attempt ending in the manual flapping like a seagull, Hilda gave up and slumped into her "great for your lower back" chair. A chair as comfortable as lower back pain and pretty good at causing it.

Hilda shifted uncomfortably.

"There has been talk of motorizing windows," said the H-Pad.

"What would you know," said Hilda, rubbing her back. She had forgotten how uncomfortable the chair was, and why she had commissioned the inventing of it. It was designed to keep sitting workers awake and came with a leaflet called "Pain is Healing at Work." The chair wasn't exactly a hit and sparked a frenzy of leaflet tossing, despite windows not being motorized. Now it was used for interviewing, one of Hilda's favorite pastimes.

Hilda stood up and began to pace the floor while swinging her earphones in her hand, the only thing they were good for.

"Mex is an expert blocker."

"Ma'am, it is a given," said the H-Pad.

She sighed. She had tried to read Woody's mind and got a series of Terry Pratchett readings. And as for Bunnie's mind, that was all over the place, one minute looking at men's groins, the next thinking about food, or jokes—that woman had more jokes in her head than the Voted In had cushions.

She went back to the screen. "What have you got visually, H-Pad?"

"Woody's Nokia," said the H-Pad.

"Nokia?"

"A phone, ma'am, but not as we know it."

Hilda looked questionably at the H-Pad.

"It's as open as a three-day-old sandwich, clear view—even in his pocket."

"Excellent," said Hilda.

"Excellent," said the footman, heading out for more sparkly.

Don drove the people carrier under a series of mutters. He had planned a fun trip with blankets and AC/DC music, and now it was all ruined.

Bunnie looked across at her man of the hour with concern. "Something wrong?"

"Wrong? My car has a dent the size of an elephant's arse. And now my so-called pal is moaning about insurance not covering old ladies in car parks . . . you entered at your own risk," Don huffed. "And my piles are playing up."

Bunnie rolled her eyes.

"Piles," muttered Hilda, "what the gherkin is that?"

"Grape-like growth, ma'am," said the H-Pad, "reputed to forecast the weather."

"Growth?"

"Yes, usually on one's butt, ma'am,"

Hilda, without even thinking, clenched hers.

Mex stared out onto the motorway. The spark plug jokes had cut her to the core.

"I used to slay," she muttered.

"The slaying was more a story for the masses," muttered Pete.

"Great giants too," said Mex.

"The slaying of giants was more a rounding up of tall men," said Pete.

Bunnie turned to Mex. "To be honest, I can't imagine you slaying a mosquito, let alone tall men."

"You know nothing about me," muttered Mex. "I was a hero—I saved the planet."

"Not everyone would agree with that," said Don.

Woody looked at the back of Don's head and began to feel a sense of his thoughts—like when he was with the Identities in Glasgow.

Don's mind was in turmoil and it had little to do with car insurance.

When Don first met Mex in the rain, he was embroiled in the ways of man. He was an Identity who lived two lives.

Years ago, before there were many second-generation Identities, Don had met Bunnie and allowed feelings for her to grow. Archie warned him against such feelings and they had words.

"The way of an Identity is different to an ordinary man," said Archie.

Don laughed at him, just as he laughed when Archie retold Legless stories.

Especially the ones about women from Planet Hy Man with thighs that could crush a walnut.

He encouraged others to question. He talked of pubs, casinos, and other places a cabby took people in the middle of the night—cheesing Archie right off.

"We don't need that," said Archie. "We have our stories, dancing, we make women happy—is that not enough for you?"

The Identities began to argue, many, like Don, having become more man than Identity. And Archie blamed Don.

Now it seemed that that damnable Archie was right and he, Don, would have to eat his words. He was driving part of the legend about, the legend he had laughed at, and now there in front of him was she who captured men like Legless.

And quite frankly, she was a disappointment.

It had taken a while for it to sink in who Mex really was. It was clear she had no idea about sex, an intense dislike for men, plus a taste in clothing not from Earth. But she did have thighs that looked like they could crush more than a walnut.

He shifted uncomfortably in his seat. And now someone was rummaging in his head.

He looked in the revision mirror to see Woody staring at him. It had to be Woody, DJ was too wrapped up in Beryl.

He decided to stop for a smoke.

Chapter Fifteen

DISCOVERY

"Spying is but a fickle game."–An ex man spy

oody followed Don they stood together and talked with their thoughts.

Don began to relax into the flow of ESP conversation. It wasn't so bad; in fact, it felt comfortable, and Don was just about to ESP DJ to join when Woody felt a rumbling in his pocket.

He pulled out his Nokia and stared into the unrecognizable face of DBO.

Hilda threw aside the earphones and the manual. She felt an exasperation she hadn't felt since living in the complex.

Who is interfering with Woody's Nokia?

She headed into her room, stripped off her cape, and tossed it on the bed in disgust.

"Beryl's on the move, ma'am," said the H-Pad. "The tablet is wearing off."

"And is someone going to block that connection too?" snapped Hilda.

"Ma'am, spying is but a fickle game."

"Tell me about it," muttered Hilda.

"But you have averted a crisis."

Well, that's true, thought Hilda.

She heard the shuffle of her footman followed by a grunt.

"You got the Voted In moving," said the H-Pad.

"True too," said Hilda. She looked up from her bed and caught a glimpse of the footman picking up the manual.

"The cleaners prepped," said the H-Pad.

"Totally," muttered Hilda, watching the footman open the manual and begin to read. She let out a "what are you doing" cough. The footman started, caught Hilda's eye, and fumbled with the manual.

"Thank you, H-Pad," said Hilda, entering the room.

The footman tentatively placed the manual back on the bench.

"Ma'am," said the H-Pad, "the Operators are getting fidgety . . ."

Hilda stopped in her "about to reprimand" tracks. "The Operators?" Why didn't she think of them before?

She snatched the earphones and the manual and, with surprising strength, thrust them into the footman's arms. She had an idea, and she was annoyed at herself for taking so long to think of such an idea. What was she playing at? She may not be a master of technology, but she was a genius at spotting others who were.

"Follow me," she told the footman.

"But ma'am, I am but five minutes from sleep time . . ."

Hilda looked at him. "Sleep time? Don't think so. I need to find the blocker. And I need something better than that pickle-forsaken manual and earphones . . ." She wrapped her cape around her. "And the last thing I need is you spreading *that* about like hemp effluent."

Hilda, after a quick pose in the mirror, picked up the H-Pad and pushed the footman in front of her. "You're both to come."

"What have I done?" muttered the H-Pad.

"It's what you can't do," said Hilda, "and I know a place where you can."

She headed for the basement, the place no one went (apart from Beryl).

❄

Hilda marched through the kitchen, waved to the security cameras—as she now controlled them—then pinched one of Lidia's dairy-free, lead-like-cheese scones.

She didn't necessarily need to go to the kitchen, but Hilda felt it her duty as the de facto dictator to be seen effortlessly ruling—something she had learnt from a younger Beryl. It took a bit of getting used to, as Hilda had spent her whole life ducking and diving; flagrantly marching about the place with not a bribe in sight took practise. Besides, she had promoted Lidia to head chef and demoted the chef to veg and herb duties, a sort of divide-and-conquer experiment, and she had heard rumors about scones you could build a wall with.

Lidia slapped the footman's hand as he copied Hilda.

The footman rubbed his hand as Hilda took a bite and pulled a face.

"Where's that old yin?" shouted Lidia.

The other cook pointed to the doorway where a sorry-looking elderly woman was plucking thin whispers of hairs from herb leaves for a stew.

"What's she doing that for?" said Lidia.

"You should know," said the other cook. "That used to be your position."

"Oh, so it did," smirked Lidia.

"Enjoy your scone, ma'am?" said Lidia with a "comrade to comrade" stance.

The kitchen fell silent. The older woman looked up from the doorway; no one dared ask Hilda if she liked a scone. The trick was to look busy and hope.

"Another scone like that and you'll be back to plucking hairs," Hilda snapped and was about to say more when she heard a twinkle in the wind, coming from the back door.

Was that a wind chime?

"A mere wind chime, ma'am," said Lidia, "We love 'em, don't we girls?"

Hilda held up her hand to silence, she stared out onto the grounds. *What a fool she had been . . .*

Fenced from the public the grounds were designed to camouflage the shed at the other end. Years ago, when Beryl was still a voted in and trying to impress she designed the grounds-inspired by Zen (all the rage back then) using rocks, sand and wind chimes.

The wind chimes hadn't chimed since Hilda left the shed. She had cemented them together with an experimental tofu which, when cooled, had the consistancy of concrete. The last thing Operators needed as far as Hilda was concerned was peace and tranquillity.

Now they were chiming again?

Hilda looked at the shed.

The blocker of course . . .

She turned to the ex-chef, now on her fifth bucket of herb plucking. "How are you with egg sandwiches?"

"Egg?"

"Pseudo egg."

"Oh, that. Very doable, I pride myself in my egg sandwiches, there is not a corner uncovered in my batch, not a—"

Hilda with a "that's enough" gesture muttered a "Good, I know a footman . . ." The ex-chef looked at the footman. ". . . another footman, who could do with a little persuasion."

"Just say the word, ma'am."

"I do a mean salmon if called for—soya is putty in my hands," shouted Lidia with a hopeful smile.

Hilda, with a comrade look at the old woman, said "Salmon is not called for. He is but an egg man."

Chapter Sixteen

THE FACE READER

"Why the beetroot did Beryl fall for him? Sure, he was short, looked good in Lycra, and had a sort of something, but then so had many."—A Voted In no longer employed

Hilda thrust the H-Pad into the footman's hands who, balancing the manual while trying to keep awake, staggered, regained his balance, then regained his leaning pose until told otherwise.

Then she told the H-Pad to make sure he did remain in said leaning pose.

Hilda entered the basement and, like Beryl, walked past the *buggered equipment* shelf, the *you're having a laugh* equipment display, and the *when men ruined the planet* sections. She entered the recycling area, scouring through the same shelves of obsolete phones and cameras that Beryl looked at.

In fact, Hilda was sure she could detect a slight whiff of Beryl's hairspray.

She smiled. All those years in the shed, what a bonus; it had given her the edge over Beryl. She knew those Operators like the inside of her onesie. Hilda, like Beryl, knew not only what they could do but how to make them do it. Hilda, however, also knew what women thought they could not do, and she had ways of making them do it anyway. A talent way beyond Beryl's understanding.

And she knew the Operators could make a caffeine mug, talk if pushed.

Finally, she came to what she was looking for: the C-Pad shelf.

Hilda knew the frustrated industrialist who had designed the C-Pad, which preceded the H-Pad. He had, in a last-ditch attempt to control women, invented the face reader with amazing "just in case" attachments. And there it was behind several out-of-date debunked C-Pads.

Hilda picked up at the face reader (plus applicator attachment)—a failure from the start.

The face reading applicator was hailed as the new security—better than fingerprints, way better than handwriting, and ten times better than voice reading. It was used on limos, door entrances, and for signing documents. It was devised at the time when women were becoming more than breeding machines, educating themselves and moving up in the world. Some say the face reader was designed to put them off, because it required staring into a small screen and snorting.

Men were comfortable with snorting; some even relished it, and most did not care that the camera magnified the face to show every open pore. Women, however, did. And when magnified images were obtained by the then-male-run media, all hell broke loose.

In the end, the frustrated industrialist lost his funding and his lab, and he went from a famed designer to a footman manning the room with a view—observing some his designs being used to work against men.

Hilda looked at the face reader. It read and interpreted expressions particular to that person—not a stone's throw from mind reading. Perhaps with a bit of tweaking—and a connection on the H-Pad?

She turned it about in her hand. It was big, flat, and bulky, with one of the industrialist's famous attachments for further inventions on it. Hilda dropped the face reader into her extra-large pocket in her cape, making it lopsided.

She smiled to herself—Beryl bragged about her out-of-the-box thinking. *Well, suck on this, sister.*

She laughed a maniac laugh, which thankfully no one heard, and headed to the room with a view.

Chapter Seventeen

THE ROOM WITH A VIEW

"A room with a view is worth two in a basement."—Operator One

Hilda burst into the room with a view on her flying platform. "Stop what you're doing," she shouted.

The Operators looked up.

They weren't doing anything apart from wondering what they were supposed to be doing. Once Hilda had installed the Operators in the room with the view with her infamous platform-descending meeting (now out of action for servicing), they had heard nothing.

The Operators had spent nights in the room with a view in a state of suspended confusion, wondering.

Apart from the third in command, who, having discovered the voice-operated curtains, was still having a ball.

The flying platform filled the room with a low hum as Hilda entered the room. The Operators stared; they had never seen Hilda's Darth Vader entrance on a flying platform before.

"It's time you did what you're paid to do," said Hilda.

The Operators looked from one to the other . . .

"Paid?"

"Who gets paid?"

"We're getting paid?"

"In a manner of speaking," said Hilda, hovering, which she had now got down to a T.

"Was that a yes or a no?" muttered an Operator.

"No idea," whispered another.

"Shhh . . ."

"Now that Beryl has left the building," quipped Hilda (a quip being the closest Hilda got to a joke), "We need to take the H-Pad to the next level."

Hilda mastered a twirl, pulled the face reader from her cap, and thrust it on the table.

"A prototype," she shouted, demanding tweaking "and more."

The Operators looked at her with a *she who must be mad* look. Hilda's idea of "tweaking" was anything but tweaking—"reinventing," "starting from scratch," or "a complete overhaul" was more what she meant.

Hilda reversed around the table, eyeing each face. No one looked at her but rather focused on the "face reader" in the center of the polished table.

Hilda, after a small skid, nodded at her personal footman, or PF as she had taken to calling him. He jolted awake and put the H-Pad beside the face reader.

"I am giving you seventy-two hours," she said, reversing an exit.

The Operator watched as Hilda attempted to reverse through the door.

PF fumbled to help.

"Little to the left, ma'am."

"Not quite so sharp, ma'am."

"Here, let me help, ma'am."

Which was followed by a slap, a scrap, a slamming of the door, followed by a "for pickle's sake."

The Operators pushed so-called prototypes about the table.

"Getting pictures from Earth was one thing," said the first in command, "but ESP-ing through equipment"—she sighed—"even in the shed would be a mission impossible."

The second in command turned the H-Pad in her hands. "There's nowhere for the attachment."

"You only have to ask," said the H-Pad.

The others looked at the face reader; it was anything but sleek, and as for the attachment, it was as out-of-date as a footman's uniform. She tugged at the old-fashioned "stickies" on the back to hang it on a wall. *As useful as Beryl's face cream.*

"It is doable," muttered the secretary.

The first in command looked at her. "You haven't spoken in years and now you're telling us the impossible is doable?"

"We're smart, and there's what, five of us?"

"Five?" said the first in command.

"If you include the third in command," said the secretary.

The first, second, and fourth in command looked at the third in command, who, having spent most of her time commanding the curtains to open and shut, was now pushing them open in the hope that no one would know they were broken.

She stopped.

"I make good coffee."

"And we have the footmen," said the secretary.

"What?"

The door footman coughed. "Ma'am, our back massages are at your disposal."

The first, second and fourth command looked at each other with a "what's a back massage got to do with it" gesture.

"Blood to the brain, that's what that does," said the third in command with a final tug at a curtain.

"Don't forget me," said the H-Pad.

That night the Operators worked as a team. Spurred on by Brazilian coffee, luxury whipped soya cream, and hemp biscuits, which thanks to the third in command was "pilfered" from somewhere, the Operators tweaked like their life depended on it (which it probably did).

They excelled themselves.

Turned out that the third in command, who no one thought had any talents apart from breaking robotic curtains, had pilfering (as opposed to stealing) down to a fine art. And not only could she pilfer like there was no tomorrow, but she was damn good at sneaking into locked rooms, opening drawers, and putting everything back the way she found it.

The Operators worked into the night, and when their hope faded, the footmen back-rubbed along with a "come on you can do it" mutter.

At first the Operators tested the prototype H-Pad on each other. Which caused nonproductive conversations such as . . .

"That's not what I was thinking."

"So, if that's what you think, you can stuff it."

And . . .

"If my hair's a bird's nest, yours is a cow pat."

The H-Pad almost ended up smashed against a wall until the secretary suggested they try the H-Pad on the footmen.

The first in command laughed, the second poked fun. The footmen were half asleep, exhausted from massaging. "Their heads will be as empty as our wage packets," muttered the second in command.

"Exactly," muttered the third with an arm full of matching cushions pilfered from who knows where.

You've taken the whole pilfering thing too far, thought the secretary.

You think? thought the third in command with a glare.

A footman intervened and grabbed the almost finished prototype. "Knock yourselves out, ma'am, I am off to sleep."

Hilda, disregarding her seventy-two hours threat, arrived the next day (surprising no one). Ignoring any "there are a few things to be ironed out" comments, she grabbed the H-Pad, called it the H-Pad 11, headed back to her room, and tossed off her cape.

If her timing was right (which it always was), then she was in for the show of a lifetime.

The secretary watched Hilda leave with a sense of smugness. As her job description stated, she had made copies of the template and hid them—just in case.

Chapter Eighteen

THE MOVE

"The size of an earphone has nothing to do with volume."–DBO

The Voted In stood, mute, in the corridor. It had been years since the Voted In had ventured south of the upper level. In fact, it had been so long they had nothing to wear, and no idea where the bags were. They had been told they had a day and to wear their earphones.

"The big clear-out commences at sunset," said Hilda. "A day to pack is more than generous."

Which was seriously a joke . . .

Hilda could have given them a week and it wouldn't have been long enough, the Voted In had no idea how to pack. And as for the art of finding, folding, and knowing what to leave behind, they hadn't a clue; the only thing they knew how to do was make coffee.

The Voted In stared at each other. Hilda had turned liked soya cream in the sun; had she not been one of them? Where they not comrades?

"One day," muttered a voice from the back, "it will take us that long to find the earphones, let alone unravel them."

The Voted In started to rustle through their cupboards with a sense of panic. Who would help them? The robots had been relocated, while the footmen had begun preparing for the *"big clear-out."* Which involved shuffling like half-asleep sloths from room to room airing things.

"Will we need this?" said one Voted In, thrusting a ten-geared, super hygienic, automatic foot massager in a footman's face.

"Will it be hot? Will we need creams?" said another.

"What about my coffee mug?" shouted another.

Finally, Baby (called Baby because she, unlike many, had not reached the wrinkled stage) burst into tears. "What about Woody? Will we still be able to watch him?"

Senator one of the Voted In turned to console, an action unfamiliar for the Voted In. The others stopped in their tracks and gasped as she gingerly patted the arm of her comrade.

Touching? Had things got that bad?

"We could take the H-Pad." Senator glanced hopefully at the footman.

He coughed and shook his head. "Regulation ninety-six zero zero zero, ma'am, H-Pads must remain in designated areas."

He looked at her with a blank face. "Passed by yourselves."

"Oh . . ."

"Or maybe there is one there?" said Baby.

The footmen shuffled uncomfortably.

"What would Vegas do?" shouted a voice from the back.

No one answered, as it was accepted by many that Vegas was now Hilda's personal puppet.

Finally, the Voted In found their earphones and slid them in. Elevator music filtered through, interrupted by an automatic voice: "Please make your way to the exit in a march-like fashion."

"It is time, ma'am," said a footman.

"When in doubt, queue," muttered a voice from the back.

"Yes, that makes sense," said Baby.

"Come on girls, look lively," said Senator.

Downcast, the Voted In ambled to the elevator and queued.

"Open!" said Senator.

A footman coughed. "Ma'am, the elevator is out of action—budget cuts."

"Oh?"

He looked at her with a blank face. "One of your amendments."

"Then what are we to do—fly, jump, use the stairs?" snapped a voice from the back.

"Stairs," came the voice from the earpiece.

"Stairs?"

"Only robots and footmen use the stairs."

"One has been told to march down them," muttered another footman.

"Stairs? Marching? What next? Parading?"

"Parading is no longer legal," said a footman.

The Voted In walked through the door and huddled at the top of the stairs. It was a small platform, making it impossible not to touch. They looked back for one last glimpse of their home, their footmen.

A footman stretched out his hand with a sock.

"Ma'am, don't forget . . ." And the door snapped shut, cutting off the sock from the hand and the soothing elevator music.

They silently watched the sock plop to the ground as the noise of the wind whirled up the stairs. It would take them hours to reach the lower level.

The lower level was the bottom of the Building of Opulence. It was full of ambitious young women working their way up, women like the Voted In were decades ago.

Finally, they arrived at the lower level door, puffed and sweaty.

Senator pushed the door open. The Voted In shuffled onto the floor and huddled together as cool air blasted onto their faces and through their silk shirts. The change took their breath away; it was nothing like the perfumed, windless, temperate atmosphere they were used to.

The passage was full of young women walking while speaking into earphones, and as the door jolted shut with a loud thud, the younger women stopped. No one had seen the Voted In for years, except on screens when a new amendment had been passed. They stared at the flat-faced older women dressed in the finest silk black suits with uniform short back and sides. They all looked the same and so ordinary—much smaller than on-screen.

"I want Woody," muttered Baby.

"Hello," said Senator. She stretched out her hand to a young woman; a few of the Voted In gasped.

The younger woman blinked, confused; the Voted In were known for their extreme off-handedness.

Senator walked forward knocking a water cooler. Water spilled out onto the floor. A united gasp filled the corridor as Senator tried to straighten the cooler. She skidded and grabbed onto the cooler, sending it tumbling to the floor. She balanced herself looked about with a weak smile then attempted to pick the water cooler up.

Some, embarrassed, looked away as she groaned at the weight.

"Let me," said the younger woman.

Senator let out another grunt as the voice from the earpiece told her to "leave it and make for the door."

"Best do as she says," said the young woman, gesturing to the exit.

"Yes, best," muttered a few of the Voted In.

Soon they squinted into the natural light at the top of the entrance stairs, staring down at a flock of reporters in front of them.

"Is it true the seaside is up and running?"

"The stationaries—are they being oiled?"

"What about new amendments—are there any?"

Deirdre, the top reporter who spoke in an annoyingly urgent voice, was at the head of the pack. She turned everything into a drama; even the unveiling of a new statue at the courtyard of greatness was reported like a hurricane was about to arrive. She shoved an H-Pad into Baby's face. "Will you be wearing Lycra on the stationaries?"

Baby stuttered. "Lycra?"

The voice from the back was about to tell Deirdre what she thought of Lycra when a fanfare blasted through the air, followed by the appearance of the announcement robot. A seven-foot-seven gleaming machine with an eagle-like face and American footballer-type figure. It towered over the woman.

"Hear ye, hear ye: the Voted In are on the move, please let them pass, no interviews required."

The Voted In shuffled with embarrassment. They were hoping for a more dignified exit, or at least an incognito one.

"Continue in a march-like fashion," said the voice from the earphones. "Through the market."

"The market?" muttered the voice from the back. "They'll have us for breakfast."

Chapter Nineteen

THE MARKET

"Never underestimate a cleaner."–Cleaner One

The Voted In had spent a lifetime stamping approval on amendments with no thought of the results. And the market, so they had heard, was one of the results of careless stamping. It was a place the Voted In had looked at from on high, a place talked about by many, and now filled the Voted In with dread; apparently it was full of mechanical monster rats and loud, Earthy women selling things and not taking no for an answer.

Opposite the market hidden behind a hedge was the courtyard of greatness: a courtyard with statues of past leaders and the odd great hero. Beryl's was covered up and Hilda's was in the making, while any male statues had been moved to the dark corners with "no flower" scrawled across the bottom. To enter required a couple of hemp biscuits for the footmen at the entrance. The Voted In hadn't been for years due to the inability to visit incognito along with the possibility of rubbing shoulders with the workers or said monster rats.

They looked longingly at the footmen dozing at the courtyard entrance.

"If only," muttered Baby.

"Come on, girls, best foot forward," said Senator.

The marketplace was full of women, all colors and shapes with just a whiff of cooking. Their skin was sun bleached with laughter lines and their hands as wrinkled as a bulldog's face, despite being much younger; even their hair was different lengths, and colors. The Voted In walked past stalls jam-packed with unrecognizable objects. Nothing matched, everything was botched together. And it was so crowded that touching was inevitable and, it seemed, often welcomed. The streets were clean, covered in murals, painted-over broken sheds, and misshaped stalls, and there wasn't a rat in sight.

The Voted In's pale skin and silk outfits stood out like a stuffed pig in a vegan restaurant, and yet no one noticed—they carried on selling.

The gym was below the Building of Opulence. Which required walking through the market to get to the tunnel entrance and then walking through the tunnel back under the market. It was all designed to confuse and distract, to put off any thought of leaving, resigning, or "taking a break."

The Voted In had walked their shoes off, which in truth were only suitable for sitting in a limo.

The Voted In lived in luxury; the air circulated at a temperature perfect for wandering around in PJs, keeping skin smooth. The tunnel was not so kind; it was dark and hot, with no windows, just ceiling fans circulating muggy air that smelt like a used jockstrap. As they stumbled through the tunnel, the Voted In had a sense of what was to come. They were beginning to realize that packing their silk PJs had been a waste of time.

Basking in her amazingness, Hilda watched the Voted In enter the gym. She, lounging on her bed in her onesie, enjoyed the cool scented air. She took a sip of her sparkly and turned the volume up on her earpiece . . .

Soon she would make promises to the Voted In to entice them to do their best.

"Seaside," she yelled at the PF, "is it ready yet?"

"Ma'am, waiting on the last polish."

Hilda smiled. *This will do the trick, keep things at bay at least till Vegas is back with the formula . . . come to think of it, where is Vegas?*

Hilda flicked through her log; it had been ages since she had heard from her.

Chapter Twenty

THE CLEANERS

"The end of the beginning is not the beginning of the end."– Manifesto the Great, Planet Hy Man's National Geographic, last edition

The gym had been empty since the last man climbed off his stationary and donned the footman uniform. For years the doors had been locked, the stationaries dormant, collecting dust and robotic mice. Hilda had sent in the "squat team," robots of all shapes and sizes who cleaned with a robust intensity (which the Voted In had never seen before).

They were busy oiling when the Voted In arrived.

Beside the robots were a couple of cleaners with a solidarity also unseen by the Voted In. Cleaner One was in the middle of scrapping a smashed robotic mouse into a dust brush when Senator staggered in; by now marching was too sore on her feet. Cleaner One looked up, eyed Senator, then turned to Cleaner Two.

"A few new chains and we're good to go."

Cleaner Two nodded.

Cleaner One gestured towards the stationary bikes with an eye towards Senator. "You ridden one of these before?"

"No," said Senator with a stiff smile.

The cleaner sniffed, dumped the broken mouse into a bucket, and surveyed Senator like she was the next mechanical rat to be squashed. "Thought as much."

Baby, fast on the heels of Senator, stared at the row of stationary bikes. "What are they, anyway?"

Cleaner One threw her a look. "Thought as much about that too!"

"What do you mean?" Baby muttered.

Cleaner One walked up to Baby and stood an inch from her nose; Baby got a whiff of soap—hemp, the cheap, scratchy kind. A lump formed in her throat.

Cleaner One fingered Baby's collar. "Silk, huh?"

Baby swallowed the lump and nodded.

"The finest, I expect."

"Well it . . . it's up there, not the finest of fine but . . ."

"Well, you won't get far wearing that *gherkin* trash here."

The other Voted Ins stumbled into the basement. "What I'd give for some caffeine," muttered one.

(Voted Ins didn't operate without at least three in the morning.)

"You can't run a stationary on caffeine *or* sugar," said Cleaner One. "You need pork lard."

"What in the beetroot is pork lard?"

"Hemp lard that tastes like pork," said Cleaner Two, looking up from the wheel of a stationary.

"Pork?"

"It's a man thing," said Cleaner Two, straightening up.

"A day on a stationary and you'll soon be screaming for it," said Cleaner One.

She handed an instructions manual to Senator—"Read it and weep."—then turned to Baby—"Oh, and here's a hint: you sit on it."

"What?"

"Make like a Voted In and sit!"

"I am not sitting on that," said a Voted In.

"According to she who must be obeyed, you'll be sitting on it all day with standard tea breaks," shouted Cleaner One from the door.

"Tea—who drinks that stuff?"

"When I say tea I use the term loosely," said Cleaner One.

"No more Woody," muttered Baby.

"Will you shut it with the Woody," snapped the voice from the back.

Cleaner Two followed Cleaner One to the door carting a brush, a bucket with a catlike robot in it, and another catlike robot under her arm. "Here, help us with this will you," she said.

"Helping is not my job," said Cleaner One, filling the doorway with a hands-on-hips stance. Cleaner Two rolled her eyes and tutted.

"Cleaners do more than clean; we restore, recycle, and boss robots. You should get the robots to take that stuff."

A few of the larger robots shifted uncomfortably. One grabbed a bucket, another tugged it off him, a third got in on the tugging as the bucket clattered to the floor; water, suds and a broken mouse spilled out. Cleaner Two, with a glare at her comrade, began to tidy up.

Senator tried to open the manual but it weighed a ton, she staggered under the weight of it and dropped it on the ground.

"Here here, you can't treat manuals like that, that's the property of the Voted In—they'll charge you," snapped Cleaner One.

"We are the Voted In."

Cleaner Two stopped in her tracks. "What?"

"The Voted In—that is us."

"You sure you're the Voted In?" said Cleaner One.

"What sort of question is that?"

"It just that I thought you'd be more . . ."

"Concise?" said Cleaner Two, slapping the hand of a robot attempting to help with the bucket.

"Neater," said Cleaner One.

"We have just walked through some pickle-forsaken tunnel you know," said a Voted In. "And we have been told nothing, zero, zilch, not a pickled egg of a thing."

"Instructions soon, please wait, you are third in a queue, please wait," said the voice from the earpiece.

"That explains the silk," muttered Cleaner Two.

Cleaner One sucked in her breath. "No one told me it was you lot coming, there's regulations and things." She turned to Cleaner Two. "Isn't there?"

Without waiting for an answer, Cleaner One launched into a tirade of "inefficiency speech" that had been bottled up for years—instigating a long-suffering look and eyebrow raising from Cleaner Two.

"What you have," said Cleaner One, taking a sermon-on-the-mount stance, "is the city on one hand, the suburbs on the other, and hemp farms up the sewer—they all have a purpose. And your . . ." Cleaner Two thrust an accusing finger at the Voted In. ". . . pickled egg regulations balls it up; where we need to communicate, you put in rules. Delivering must be done at dawn via dusty roads, which you refused to pay due to "organic regulation." Hemp is passed to the marketers who need a license before selling "to protect us" the buyer. *From what I ask you?* Which you can't get cause the office is always closed. Who then sells to footman who are too old to carry things, so robots—under the instruction of cooks—take them, but then they get their wires crossed/blow a gasket cause they're doing things "out with their remit."

Cleaner Two let out a sigh.

"Ma'am?" said a robot.

"And we have to sort things, and there is no budget for overtime."

The Voted In began to shuffle. They were lost at the hemp farms.

"Now you're here and you can't even hold a manual properly," she tutted. "This planet is as mashed as a hemp pad."

"We were told about the stationary," muttered the voice from the back.

"And the seaside," said Baby.

"Seaside? Oh that, everyone is promised that."

"Seaside," muttered the robot rubbing his hand, "is but a mere mirage."

Senator fumbled with the manual. "It doesn't say anything about a mirage in here."

Cleaner Two pulled a leaflet from her back pocket and handed it to Baby. "Here, this is far better, tells you all you need to know, including oiling."

"Oiling?" muttered Baby.

"That's right, if you don't get the oiling right the whole thing will seize."

"Seize?"

"Told you . . . told you," muttered Cleaner One, as Cleaner Two steered her out of the gym.

"It's pretty straightforward," Cleaner Two said over her shoulder.

"For a robot," yelled Cleaner One.

"What's seizing?" said Baby.

Nobody answered.

Chapter Twenty-One

THE MAP

"Never had so many suffered for so few and never had so few had so many leaflets."–Deidre

In the early hours of the morning, DBO slipped out to Verruca's kitchen. She was running out of food and info.

From the moment she heard Hilda had shut down the shed, she knew she had to do something, and as time went on she was getting better at knowing what that something was.

DBO had learned many things from sneaking around Verruca's kitchen, even whispers of the library. It was amazing what Verruca stored in her fridge: slips of paper, maps, leaflets with the odd technology info. DBO had brains when it came to reworking instruments in the shed, but Verruca? She seemed to second-guess any issues DBO came across. Sometimes DBO wondered: was Verruca all she was made out to be?

Verruca, on the other hand, was pleased to see the back of her food. She was fed up with the soups for the infirm left by the robot, and completely fed up with Hilda's "so-called gift." A robot beyond any *tweaking* to improve, so old its serial number was in the single digits, and so old it had no idea what an H-Pad was.

Verruca would give anything to palm off the damn thing. The last thing she needed was a hopelessly clumsy robot poking its nose into her fridge, knocking things over, and pouring tea into her underpants.

After one of Hilda's many visits, she assigned a robot to "take care, keep the fridge full, and watch for anything untoward" . . . i.e., the missing Operator.

Hilda had come across the robot in the basement, and like all good ideas it hit her instantly. The robot was like something out of a fifties sci-fi; grey, rigidly tin-like, and, well, robotic.

Verruca would welcome it like a set of heated curlers, thought Hilda. Hilda switched on the robot; it rattled into an incognito pose.

"I have a mission for you," said Hilda. "A woman—she must be watched."

"Ma'am . . ."

"Her name," said Hilda, "is . . ."

"Name immaterial, ma'am."

"Gran."

"Immaterial, ma'am."

"I mean Verruca," said Hilda.

"Foot complaint, fungus issues, scabby skin? Try oils from the tea tree past the Black Hills . . ."

"No gran's name is Verruca," said Hilda.

"Code Grannie, now embedded."

"No," said Hilda, "the code is *watch at all costs.*" She looked at the time and sighed. "I'll connect you to my H-Pad."

"H-Pad, ma'am?"

"Yes, so we can communicate—what do you think I meant?"

"Think, ma'am? Doesn't compute."

"Communicate, we need to . . ."

"Watch and report—report and watch."

"Yes, *communicate.*"

"Watch and report—report and watch Grannie Verruca."

She sighed again. "It's Verruca, not . . ."

"Verruca growth on foot, oil from tea . . ."

"Look, just go in there."

"Trees from the black hill, slag heap . . ."

"Forget the oil."

"Oil forgotten, tossed, blanked but stored."

"Just keep an eye on Verruca's fridge . . ."

"Oil from tea . . ."

"And wait for further instructions."

"Grannie Verruca's fridge now under observations, ma'am."

Hilda watched the grey robot disappear into Verruca's home. She heard a squeal, a crash, and a "get out of it" slap.

It wasn't exactly how she planned, but not much will go in Verruca's fridge unnoticed now he/it was about.

DBO slipped into the kitchen, making sure to pull the wire door closed without a sound. She prised opened the fridge and spied a wrap full of hemp leaves and soya beans beside the pickled pseudo eggs. She made for a gentle pull. It was lodged hard against a slab of soya (date unknown) and a slimy robot mouse that had found its way in and never made it out.

Mother of beetroot . . .

She tugged again, this time harder—nothing happened.

She slid her fingers further into the fridge and when her fingers touched the cold Teflon of the mouse, she jumped. A bottle of soya milk (date unknown) crashed to the floor; she bent to pick it up at the same time the fridge door was closing.

Thump

Crash

Mother of beetroot!

Whatever was on the top of the fridge clattered to the floor via DBO's head.

"Mother of pickled egg!"

The light flicked on.

DBO, rubbing her head, turned to see Verruca glaring at her in curlers and a dressing gown.

"I was hungry," she was about to say, when Verruca gestured to her with a "shhh," pulled a rolled-up map against the said mouse, and handed it to her.

"Is this what you were looking for?"

"Actually, I was hungry."

"Shhh, I will say this only once," Verruca whispered.

"What?"

Verruca cupped her hand over DBO's mouth and whispered into her ear. "The library is the key"—she shoved the map into DBO's hands—"and with that thing, finding it will be a piece of beetroot."

"Piece of what?" said DBO with a confused look.

"Piece of beetroot—play on Earth's 'piece of piss,' ha ha ha . . ." said the robot.

"Oh, right," said DBO, looking about the kitchen.

"Thought you were asleep," snapped Verruca.

The robot appeared at the door: "Shut down, ma'am, not the same as asleep."

Verruca tutted.

"Must clean floor—remove mouse."

Verruca looked at DBO. "You don't want a robot, do you?"

Verruca was the last generation to have a real father. Verruca's father, like all fathers of that time, were part of the filtering scheme.

Romance had been given the big flick. Instead, pairing up was based on the talent gene.

After all, if Earth could breed a dog that rounds up sheep with a silent whistle, what could breeding do for those of the great Planet Hy Man?

Women with the right body produced babies; women with the wrong body were assigned to farming and cleaning duties. Men with brains were paired with strong everlasting women who had the *I will die of old age in my sleep* genes.

An idea some men saw as possibly flawed.

It was called *work in progress* by men and *a pickling stupid idea* by women.

Who wanted to procreate purely for offspring? Who wanted an offspring from an Amazonian man with no interest in making said procreating pleasant? And what would his offspring be like? A child with as much feeling as a Neolithic dad?

Men changed, procreation was seen as well, mere procreation: *sex on tap*, foreplay optional. And as for romance, it was as obsolete as a set of rollers for a bald man.

The women had to do something, or rather not do something, and soon *slap and tickle* became as easy to get as a decent burger.

Fanny, Verruca's mother, was a vital yet forgotten part of the movement. She started what others like Beryl finished. A grim, determined woman who never gave up, she joined—some say started—the fight with gusto.

While the smarter ones like Beryl watched, waited, and planned, Fanny let her passion get the better of her.

She scrawled "no procreation on demand" on the walls of the Building of Opulence, poured semen on the flowers at the foot of the male statues. And finally, during a "things are going great" speech in the Courtyard of Greatness, Fanny climbed to the top of Manifesto the Great's statue. She pulled her bra from her shoulders and, using it as a slingshot, pummelled the leaders with hard-as-nails hemp balls and soya effluent—which, in the end, was her downfall.

She, tripping over her *foreplay or no play* banner plummeted to the ground, followed by a cascade of leaflets.

"They can lead us to the kitchen, but they'll never make us swallow," she muttered before her eyes fluttered shut and she fell into a coma.

She never woke up and spent her last three days cared for by the innovative but highly criticized robotic care team who provided four-hourly flipping of sides and a daily *hosing-down*. Their speciality was setting alarms for the infirm and comatose—*for safety purposes, naturally*. An alarm was set at her door, in case she managed to *resurrect* to her feet and *wander*, and at her bed, in case she overreached a turn and fell.

Not the most dignified of endings for such a heroic woman who spoke in metaphors that many chose to misunderstand. After two days, she passed to another life, and Verruca drowned her sorrows with a ritual burning of leaflets while wearing her mother's bra.

In fact, she never took it off until the underwire broke and discomfort got the better.

Verruca watched the fall of man, the tumble of Legless, and the rise of Beryl. Never was her mother mentioned. And it niggled like the said loose underwire.

They were promised freedom, intellectual stimulation, and a decent pension and they were still waiting. Sure, the planet was a little cleaner, the wars had stopped, and recycling was all the rage; but what about food worth second helpings and houses worth decorating?

Did taking care of the planet have to be so . . . dreary?

The only bright spot in the new Beryl-and-Co. management was the *care for our grans* scheme. Runts from the compound were farmed out to grans like herself, a sort of *you scratch my back and I'll scratch yours* idea.

H2 was farmed out to Verruca. H2, like DBO, came from the compound; however, when she was there, the compound was full of Hilda's pictures and other inspirational Voted Ins who rose from the compound.

"Never underestimate the power of body watching," Fanny used to say to Verruca, "learn to read women and the world is your soya."

At the time Verruca thought Fanny had been on the caffeine. Until U2 brought DBO home.

U2 and DBO sat at the dashboard in the shed talking about knowledge, ideas, and all things mechanical, political, and futuristic. No one noticed them except to shout orders.

Verruca watched a friendship blossom and realized that a duo was in the making that could lead to many things.

Chapter Twenty-Two

VEGAS'S JOURNEY

"Besides, robots were being developed, used, advertised; how long would it be before they developed a robotic womb and got rid of women altogether?"–A scientist in the fertilizing plant

*V*egas looked at her trusty, "only available for the Voted In" transportable H-Pad. It had a tiny screen and was of the waterproof variety. She toyed with the receptor, flicked it on and off (which was a waste of time as Hilda could override all flicking of switches), and sighed.

Hilda would want an update soon. In fact, Vegas wondered what was holding her up.

She let out another long sigh. What the pickle was she going to say?

My map dissolved quicker than a salt tablet, no idea where I am—not to worry, fairy godmother's here!

She could just imagine Hilda's reaction—her short, spiky hair bristling with agitation.

She needed a story, a diversion, and had been walking for the past hour with a mind as blank as the hemp and soya fields she walked through. Hemp and soya were used for everything and claimed to be one of Planet Hy Man's last natural beauty. Vegas couldn't see any beauty. All she saw was miles of green-grey bushes rustling in the wind, with the odd worker poking her head through.

Like most women in the city, she never questioned where things came from, she just moaned about the monotony of it. And now, as she looked about, she understood why. The only thing that grew was hemp and the occasional soya field. Even Vegas with her minimal understanding of farming knew there were only so many ways you could make hemp eatable, and as for soya, who enjoyed soya?

Her silk shoes were ruined from the dirt tracks. They were as equipped for walking as a footman for running. And as she crunched and stumbled along the stony path, she noticed the odd head appear from the hemp bushes and the odd stooped figure look up from the soya fields.

Vegas could not imagine spending an hour in the fields, let alone a day. The soil was so soft in places you lost your shoe, and then so hard in places you tripped. It rained a downpour only to stop for a wind to pick up and whip through your wet clothes.

She felt as comfortable walking on the dirt path as a Voted In on a stationary. And for the first time in a long time, she grasped how privileged she was.

The roads outside the city were dirt tracks to discourage country farm workers from traveling near the city. Not that the farm workers need any discouragement; they had their own stories about the city, which combined with the noise and the view of the city had them convinced they were better off.

Vegas had never seen the city from the outside before. The skyscrapers filled the horizon, piercing through the mist, at times blocking the sun. And the noise could be heard everywhere, the radio blaring news, music, and the odd blast of Hilda's latest orders.

"Keep going," said the voice of the fairy godmother.

Vegas continued.

"Don't stop," said DBO to the footman, who had taken a breather from massaging her feet.

"You try walking in these shoes—they are as helpful as a footman with gloves."

"Tell me about it," said DBO.

Crop rotation was one of Hilda's pet subject, along with bin collections and the plight of the cleaners. Which when talked about cleared the room with a view in seconds—apart from Vegas. Vegas's seat was scrunched in the corner next to Hilda with no means of escape-until Hilda moved. And Hilda had the bladder of an elephant. Waiting for a loo break from her was like waiting for a footman to shuffle in with coffee: by the time they had made it down the passage it was usually cold with a rim. In fact, the Voted In often had bets on who would beat whom.

Whenever crop rotation was mentioned, Vegas knew she was in for long, dry hour with an empty mug, empty percolator, and no hope of a refill in sight. And as the others drifted from their seats, Vegas drifted into open-eyed sleeping.

Now, as she looked at the crops, her mind as blank as a footman's purse, she wondered—could she remember anything, and if she did, would any of it be any help?

DBO told her to use her instinct, think out of the box; all advised against it in the complex. DBO said it felt good. Vegas had yet to feel anything good, and as for thinking out of the box, having field workers staring at you while ploughing your way down *path unknown*—that was impossible.

She threw a wave at one; another worker appeared from nowhere and stared. She tried a smile, she got a glare. The longer she was on the track, the more appeared; soon there was a whole row of workers watching in their grey and blue itchy-looking overalls. Vegas's pity began to turn to discomfort as they started to point at her shoes and snigger.

"What, you got gloves for feet?" shouted one of the workers.

"Not get far in them."

"May as well put a hemp leaf on your foot."

A few laughed.

"These are the latest," muttered Vegas with a mild stomp; she staggered, stumbled, then regained her balance.

"For what, polishing a floor?"

"A robot's head."

"A footman's bum?"

"Yes, well, where I come from they are the envy of all."

"Were you come from must be the inside of a cushion."

The Operators began to tentatively explore the room with a view.

Operator One surveyed the extra-large table, which involved a lot of squeezing past dozing footmen, excuse-me's, and face pulling, while the footmen remained statue-like apart from the odd stagger.

Operator Two, who had found a concealed set of drawers, pulled open several and found pictures of Woody in various shades of grey. She looked up. "Do you think we should be doing this?"

The others looked at the footmen.

"Perhaps we should stop," said Operator Two.

She slammed the drawer shut, setting off the table screen. It began to rise from a slit.

"Who did that?"

They all looked at Operator Three still by the curtains.

"Wasn't me."

Woody appeared on the screen as he was the default setting. For a moment they stared; Woody was even more impressive close up.

"Turn it up," said someone.

"Do you think that's a good idea," muttered Operator Three.

Operator Two slid the drawer in and out, looking for some sort of control button.

A loud *thump* came from the door.

The Operators jumped.

"Turn it down!"

"Switch it off!"

Thump!

Operator Two slammed the drawer shut looked at the screen, unmoved, then eased the drawer open again.

"Hilda never knocks," muttered Operator Four.

"Is it an enemy?" whispered a voice from the back.

"A spy?"

"Should we answer?"

Operator Two looked underneath the drawer and saw a *do not touch, press, or twist in any way* switch.

"You answer," said Operator One.

"No. You answer," said Operator Three.

The Operators looked at the footman. He nodded, sauntered to the door, and before he had the chance to place his hand on the handle, it burst open. A large silver ball suspended in the air dashed into the room with jet-like speed. It was the size of a basketball and so fast that it didn't see the screen mid rising. A footman in its path ducked.

Thump! Crash! Crack!

"Alice[1]," muttered one.

"Pickling Alice," muttered another.

Alice was the first messenger to be invented but, like the 33 Robots, was way too smart for her own good. She remained mostly unused, brought out now and then when the leader in question had a point to make, needed a stretch, or, as in this case, to keep the Operators on their toes.

---

1. *Similar to Amazon's Alexa's with many of the I know better than you bugs still intact. No metamorphizes or IT students involved.*

Chapter Twenty-Three

ALICE

"An opened gate is not always an invitation."–Verruca

egas finally left the dusty road, the fields, and the on/off rain to arrive at a gate with *no need to shut* scribbled across it. The gate led to the Black Hills, known by many as the slag heaps.

Vegas had spent the last hour watching the gate and the hills behind it loom closer, all the time hoping that DBO would stop, intervene, and send her somewhere familiar. She didn't.

Vegas could feel the eerie stillness as new to her as the infamous Black Hills. In fact, she couldn't work out which was worse: the thought of speaking to Hilda or walking through the *no need to shut* gate. The Black Hills and the silence were as foreign to Vegas as the Argyll to Beryl and filled her with trepidation.

Women from the city never ventured outside and those from outside never ventured to the city. Silence, however, was a sensation unheard in either camp. The most silence a worker got to hear was the rustling of Hilda's cape when she made herself comfortable before speaking on the radio. And the closest someone like Vegas got to silence was the whale sounds in the spar, which was probably why many stopped going.

At one time the hills had been a place of great beauty, full of animals and rare plants. Now there was just a slag heap as scalable as a mountain of slate and a few pictures of a time no woman was old enough to remember. The hills turned black during the time of men. When women took over, they thought, if left alone, the hills would turn back to their former glory. They erected a gate.

That was decades ago. Who scribbled "no need to shut" was anyone's guess.

A red light on Vegas's H-Pad flashed with urgency: *Hilda calling! Hilda calling!*

Vegas stared at the gate.

Hilda still calling! Ignore at your peril!

"You need to keep going. Get to the other side of the Black Hills," said DBO.

"Is it safe? Am I going to suffocate, explode, or worse still—never come back?"

"Verruca says it's safe."

"Verruca?"

"Gran."

"Well that's okay then, if some old-timer says it's safe, what the pickle; let's throw a meeting; bring some hemp biscuits . . . I'll just get Hilda . . ."

"Where the pickle are you?" shouted Hilda.

"Shall I deal with that?" whispered DBO.

"Can you?"

"Just say the word."

"The word is spoken."

DBO nodded to the footman.

"Interference of a weather kind," said the footman in his best elevator voice, "please try again later."

Vegas heard a selection of pickle swearing and a clatter of something solid, followed by a long beep and silence.

The gate inched open.

Operator One tried to grab the ball as it ricocheted off the screen. It slid out of her hands and circled the room, passing Operator Three. She dodged, grabbed, and missed.

"Someone get rid of the screen," snapped Operator One.

"How?" shouted another.

"I found a button," said Operator Two, neglecting the "do not press."

"Press it."

"But . . ."

"Just press it."

Operator Two pressed the "do not press" switch. The flat screen didn't move, but the chandelier folded into a ceiling as Hilda's platform inched down slower than a comatose snail.

"I thought it was for servicing," muttered Operator Two.

"Needs it," muttered a voice from the back.

"Grab that, Alice!" shouted Operator One.

The secretary lunged at the ball, overstepped, and fell into a footman.

He staggered, tottered, and then knocked into the table.

The screen screeched to a halt and began to bleep loudly.

The platform began to play a *let's hear it* for Hilda fanfare.

"Press harder," shouted Operator One.

"I'm pressing as hard as I can," said Operator Two.

The table wobbled as the platform played louder.

"Stop pressing."

"What?"

"I said you're making it louder."

"I got her," said the secretary, going for a grab. They all looked at her, still trying to get used to her speaking.

The ball slipped from the secretary's hands, stopped an inch from the top of the screen, and bounced on it. The screen slid back into the slit with a prolonged, drawn-out screech.

The ball waited for a reaction: a thank-you, perhaps even some applause.

"What about the platform?" shouted Operator Two over the blaring fanfare.

"The stop button," said the footman.

"Where's that?"

"Beside the play button, ma'am."

"Where's that?"

"The restroom, ma'am."

Silence fell . . .

"Of all the stupid places to put a button—I mean who looks in the ladies' for a stop button?"

"Security, ma'am," muttered a footman.

Alice hovered in the middle of the table.

"What is it Alice?" muttered Operator One.

A superbly manicured hand appeared from its side with a scribbled memo in it.

Operator One snatched it from Alice.

"What is it this time? Budget cuts," said Operator Two.

"No," said Operator One, "we're to wear suits." She passed the memo on.

"Suits?"

"Yes, suits."

"Aren't they a little old-fashioned?"

"I know one thing: they require ironing and who the pickle is going to do that?"

Another note appeared. Operator Two looked at it. "It says here they're made of silk."

"Silk?"

"The last thing you do with silk is iron," said the secretary. The others looked at her as both memos puffed into confetti cascading onto the table.

"Well, that's what my gran says," she muttered.

Chapter Twenty-Four

FOOT RUBBING

"They didn't get rid of men, they just didn't make any more—let them grow old—final-destination footmen."—Footmen's latest jokes

As the secretary began to sweep up the confetti, Alice moved to the curtains, adjusted what was broken, and waited for a reaction. When none came, Alice moved to the table, hovered for a bit, then let out a small cough.

"Okay, thanks Alice . . ."

"Good ball, Alice . . ."

Alice pulled oil from a drawer and silicone from another, then squirted the two into the slit of the table. After a small hiss, the slit closed and Alice produced another memo.

Operator One read it. "She said leave the screen for two hours and it will be set."

"Show-off."

"And we're to follow."

"Follow? What does she mean? Where? Why?"

Alice bobbed towards the door.

"Always with the cryptic body language," muttered Operator One.

❄

The footman teetered in front of DBO with an elevenses tray and coughed. She turned from the dashboard and looked at his wrinkled hands and sunken backside; she had never noticed how old he was before.

"A funny thing happened on the way to the Milky Way," he said.

DBO, with a sigh, turned back to her work. His jokes were as long as a Voted In shopping list and she had other things on her mind. She had just been face-to-face with Woody, who apparently wasn't impressed with the fairy godmother story.

"Beryl liked the story," DBO said to him.

"Beryl?" said DJ.

"Yes," said DBO, and that was as far as they got . . .

The connection was cut and DBO had no idea how.

The footman looked at DBO working under the dashboard bonnet. She was but a mere *slip of a lass* and yet she reworked things like a pro, like someone who been trained and was now the trainer.

DBO loved spark plugs, in fact anything technological; it was the bond between her and H2, along with the fact that no one else talked to them. They had been friends since they met in the shed. They sat at the dashboard and did all the things shouted out to do, secretly sharing knowledge of all things mechanical, political, and futuristic.

They had the invisibility of the unimportant.

DBO missed her and wanted to share what she had done . . .

DBO had taken recycling to a whole new level and had transformed the shed into a body of patched-together instruments, a pulsating dashboard, and wall-to-wall screens.

It was like *Doctor Who*'s Tardis . . . the footman was in awe, and he, a mere footman, was part of it.

How could he help?

"Years ago, connections were a given," he said.

"Hmmm."

"Hungry?"

"Sort of busy right now," she muttered.

"Some say connections took a beating when women took over. Not that I'm saying that, I mean really, when you think about it, it was the death of the four-legged species that changed things."

"Haven't really got time, " said DBO, trying to adjust the pickup range.

"Meat was a dirty word," he muttered.

DBO looked at him. "Well, that's a given."

"Women blame men, which is not strictly true, but I guess the barbecuing didn't help . . . biscuit?"

DBO looked up at the footman's tray: a plate of hemp biscuits and coffee sourced from the clear-out at the Voted In's. She shoved a biscuit in her mouth and took a slurp of coffee; for a moment she paused at the perfection of such a taste. The footman, on a roll, continued on about the past.

"Once meat was gone, it was all hemp and soya," he said.

"Well, that goes without saying," muttered DBO.

She pointed to a solar-powered miniature drill. The footman handed it to her and watched as she, biscuit in mouth, made aim. The drill silently whirled.

"It was the soya—it changed women," said the footman.

"That's what Verruca said," muttered DBO through her biscuit.

"It's in their makeup," said the footman.

"Don't think makeup had much to do with it," she said.

The footman began to talk about ovaries, soya, hormones, and how with just a few tweaks in the food chain woman changed and became more bolshie.

"Did you know it was a woman who made the breakthrough in the end?"

"Everyone knows that," said DBO.

The wife of Manifesto the Great was held by all women as the revolutionary who freed women. It was she who noticed the changes soya made to her friends. "There could be something in this whole soya issue," she said to her husband, and he ignored her for the last time.

Fed up with his *I'm too busy to listen*, angry at his *I need a shag now grope*, which was always followed by an "I'd be better off doing it myself" comment, she worked *incognito*—until she found a way to self-fertilise an ovary.

DBO slapped the bonnet of the dashboard shut with a satisfied thump, stood back, and surveyed her work with pride. She took another biscuit and finished her coffee.

"Semen was out the window and Petri dishes were in," he said.

DBO choked on her mouthful.

"Just a couple of strokes, that's all it took," said the footman with a dismissive gesture.

"You could have put that in a more . . . scientific way," muttered DBO.

The footman, seeing this as an opening rather than a criticism, continued: ". . . and man's future was doomed. Although we—they didn't see so at the time. Men thought a woman free from months of pregnancy would have time for other things . . ."

"Any more of this coffee?" said DBO.

"Like wearing leather."

DBO stopped. "Leather?"

"Hemp leather, it gives and breathes . . ."

DBO looked at him questionably.

". . . like Lycra but way better for dressing up."

"Dressing up—what are you talking about?"

"Some men thought a free woman would be happy to wait for them to come home—even talk dirty on the phone."

"Men and women talking on a phone—Verruca never mentioned anything about a phone, or cleaning for that matter." DBO gestured with her empty mug. "Any more?"

"Some men saw the writing on the walls; without meat hormones, many became indecisive and weak." He stopped and looked at her. "Many just gave in . . ." He sighed. ". . . and women took over."

"Well, it was a bit more complicated than that," said DBO. She helped herself to another cup and gestured a "do you want one" to the footman.

The footman, lost in thought, didn't notice.

She pulled a cloth from her pocket and, with a coffee in one hand, began to rub the screen clean.

The screen lit up to show the golden body of a 33 robot in an advanced yoga position.

They both stared.

"I was hoping for Woody," muttered DBO.

The 33 robot moved from a backbend to a headstand, his legs spread out into a Y shape. A small fart squeaked into the air. The robot looked around, then dropped beneath the grass.

DBO was sure she heard a chuckle.

Chapter Twenty-Five

THE VOTED IN

"Hilda's jokes are as funny as a plucked chicken."–Mex

Senator was reading a *read before you ride* leaflet to women too shocked to listen. Voted In Three appeared from behind a curtain. She pulled it open.

"I've found the sleeping compartment," she shouted, dusting her hands. "And it's not pretty."

Senator poised under the matchbox of a window for light looked up from her leaflet. It was a fold-out affair that required light to catch the small print and made as much sense as a cleaner who didn't clean.

The leaflet talked of "making oneself at home" and how "relaxed riders made better energy" while listing a set of conditions as bearable as one of Hilda's *waste not want not* lectures . . .

"Eleven-hour shifts and five-minute breaks only after quotas have been made," read Senator.

Everyone was confused; *quotas* to a Voted In were purely for caffeine purposes.

"What about our elevenses?" muttered the voice from the back.

"Think the days of elevenses and meetings are gone," muttered Senator.

"Won't miss the meetings," said Baby toying with a peddle; she looked at the label swinging from the seat.

"It says here to *sit on it and spin.*" She looked up. "That sounds like fun."

Voted In One flashed a *don't play with the equipment* look at Baby.

"Are we to drink beverages on them? And when do we sleep?" muttered the voice from the back.

"You won't be asking that when you see where we are to sleep," said Voted In Three.

Baby moved to the only rowing machine and read the label.

Row and stay young. She slid on it and pulled the oars. "Do you think this was Legless's secret?"

Voted In Two tutted, "Legless? Secret?"

"I meant the butt, the legs—I saw pictures of him, not Woody's standard, but . . ."

"We should have seen this coming," muttered a voice from the back.

"Seen what?" said Voted In One, flashing another look at Baby.

"Hilda's takeover, sending around memos requesting the whereabouts of the code for Beryl's penthouse; removing Beryl's portrait . . ."

"Thought that was for cleaning."

"So she says."

"We are to stay in the barracks like footmen," shouted Voted In Three.

Voted In One grabbed the rowing machine's handlebar and stopped Baby. They tussled, setting off an alarm.

"It says here"—Senator gestured with a leaflet—"that interfering with other riders will be treated with a fine."

Baby pulled the handle from Voted In One and with a smug look began to row again.

"It also says that riding without Lycra is forbidden and three percent will be docked from said wages."

The Voted Ins glared at Baby; she stopped and sheepishly slid off, while Voted In Two began to calculate the said three percent. Until it was pointed out that three percent of nothing was nothing.

"And if you think this is bad," shouted Voted In Three, "wait till you see the said barracks."

"Barracks? What is that?"

"Follow me." Voted In Three gestured to the opened curtain and led her comrades into a dark and dusty room which looked like it had been shut up for years.

The walls were covered with fifties-style posters at various stages of peeling of women with pouting red lips and pointy bras and men with slick dark hair clutching cigarettes. The only furniture was a row of beds, barely covered with itchy-looking blankets and a minuscule flat grey pillow. Voted In Four was busy in the corner flapping a blanket; dust flew everywhere.

"Haven't done this for a while," she said with a brave face.

Baby coughed as the voice from the back silently picked up a few stray plastic cups with a *what is this* look?

Voted In One tugged at a poster; it slid to the ground. She tutted. "If only we could burn these."

"Yes, a fire would be nice," murmured Senator.

"Put up pictures of Woody instead," said Baby.

"Oh, and some fizzy. What I'd give for one of them."

"Could ride anything then," muttered Baby.

The footman under orders to "stop talking about the past and see to foot things" was working on a new massage oil combination in the shed. It was dark-lit by the lights of the instruments plus a few candles, *thanks to him*. He breathed in the scent and looked around. On the screen was a magnified Vegas ploughing her way through the last of the Black Hills.

And on the floor was DBO sitting cross-legged, engrossed in a map like she knew what she was doing. She didn't even need to ask which way was up.

Passing through the Black Hills for Vegas had been an experience she'd rather forget.

She had been taught about animals, heard about them, but still they were a complete mystery to her. They had died out years ago, despite the great liberation of the four-legged creature. A time when animals were shoed from the farms and liberated from the zoos to stand and stare in the only place left for them—the Black Hills.

And she had spent the last hour walking through that bleak black landscape littered with the said remains. The silence was beginning to oppress her, all she could hear was her heart thumping against her chest . . .

As she passed the last hill, she saw in the distance a green field, knee-high grass waving in the wind. She moved closer, relieved to hear rustling breaking the silence. The field stretched for miles; she entered and felt the dry grass brush against her knees. She ran her hands along the tops and was just thinking about plucking a few heads when a *golden being* rose up from the heads of the grass like a swimmer from the sea and glided into a pose . . .

Two more appeared and moved in unison to the same pose.

Robots?

She stopped. She could almost make out their crow-like faces peering over their outstretched arms. She was too close . . .

She looked for something to crouch behind, somewhere to hide but there was nothing. Panting, she went for an incognito pose, a pose she had only seen and never practiced; unsure, she faltered.

One of the robots nudged the other two and they laughed.

She pulled herself together, held her ground, and made like a statue; then her H-pad flashed.

Beetroot and bugger!

Vegas tried to silence the H-Pad with a frantic fumble. The H-Pad clattered to the ground, now flashing with a loud beeping sound.

Bollocking beetroot!

She bent to pick it up, scrabbling through the grass, her heart racing yet again.

"Ma'am?" said the footman.

Fairy godmother? thought Vegas.

"Ma'am, it is but the plough!"

"Shhh, they'll hear," she hissed.

The robots dropped their pose, tilting their heads like collies listening. One gestured to the other two; they stopped, picked up their mats, and disappeared into the horizon.

"The plough position," repeated the footman.

"Plough," whispered Vegas, "in a field?"

"Yoga, ma'am."

"I see."

"Not far now," said DBO.

Vegas stared as the robots disappeared into the horizon. "How do you know?"

DBO, engrossed in the map, didn't answer.

"Don't tell me—*Gran*."

"Verruca is her name."

"I refuse to use that word."

"Grannie Verruca then?" DBO paused. "You need to look for a place called a library."

"Yes, I am aware of that, but what does it look like?"

"A library?" said DBO.

"That's not helping," said Vegas.

"Suppose you got those maps from *her* too."

"A given," snapped DBO without a glance at the footman.

"The first women to rebel worshipped knowledge," muttered the footman. "And the old ways of turning a page."

"Turning a page? What has that got to do with finding a library?" said Vegas.

"They took all the books," said the footman.

"Books? Who bothers with books?" said Vegas. She had heard of libraries, places with great big chairs, shelves up to the ceiling, and files.

"Books are the key, ma'am," said the footman.

"Books?"

"Yes, books."

DBO and Vegas said nothing. A footman stating the obvious was not something they were comfortable with.

Chapter Twenty-Six

VEGAS AND THE VERANDA

"The scent on the veranda always protects you from the sun."– Pot

Vegas continued to walk through the field. In front of her was a cluster of buildings and stiff figures swaying in the breeze. Which the footman pointed out was "nothing to be scared of being that they were scarecrows."

Vegas pointed her H-Pad at the buildings. "Is this what I am looking for?"

"Hmmm," said DBO, "it says here there is a place in the middle of nowhere." DBO silently read . . .

"And?" said Vegas.

". . . full of women who collect hemp."

"Don't see any women."

"Lunchtime, ma'am," chipped in the footman.

"Some called them units," said DBO, "others a steading."

"Think you'll find it is a production plant, ma'am, of the eco variety."

"Don't see any production," muttered Vegas.

"Lunchtime, ma'am."

Vegas stared ahead. This production eco compound or *whatever* looked as foreign to her as a beef burger.

She, like most in the city, never thought about "out there," let alone "way out there and beyond." She thought buildings only existed in the cities. In fact, she had no idea that anything existed outside the city.

Vegas, like Hilda, came from the compound, a place where little grew. It was hot, dry, and dusty—the opposite of the city—and by the looks of this damp place, here. The compound taught its girls a blanket, one-sided version of life aimed at keeping the girls in their place.

And Vegas, unlike Hilda, was spotted as a questioner from an early age.

The compound marked toddlers by their gifts: the social ones, the criers, the carers, the givers, the takers, the bullies, the leaders, and toddlers like Vegas, who as soon as they spoke asked questions. Every gran kept an eye on the questioners. They could invite riots, backchat, and a "why me" attitude.

The questioning sort were the most controlled, for their own good —*so claimed*. Grans bombarded the "questioners" with reading and writing—about the said reading, along with a "not now, dear" attitude. In short, Vegas had been fed a black-and-white political philosophy all her childhood—along with the writing of said black-and-white political claptrap. For years Vegas's questioning was stampeded, trampled, and quashed.

Then she met Hilda.

Vegas was ten; Hilda, a young woman of twenty, was in her last year at the compound.

Vegas was walking out of *the room of reflection*, after yet another lecture about "the pointlessness of questions," when Hilda spied her downcast face.

"Remember, this is for your own good," shouted the grannie from the door.

Hilda grabbed her arm. "Join me," she said, "at the recycle bin."

Vegas pulled a *that place stinks* face.

Hilda offered her a tea and, when that didn't work, an all-day soya sucker.

"Come on, there's no one there, we can talk."

Hilda talked about the shed and how it was the only starting place left. Vegas, confused about the whole *starting* issue, silently listened— her jaw cemented together with the all-day sucker.

Hilda's charisma grew on her.

"That's where I am going," said Hilda, scrapping scraps into the recycle bin. "And I will keep a spot for you." She stopped and smiled into Vegas's soft brown eyes. "You'll be my right hand."

Hilda seemed to make sense, and when she called herself a mentor, Vegas believed her.

"Choose your arguments, don't let them choose you," Hilda was fond of saying. Vegas listened, and soon life in the compound grew easier.

Vegas stared at this eco-apparition of color in her posh, useless shoes.

Watching her mentor embrace power as a caped crusader had stopped Vegas in her tracks. Hilda's change of tactics triggered a questioning in her again . . .

Her feet squelched in the moist fertile soil; she stared up at the colorful eco-whatever plant and wondered . . .

What other political effluent had Hilda fed her to file, microchip, and sell to the masses?

Vegas was fast approaching the eco plant. The closer she got, the more scarecrows she saw; she felt spooked despite the footman's "nothing to fear." Of course, black parrots the size of buzzards making themselves at home on the scarecrows didn't help.

The only mechanical birds in the city were tiny sparrows that fluttered about like feathers in the breeze. Here the birds were black, menacing-looking beings that stared for an eternity, like the farm workers, and squawked louder than Beryl's outdoor *reach every corner of the city* sound system.

Telling her not to worry was like telling Hilda not to shout, order, or dress up.

She passed the tallest scarecrow she'd seen—at least six foot. It was flapping madly in the wind, which didn't stop a parrot landing on it.

The parrot dug its talons into the scarecrow and regained its balance, then from under it heavy eyebrows peered at Vegas.

"Which way did it go?" *hiccup* "Which way did it go?" *belch* "Which way did it go?" *Burb, belch, hiccup.*

The parrot's head turned a full circle.

A scone flashed past the side of Vegas's head; the parrot squawked and thudded to the ground.

"Which way did she goooooo . . . ."

Vegas stared at the bird as its eyes rolled back into its head. "Incoming; incoming, goooone . . ." A flock of birds descended onto the scone.

She looked up to see a robot with a slingshot by his side. He turned and headed for the buildings, his fluid movements gliding across the field—typical of a 33 robot.

Vegas looked back at the flock of birds; a crumb lay where the scone had been. The birds glared at her.

She decided to move—quickly.

"Act casual," said DBO. "It says here whistling helps."

"How the pickle am I to whistle and run?"

"Walk."

"It confuses them," added the footman.

"What shall I whistle?"

"Anything."

"Anything?" said Vegas.

"Yes, anything."

Vegas, whistling the national anthem, wandered across the field with her eyes firmly fixed on the eco plant/whatever. She figured if she didn't see the birds, they weren't there, and if she whistled loud enough, she didn't hear the squawking.

Neither worked, but the large sprawling wooden steadings were getting nearer. She told herself to keep going, concentrate on the buildings. In fact, as she got closer, she couldn't take her eyes off the settlement (which she had now chosen to call it).

The roofs were green, full of nesting birds, some small and almost musical. The walls were brightly painted, decorated with graffiti and broken bric-a-brac. And there were verandas everywhere, cluttered with hanging plants swinging in the breeze and piles of books.

The largest veranda had two 33 robots working their way through several yoga poses.

The robot with the slingshot stepped onto the veranda, hit its head on a swinging plant, and cursed. The two other robots stopped mid warrior yoga pose and laughed.

Vegas watched a parrot squawking like a hungry seagull fly onto the roof, knock a few smaller birds to the ground, and nest into a green patch. One of the robots threw a shoe at it; the bird looked up, squawked, and then returned to its nesting.

Another bird flew inches from her head, almost knocking her over.

She gained her balance with a few dramatic breaths.

"Keep moving," said DBO.

Vegas was about to moan about DBO's lean description and useless whistling when she was tripped again, this time by a passing rat. She squealed, then when she saw it was the size of a dog, she jumped into her incognito pose.

One of the robots laughed and waved her in . . .

She switched her H-Pad on silent, slid it into her pocket, and for the first time ever wished she had earphones . . .

Chapter Twenty-Seven

MORE THAN A PICKLE

"He was a man who spent most of his time plotting against Beryl, who in truth had never heard of him. In fact, that was all he seemed to talk about: the overthrow of that upstart Beryl."– Manifesto the Great, Planet Hy Man's National Geographic, last edition

Vegas stood on the veranda waiting for the door to open. She had knocked several times, tried the handle, then looked at the robots.

"Just go in, I told you no one gives a pickle here."

"This is a 'one rule for all' camp."

"Anyone can walk in."

Vegas, still unsure, stared at the graffiti for what seemed the fifth time . . .

Freedom,

Your choice,

Animals rock.

Books a women's best friend.

Paint your own wagon, leave mine alone.

Take charge or someone else will.

Make bread, not sausages.

Let sleeping parrots lie.

Growing bolder, she read each one out aloud, *making her presence known . . .*

"No point being subtle, just go in."

Vegas surveyed the books stacked about in piles, some holding windows open, some piled up to use as coffee tables, and other just opened to, perhaps, read? She flicked through a few, read aloud a few titles.

"'Here lies the truth for all men: the womb is twice as big as a man's scrotum.'" Vegas looked at the robots. *Scrotum?*

"You're wasting time. Just go in, they won't hear you out here."

Vegas, still wondering who *they* were, walked around the side.

She looked in the window. There were robots packing and laughing women—dancing. She looked closer: they were wearing earphones, while the robots were packing boxes with great industry.

Vegas knocked on the window. A robot looked up and gestured her in.

Chapter Twenty-Eight

THE SEASIDE

"Sand at the seaside is not always a given."–Cleaner One

Baby looked at the only window in the barracks—a tiny patch of light in the ceiling laughingly called a skylight.

"Where is this so-called seaside?" she said. "We were promised one, it must be out there somewhere."

When no one paid any heed, she looked about, then nudged a bed. *Light as a silk hanky.* She pushed the bed under the window, tried to reach, then spied a large box in the corner. Ignoring the *what do you think you're doing* glance from the others she pushed the box to the bed and, with a grunt, balanced it on top of the rock-hard bed.

The Voted Ins rumbled with disapproval as they watched with a dismissive air.

Baby clambered to the top and stretched to peer through the *slit.*

"You won't see anything from that thing," Voted In One said. "The angle's all wrong, and look at the size of it. I mean, could a window *be* any smaller?"

"It's regulation size—standard," muttered Voted In Four, mid blanket flapping. She was working her way through the beds.

"And who's the idiot that set *that* regulation?"

"Um, us," said Baby with her back to all.

"Oh."

Baby looked out and saw the Zen garden, the shed in the distance, and the kitchen. A light in the shed flickered on. Baby didn't notice; the kitchen had caught her attention. Its large patio doors were open, giving a perfect albeit soundless view of the cook, who, leaning over a bench, was rolling something across something else.

Baby squinted for a better view.

The cook was covered in white powder and working with great industry . . .

Baby watched, mesmerized, at the speed of such a round woman talking with great animation. Baby waited to see to whom all the animation was aimed at—finally the apprentice appeared.

"It's a young woman," she shouted with her back to the Voted In.

Voted In One tutted, "get down."

"No good will come of it," muttered another.

Senator, now blanket-flapping alongside Voted In Four, looked up. "That'll be the *used to be* apprentice."

"What?"

Senator turned to Voted In Four. "Hilda, she made the cook the apprentice and the apprentice the cook."

"That explains the flat scones," muttered Voted In Two.

"Changing *roles*?" said the voice from the back.

"It's all part of the mixing things up project," said Senator.

"Next she'll be *rolling* out orders and making us butter our own scones . . ." said the voice from the back.

The pun fell on deaf ears.

Baby watched as a robot came into view with a large bag slung over its shoulders.

"It's one of the old style," said Baby, "for cleaning."

"Built like a statue, so I've heard," muttered a voice from the back.

"Exactly," muttered Baby. "It's sliding a bag onto the bench. That bag must weigh a ton."

"Those robots are strong, alright."

"It has pulled a round *something* from the bag," said Baby.

"That'll be a beetroot."

"Or an egg?"

"Or one of those flat scones," said the voice from the back.

Senator chuckled.

"The robot," said Baby, "is starting to circle a knife around it."

"Peeling?" said Voted In Two.

"What?"

"It's called peeling," shouted Voted In Two.

Baby continued her commentary of the kitchen, describing the arrival of Alice.

"Alice? They still use Alice?"

"She's handing a message—the young thing—looks angry, and the cooks are laughing," said Baby. "Wonder what the message is?"

Senator stood back to admire the blanket handiwork. "Almost sleep-able," she said.

"Almost," muttered Voted In Two.

Baby watched the cook point the rolling pin at the apprentice with a *you do it* gesture.

If only she could hear, thought Baby. She tugged at the lever. "If I could just open this window."

"I wouldn't do that," said Voted In Two.

"Mind," said a voice at the back.

"Just get down," snapped Voted In One.

"There must be a way to open it," said Baby. "I mean what is the point of a window if you can't open?" She pushed and pulled; the lever came off in her hands.

"Oh, beetroot and bugger."

"Told you."

"Never listens."

Baby tried to click it back in.

"It says here that all opening of orifices, without a request on appropriate paperwork, is strictly prohibited," said Voted In One with a crisp shutting of the *how to sleep in a barracks* leaflet.

"What is an orifice?" said Baby, turning the lever in her hand.

"It is what that should be attached to," said Voted In Two.

"And a ten percent fine," added Voted In One.

"Well in that case," said Baby, "I may as well get my money's worth." She dropped the lever and made an all-out effort to force the skylight open. She jiggled, pushed, and even tried a ramming action with her shoulder.

"Maybe it seized," said the voice from the back.

"Seized? What the pickle is that?"

"Stuck, you gherkin head."

Baby, in desperation, grabbed the windowsill and shook it. "Maybe this will unstick it then."

"Careful . . ."

The sill, being made of super-absorbent expandable foam from hemp/soya/substance unknown (some call dough-like), expanded with each pulling, until Baby overbalanced and tumbled to the floor.

The box followed as the sill retracted back with remarkable speed.

The box crashed opened and Lycra cycling outfits spilled out, filling the room with the smell of man. The smell confused, then aroused the women. They inhaled, coughed, spluttered, inhaled some more, then sighed.

Senator pulled the box upright and a C-Pad clattered to the floor from a side pocket. The Voted In, mid inhale, gasped as Senator picked it up.

"Haven't seen one of those in decades," whispered Voted In Two.

"Nor these," said the voice from the back, pulling a face reader from beneath a jockstrap.

In the distance, unbeknown to all, the shed light flicked off.

As Baby crashed to the floor, the old cook tossed the rolling pin at the young cook.

"Stick to your scones, I've got sandwiches to make," she yelled.

The young cook, with a downcast look, lifted the rolling pin as the old cook began to peel a synthetic egg.

"I was born to cook," muttered the older cook.

The younger cook said nothing—another batch of scones like last time and she was done for.

Chapter Twenty-Nine

GINGER

"Chipping away at the granite of life is apparently what gets Hilda up in the morning."—Voted In One

Vegas woke up to a scratchy, rough sheet rubbing against her skin and the smell of ginger. She coughed; she hadn't smelt ginger since her compound days, and even then it made her gag. It was used for many purposes but never for cooking, more a rubbing into areas for colds and chills, along with other burning spices and a rough-handed massage.

Smart girls in the compound soon learned never to complain about aches and sniffs.

A delicate-looking bird appeared at her window and let out a robotic chirp. Vegas watched it dance about the sill.

She had slept or rather dozed with one eye open, like the nights she slept under the great phallic chandelier in the room with a view, when working overtime on speeches. In the shadows of the night, the chandelier would play on her mind, putting her off her sleep, and making her think . . . Hilda told her she imagined too much, but then Hilda had a mind like a mouse trap.

What you saw was what you got, until you prodded the wrong way.

Vegas wondered if she had imagined things last night too. She stared at the bird and thought about prodding. Its chirping was not so delicate, loud enough to cause Vegas's head to thump. It started to flutter about the window, working up to a frenzy. Vegas looked about for something to toss and grabbed a book just as a worker walked in with a tray of hemp tea and biscuits.

"Sleep well?" she said.

Vegas didn't reply. She had been woken several times by noises she had never heard before, noises of intensity and sighing, which infiltrated her dreams. And Vegas never dreamed; something else drummed out of a woman at the compound.

The worker tore a crust from the biscuit and tossed it at the bird. The bird sidestepped, and the crust landed by its feet. The bird grabbed the crust and took three attempts to fly off, staggering under the weight. Finally, it gave up with a glare at the worker.

Vegas stared at the bird as it now stamped the crust into pieces, then gulped like a fasting Labrador.

"What sort of birds are these? I mean who designed them?"

The worker slammed the window shut. "I'd keep the questions to 'when's tea?'"

"What?"

"Just mind what you say, that's all. I can't say any more than that . . ." She paused, then took a sip of Vegas's tea. "But you are welcome to look around."

Vegas eyed the young woman's eager face. "Can you tell me who you work for then?"

"Work?" laughed the worker. "Dude, what are you on about?"

Vegas spent the morning exploring the verandas. Tentatively she walked from one to another, avoiding the 33 robots. She had been told by the young worker to "feel free," "chill" (whatever that was), and "listen to the wind blowing through the chimes, it always has something to say."

The place seemed dead; yesterday's women seemed to have disappeared along with the robots. Every window she looked into showed cluttered rooms full of books, half-drunk cups, plates with food half eaten—but not one woman, one robot.

The verandas were full of wind chimes, and under the verandas were waterways. She could see through the spaces between the slats in the floorboards. Twice she saw something flash by. *Orange? Yellow? A fish?*

The third time she stopped to look over the side of the veranda.

She squatted, dipped her finger in the water, and felt a push. "I wouldn't get too close, might fall in."

Vegas looked up to catch a glimpse of an orange cape disappearing behind a door.

Vegas followed and walked into the commons room.

There were books everywhere, books used to leave mugs on, lining the walls, and some even on bookshelves. There were also two huge aquariums full of water plants. And a woman lounging on a pile of cushions, munching on what she called a "hemp-infested cake."

A dwarf robot entered on rollers, like a tank crunching over everything, until it stuck at a mat. After several attempts it reversed and turned to the right, avoiding the mat like nothing happened.

The woman laughed. "Welcome to the commons room, duckie," she said to Vegas.

The robot began to lift empty plates and mugs.

"Be a love and bring me another coffee?" she cooed to the robot. Then looked at Vegas, "supposed to do my yoga fat chance after all this cake."

"The last time you did yoga we didn't even have robots," said another woman entering.

"What's the point, who cares if I can bend backward to pick up a shoe," she cut another slice. "You see any grans here?" she gestured with her slice.

"Are you looking for something?"

"Sort of."

She eyed Vegas's dark suit, "not much good out here is it."

"Not really."

"You're a Voted In, aren't you?"

"Yes."

"My, my, they get younger every day."

"Well, not if you saw the others. I am just an apprentice for Hilda."

Vegas watched as the other worker scattered crumbs into the aquariums and fish appeared from nowhere. Vegas was gobsmacked; the fish looked healthy, robust, and darted about the water with an energy she had not seen before.

"These are our hope," muttered the worker.

The laughing woman with a *shut it* look nudged the worker with her foot.

"She's the same as us, isn't she?" said the worker.

"Hard to say," said the laughing woman.

"Ask her."

"No, you ask her."

The robot stopped in his tracks, paused, changed direction, and moved to a curtained doorway. He pulled it open and a tuning fork was played.

"You first."

"No, you."

"No, you."

The robot reversed, wheeled back to the laughing woman, and began to shoo her off the couch.

"All right, I am going, don't push," snapped the laughing woman.

The robot turned to the worker, and both women disappeared behind the curtain.

Vegas listened to the whispering . . .

"You don't know where she's been—where she's going."

"Looks okay to me."

"Shhh."

"Well I'm sorry, but she does."

"There is okay and there is okay."

"What about the comrade policy?"

"Dude . . . she's wearing silk, for *pickle's sake*—who do you know who wears silk?"

"So much for the comrade policy then."

"It doesn't apply with silk!"

"Oh, forgot about that."

Vegas fingered her silk collar, wondering what to do. She walked onto the veranda, her eyes blinded by the sun, and smack into a robot mid sun-saluting. She bounced off him with a "Ooops pardon me?"

"Ma'am" said the robot, the other two chuckled.

Vegas looked closer. They were all definitely the last three 33 robots. The swagger gave them away.

Vegas could feel the H-Pad vibrating—DBO was trying to contact her. Vegas walked out into the field, pulled the H-Pad from beneath her shirt, and gave DBO a quick scan of the building.

She told them about the two women and the fish.

"Hippies, ma'am," muttered the footman, mid foot rub of DBO's feet, "who have gotten away from it all."

"All?" said DBO.

"The rat race," said the footman.

"Oh, that," said DBO.

"And took the 33 robots with them," added the footman.

"I think you'll find the robots followed," said DBO.

The footman stopped and looked up. "I think you'll find they were taken."

"Followed."

"What the pickle is a hippie?" said Vegas.

"Women who make art out of garbage, don't shave their armpits, and hug a lot," snapped DBO.

"I see," muttered Vegas. "I didn't get a look at their armpits."

Chapter Thirty

THE KITCHEN

"Stirring the pot does not always get rid of the lumps."– The cook

Vegas finally found the kitchen; it was massive. It had at least one door on each wall and was controlled by a large cook, who stood at the stove stirring while singing in an eardrum-breaking, high-pitched squeal.

As Vegas walked in, the cook stopped. "Fetch me that ladle," she said.

Vegas picked up a spatula.

"No, not that, my little cupcake,"

Vegas went for a sieve.

"No darl, not that one . . . it's swinging to your right."

Vegas went through a whole array of items, including a fry pan, a pepper grinder, and a cheese grater, staring at each like it was a weapon of mass destruction.

"It's like a soup bowl on the end of a stick," said the cook without a hint of impatience.

Vegas finally lifted what the cook seemed to want.

"Don't know much, do you?"

"Well I never cooked, if that is what you mean."

"Everyone should cook," she said.

"Where I come from it's not necessary."

"You're not there now though, are you, young lady?"

"Young?" said Vegas.

The cook tutted, engrossed in her stirring.

Vegas looked at the cook's wrinkled hands and figured even Hilda would seem young to her.

"You're needing to go to the library," muttered the cook.

Vegas's ears pricked up.

"Learn a few things." She handed Vegas a hemp sweetie, pulling her close. "And lose the silk—no one's impressed with the likes of that here."

Vegas shifted uncomfortably as the sweetie began to melt in her hand; it felt as much like a sweetie as Hilda looked a woman.

"Yes, luvvie, there'll be lists galore in that library."

"Really, and where do I find this . . . library?"

"You don't find it—it finds you."

"What?" Vegas looked about the exits.

She tapped Vegas's chest with her spoon. "It finds you."

Vegas fingered the red stain on her shirt and looked at the cook in confusion.

The cook gestured with a dripping spoon. "It finds you!"

"I don't understand," said Vegas.

The cook tussled Vegas's hair. "Just kidding."

Vegas with a glare straightened her hair.

"Wrong side of the bed, cupcake?"

"No."

"Bird got your tongue?"

"No!"

The cook sighed, gesturing to a door. "It's that way."

"Thanks."

"Or is it that way?"

"Cheers."

"No, no, my mistake, that way."

"It's that way," shouted the apprentice, walking out of a large fridge. "And that," said the apprentice, pulling the instrument from Vegas, "is not a ladle but a saucepan."

The apprentice looked at the cook. "Must you go through this every time?"

The cook shrugged with a smile as Vegas headed through the door.

Within minutes, Vegas was confronted by a door marked "library."

She stopped; the door opened, triggering a relay of lights flicking on down the passageway. She watched as the light-flicking went on for an eternity. After several minutes, Vegas gave up waiting and entered.

Vegas inhaled the musty smell of books, coughed, then moved in to browse.

There were corridors, sub corridors, steps down to dark places, and shelves so high you couldn't read the spine of the book. There were shelves that pulled out, shelves underneath shelves, and glass cases full of objects, many handmade.

She had heard of such things.

Vegas came across a side room lit up in red, with DIY on the door frame.

She had heard of DIY. She entered. A light flicked over a cabinet she passed . . .

Vegas jumped.

"Something extra for the weekend?"

Vegas stared. *Where did that come from?*

"Pick your size."

Size?

The shelves were diagrams of unknown contraptions. At first Vegas thought they were kitchen instruments until she looked closer. They were old-fashioned Victorian drawings, some framed in gold, hung on the walls with red velvet scarves looped around them and a candle underneath. There was a sense of reverence about them.

In glass cases were the instruments themselves, complicated, phallic-like instruments—like the room with a view's chandelier, except you could pick them up.

Which Vegas did.

She opened up one of the cases and lifted out the instrument. It was light, with buttons. She pressed, and a noise similar to what she heard the night before began as the instrument lit up and pulsed.

"What are you doing with that?" shouted a worker.

Vegas stopped as the piece clattered to the ground.

DBO blew out the last of the candles and waited for the footman to finish his foot rub.

"Well done," she said. "Your timing is impeccable, footman." She still didn't know his name. "How did you do it and when?"

He looked up. "We aim to please, ma'am."

"But I mean, how did you get into the basement unknown, and how did you know they'd open the box, find the C-Pad?"

"Women can never leave a box unopened." He stood up. "I will be back with an update."

"Better still," she said. "Take one of these—why wait?"

He looked at the earphones and pulled a face.

"Look, I've made some adjustments. It slides in, and you don't feel a thing."

"Sliding in and not feeling a thing is a promise broken by many a footman."

"And it's wireless; here, let me."

Her soft fingers caressed his ears, and the footman didn't feel a thing.

Chapter Thirty-One

PATSY

"A beehive is only as tough as its hairspray."–Beryl's hairdresser

*P*atsy watched as Archie drove off. She stared at Beryl's beehive through the back window and wondered what she had just witnessed.

Archie had fussed over Patsy, saying there was nothing to worry about—setting seeds in her mind that there *was* something to worry about.

Well, that and the broken window . . .

Broken windows were two a penny in Patsy's neighborhood, but usually by teenagers with hooded heads, not a gran dressed in leather sporting a miniature whip.

"She's fallen on hard times," said Archie. He threw Patsy his best Identity look. "And she's not quite the full shilling."

Archie's Identity eye contact had little effect on Patsy.

She was a content middle-age woman who, thanks to Bunnie, appreciated what she had. Bunnie was a constant reminder of just how lucky Patsy was. While Bunnie lived in a house that was not in the best of shape with a constant stream of unhappy people looking for love, Patsy lived with her best friend/partner, Eunice, who was a dab hand at DIY and, if you ignored the rough edges, a dream to live with.

Bunnie was also a great source of material.

Patsy wrote cosy mysteries, and Tallulah, an ex–lady of the night, was her most popular private detective. Tallulah from the *I Didn't See It Coming* series made Patsy enough money for a conservatory, holidays in Florida, and for Eunice to give up work and potter. Tallulah was inspired/based on—or as Eunice liked to say *is*—Bunnie and was the only reason Patsy still lived in the run-down estate.

Patsy was fond of Bunnie and regularly visited for wine, cheese, and a rummage in Bunnie's memoirs, which she had even promised to help write—if she ever felt the need.

"Not in my lifetime," said Bunnie. "I make enough from keeping my mouth shut."

Within minutes of seeing the beehive gran's stone throwing, Patsy was on the phone, and when Bunnie didn't answer, she texted.

Gran break-in—possible ex–porn star? Call police, or the usual?

After which Patsy handed her phone to Eunice and with a "start videoing honey" boldly marched outside.

She owed it to Bunnie to do what she did best: interfere. It's what Tallulah would have wanted.

Patsy watched Archie's car disappear around the corner, then ruffled Izzie's head, which thanks to years of treats she got away with . . .

"Alright, pet, mummy is hear," she muttered, and walked back into her home to find Eunice preparing for a spot of DIY on Bunnie's porch.

This time the break-in felt different—surreal, like something out of her novels.

"Did you get it all on the phone?" she shouted to Eunice while opening a tin of chum.

Eunice, rummaging in her toolbox, looked up. "Of course! Nice bit of you at the end."

"That's sweet, dear, but did you get a good picture of the gran?"

"Naturally," muttered Eunice. "Now I just need a hammer and . . ." She pulled out a box of nails. "Some of these babies, and we're in business."

Patsy looked out the window. "I have this feeling," she muttered, "that that was not your usual vandalism."

Izzie sniffed her food.

"Not often you see a gran dressed as a porn star," muttered Eunice, counting out her nails.

"Wonder what she was looking for—Izzie?" muttered Patsy, stroking. Izzie growled.

"Bloody dog," muttered Eunice, "who'd want her?"

Izzie growled again, followed by a cough.

"What's wrong, not like your chum?" cooed Patsy. She pushed the plate under Izzie's nose. Izzie let out another cough, then started to gag.

"My wee pet?" said Patsy. "Probably scared."

Eunice looked up from her nail collection. "Scared? She's a dog, what's she got to be scared about?"

"Poor thing," said Eunice. She stopped and stared at the dog. "She does look a bit peaky."

Cough, splutter, gag!!!

She dropped her nails. "She's gonna spew!"

Cough, splutter, gag!!!

"The carpet!"

"My wee pet."

"Get out of the way!" yelled Eunice with a dramatic lunge at Izzie.

"Easy," said Patsy, "she's not nuclear waste."

Eunice, faster than a rattlesnake, whisked Izzie up like she was a leaking nappy and raced to the door.

Cough, splutter, gag!!!

"There's something in her throat," yelled Patsy from inside.

"You reckon?" shouted Eunice, holding the dog at arm's length. "Whatever it is, it's not landing on the carpet. That's a bastard to clean, and from the looks of . . . oh, fuck!"

Cough, splutter, gag!!!

". . . it'll stain like beetroot."

"Do you think those so-and-sos have poisoned her?" said Patsy, now by the sink trying to keep her breakfast down.

"Who could blame 'em," muttered Eunice.

"What?"

"I said I'll give her a hard slap, that'll do it."

"Not too hard, she's fragile."

"Fragile my arse," muttered Eunice.

"Be gentle, darl," said Patsy, muffling a retch.

Eunice, with a robust flip, turned Izzie upside down and thumped her back.

Cough, splutter, gag . . .

Eunice slapped harder, and after several gags and a pile of half-digested cheese and biscuits later, Eunice was staring at an erect bit of *something wiry*, in a pool of goo.

What the fuck?

Don headed onto the M9 towards Edinburgh. He knew it like the back of his hand. Bunnie beside him was engrossed on her phone, looking for a place to stay.

"You won't find much," said Don, "it's the festival."

"I have a pal," she said . . .

After the fourth *so-called pal* she stared into the windscreen. "Do you have a pal, Don?"

"It's the festival . . ." he said.

"Surely you must know someone . . ." Bunnie sighed. "Thought you knew everyone, a cabbie like you . . ."

"I do," said Woody, "my uncle; he's got a campsite near Edinburgh."

"Camp?" said Mex.

"You want to go camping now?" said Bunnie. She looked pissed. "I hate camping."

"What's camping?" said Mex.

Pete, thinking of the *Carry On* film, made a joke about Barbara Windsor's bra-flicking, and then talked of places where the john was a week's walk away but was acceptable to do in your PJs. "Perhaps yoga is also possible," he muttered.

Woody waffled on about peg-less tents, gas stoves, and inflatables until he realized no one was listening. "I can let him know we're coming," he finally said.

"Good idea," said Don, "can't wait to see Buns in a tent."

Bunnie looked at her phone. *Patsy had left a text.*

Eunice poked the *something wiry* with a stick . . .

Perhaps with a wash . . .

Eunice, balancing the *something wiry* on the end of her stick, headed for the kitchen.

Years of helping her ex in the building trade had taught Eunice many things, including the ability to never be disgusted or fazed—by anything. Her ex was a man with a temper who worked alongside the sort of men whose sense of humor involved dead rats in lunchboxes and locking comrades in toilets that didn't flush. She had spent her years of marriage fixing what her ex broke in a temper while developing a talent for selective breathing. Nothing made her sick. She could scrape mold from roadkill, unblock a sewage pipe without the slightest hint of eye watering, and had even stood by Patsy holding her hair during a bout of food poisoning without one silent retch.

Nothing revolted her, apart from porn—which was one of the reasons why she left her ex, but that is another story.

She swung the wire in front of Patsy's face. "Look what was causing the trouble."

"Rather not."

"Never seen anything like that before," Eunice said, now washing the wire under the tap.

Patsy tossed a treat at Izzie. "Do you have to do that in the sink?"

Eunice, engrossed in her examination, didn't answer. Finally, with a robust tap on the kitchen sink, she looked at the love of her life. "All gone," she smiled, planting a kiss on Patsy's head. "You ready to inspect the damage?"

Patsy and Eunice headed back into Bunnie's patio.

Patsy pushed opened the door to a clutter of broken potted plants blocking the entrance.

"What the fuck?" said Eunice.

Chapter Thirty-Two

THE BREAK-IN

"To break in requires force, to break out requires, know how—
unless you're a pimple."—Woody

Bunnie stared at Patsy's text, then turned to Don. "There's been a break-in."

"What again?" said Don. "Told you; you should call the police."

"I'm not having them rummaging through my personals."

Don tutted. "Police don't rummage."

"What about Izzie?" said Mex.

"Izzie's OK." Bunnie looked at Don. "In case you were wondering."

"Izzie's always OK," he muttered.

"Thank heavens," said Mex.

Bunnie looked up from the text. "She said it was a woman with a beehive."

"Beehive?" Mex looked at Pete.

"What do you mean a beehive?" said Don.

"There is more than one beehive, ma'am," said Pete.

"In purple leather with a whip?" said Bunnie.

"Not so sure about the purple leather," said Pete.

Bunnie flicked through the text.

"She wants to call the police . . . she says the burglar must be on drugs, kept talking about pickles."

"Or the pickle," muttered Pete.

Mex, with a sharp intake of breath, turned to Pete with a *she's here* look.

"She's such a panic merchant . . ." said Bunnie. "Eunice says she looked like a porn star."

"What's a porn star?" whispered Mex.

"I'll tell you later," said Woody.

"Sorry, porno gran . . . don't know any porno grans; do you?" She continued to read. "No money in porno grans . . ."

"Pity," muttered Don.

Bunnie threw him a look.

"Just saying," said Don.

Bunnie's phone rang; she answered it.

Don heard Patsy's muffled *finally* and shouted, "Call the police."

"No," said Bunnie with another glare at Don.

Bunnie sighed over the muffled hysterics of Patsy. "I told you I don't do that sort of thing anymore . . . and no I am not selling drugs."

Bunnie turned to the back seat. "Anyone know about a gran with a thing for salads, six-inch heels, and matching beehive?"

Pete and Mex said nothing.

Bunnie began to huff as a strained Patsy continued, droning on about *feeling things in her waters* and *Izzie not being quite right* . . .

Bunnie finally snapped, "Oh for heaven's sake; just do what you normally do, and I'll square you up when I am back . . . oh, and can you walk Izzie?"

Patsy looked about the mess in the patio. "She wants no cops; it's because of those bloody memoirs. Told you that woman is impossible."

Eunice, with a patient smile, nodded.

Patsy sighed. "Better go and see if the *memoirs* are still standing then."

"A porn star," said Woody, "is someone who . . ." He looked at DJ.

"Don't look at me," said DJ, "you're the one that offered."

"Well, it's all to do with leather and lubrication," muttered Woody.

"Oils?" said Mex. "Pete's good with oils, aren't you Pete."

"Not quite the same thing, ma'am," muttered Pete. "Think of a no-holds-barred *Fifty Shades of Grey*."

"Hair color?"

"Porn is not all it's cracked up to be," muttered Don. "There are better things to do with a woman."

Bunnie turned to Mex. "Forget about hair dye, what I want to know is—is that woman who was on the thing that exploded the same as that woman in my porch?"

Silence.

"I knew it; bleeding well knew it! Right in my bones, didn't I, Don? Didn't I say I felt something in my bones? Typical."

"Sounds like Beryl," muttered Mex.

"Beryl?" said Don. "Who's Beryl?"

"Beryl," sighed DJ, "rules."

"Beryl rules?" said Don.

"Beryl?" said Woody. "That's an old-fashioned name; sounds like something out of Corrie."

"Beryl is a lovely name," said DJ.

"There is nothing old-fashioned about Beryl," muttered Mex.

"That face," said Bunnie, "never forget it."

"Me neither," muttered DJ.

"And she's nothing like anyone in Corrie," snapped Bunnie.

"Control yourself, Buns," said Don.

"Control myself"—she turned to Don—"is the last thing I need to do, and don't call me Buns."

"OK, Buns."

"Just wait till I get my hands on her—upsetting my poor Izzie."

"She upset Izzie?" said Mex.

"Izzie's fine," said Don, "don't you worry about Izzie, that dog would survive a nuclear explosion."

Bunnie turned to Mex with a glare.

"She was sick, you know. Your Beryl probably tried to poison her."

"She's not my Beryl," said Mex.

Bunnie turned around and stared into the windscreen. "Well whose bleeding Beryl is she then?"

"Do you need to ask?" said Woody.

For a moment Bunnie stopped, she had learned a lot with her question about this *so-called* Planet Hy Man. And Don seemed to know a lot of answers, chipping in with the odd comments about Legless, as DJ talked of *The Story*. It took a while for Bunnie to grasp the whole washing line incident, let alone Mex and her Android. Now, as she looked at her friend with benefits, she realized he was more than a taxi driver; he was part of the whole story too. Was he what DJ was?

"What's up?" said Don.

"You always were a good storyteller," she said.

Chapter Thirty-Three

INCOGNITO

"A sausage without a barbecue is like a robot without an owner."
—Mex

The worker picked up the instrument. "You're holding it the wrong way." She flicked a switch. Vegas watched as the instrument whirled and swirled with lights flashing.

"What is it?" said Vegas.

"It has many names." Said the worker, "and if you take it back with you tonight, you'll find your own."

It had been a tough night accomplishing everything *incognito*, as Hilda loved to say; *incognito* was her favorite word. She had spent a lifetime being incognito and considered herself a master. Skirting about the corridors of power had got her where she was today, and tonight was no different. She had excelled herself.

Hilda had spent the night like a silent shadow flashing past the sleeping footmen, arranging and moving. It was even better than her closing of the Voted In's beverage room night. This time she did not wait for the few hours of footman-less corridors; she did it under the footmen's wonky noses—for added panache.

And, as always, there'd be no one to notice or pat her on the back;

no one to tell her how amazing she was. All she had was the rebooted, redefined H-Pad 11 and a cleaner robot of the miniature variety. A pat on the back from them was as probable as a footman pulling off a backflip.

As soon as Beryl had *left the building*, Hilda *yellow taped* her flat, preparing those in the know that Beryl may not be coming back.

"Things must be protected," she said.

Everyone knew what the yellow tape really meant. Beryl's pad was up for grabs, and Hilda had already grabbed it. And before anyone had the chance to argue, question, or even reply, Hilda was under the yellow tape and through the rooms investigating all that was Beryl's.

Hilda looked about Beryl's fluffy mats, large dressing gown, and deluxe ice machine and smiled. Who needed a onesie in this pad?

"Look what we are moving into," she said to the H-Pad 11.

"Look what you now have the joy of cleaning," she said to the robot, then realized she was talking to robots, who were neither impressed nor unimpressed.

She walked out onto the patio and sipped her chilled-to-perfection iced water. She was pleased with the H-Pad 11, which had successfully blocked DBO without one order. While Hilda was dipping under the yellow tape into Beryl's pad, the H-Pad 11 was working miracles. And before Hilda had slipped on Beryl's fluffy slippers, the H-Pad 11 had tracked, squashed, and reported back with a curt "Connection disengaged, ma'am." And Hilda had merely thought about the disconnection, along with egg sandwiches and bribing . . . it seemed that the H-Pad 11 had faculties way beyond any before, including the art of planning ahead.

"Cleaners are here," said the robot, "with the seaside."

"Tell them to wait," said Hilda. She smiled to herself. *It's all going to plan.*

"Plan?" said H-Pad 11. "What about Vegas?"

"I have a plan B."

"If you mean DBO, I'd think again."

"What do you mean?"

"And they are using earphones."

"Earphones," laughed Hilda. "Well, I wish them luck with that one."

"Wireless."

Hilda stopped. "Wireless—who, what, how . . . ?"

"Your opposition, ma'am, has been underestimated."

Hilda silently seethed. "How do you know of this?"

"It is my job."

Job—since when did an H-Pad 11 have a job? she thought.

"Function, ma'am, is perhaps a better description," said the H-Pad 11.

Hilda stopped; no one had told her that the face reader attachment could read her mind. She shifted uncomfortably. "Yes, well, I have estimated the underestimate-able with another plan, I just need to contact the cook."

"Cook contacted, sandwiches in situ," said the H-Pad 11.

"Pseudo egg and mayo?"

"Done and dusted," said the H-Pad 11. "Thanks to the footman here."

"Chives, peppers, and a little tomato on the side," said the footman. He smiled. "At the shed as we speak."

Hilda looked at his smug stance; was he hoping for a pat on the back as well?

Vegas had left the library thanks to the lender's "no-nonsense" directions and headed back to the guest room with strict instructions of how and when to try the implement.

That night, Vegas stared at the veranda through her window as the 33 robots lit a campfire. She was intrigued.

Fires in the city had been banned years ago after the "great singe" of '74. Burning was once a ceremony held in front of the statues in the courtyard of greatness, until one overzealous worker singed the groin of the Manifesto the Great statue.

Some were suspicious, others ecstatic.

The "keep it clean, keep it safe" committee, however, called for the removal of any bulging groin and put an end to all fires, including *the barbecue*—causing a plummet in soya sausages sales. The "keep it clean, keep it safe" committee had suggested open-air grilling, but with no flame, no smoke, no eyes watering, it hardly seemed worth the effort.

Vegas stared at the implement. She had been told to wait until everyone was asleep . . .

She pressed the button; it revved into action. *Brrrrr, zing, pop.*

One of the robots stopped . . .

"What's that?"

"What?"

Brrrrr, zing, pop.

"That?"

Vegas silenced the implement.

"A bird?"

"You think it was a bird?"

"Yes, definitely."

Vegas sighed. How long does it take for a robot to switch off? She decided to show DBO.

"What the pickle is that?"

The footman stifled a smile. "A foot massager, ma'am, but not for the foot."

"What?"

"I have some instructions," said Vegas, a little excited.

"Instructions?"

"Yes," said Vegas. "But I have to wait till everyone is asleep."

"Quite," said the footman.

"It makes a lot of noise." She stared at the flames as they cracked and flickered under the dark sky. "Heard for miles . . . across hills and beyond." She paused. "Wait—I think the robots are snoring."

"Robots snoring?"

"Can you hear them."

"A smidgen," said the footman.

Vegas stared at the motionless robots silhouetted by firelight; *not a rustle.* "I'll get back to you tomorrow," she said.

"Very good, ma'am," said the footman as Vegas flicked off with a haste unusual for her.

Chapter Thirty-Four

THE BASEMENT

"When it comes to a screen, size always matters."–The voice from the back

Hilda smiled as several footmen entered grunting. They were carrying what anyone on Earth would describe as the biggest, slimmest TV screen ever. They balanced it against a wall.

"Your seaside, ma'am," said the head footman.

He clicked his heels to attention, the other footmen followed as Cleaner One and Two entered.

They surveyed the screen with disapproval. Cleaner One tapped a corner and tutted.

"Does it have hologram facilities?"

"Yes."

"In the basement?"

"Naturally, that is the whole point . . ."

Cleaner One whistled through her teeth. "You sure?"

"It's an incentive when we need extra energy," said Hilda.

Cleaner One looked at Cleaner Two. "What do you think?"

Cleaner Two tutted. "For a start, it's way too big."

"And too slim. How's it going to stand up?" said Cleaner One.

Hilda glared at her. "Against the wall?"

"It is the flexibility that is the key," said the H-Pad ii.

Cleaner One threw an *asking the impossible yet again* look at Cleaner Two.

"It is merely a question of sticking pads," added Hilda.

"Sticking pads? We're cleaners, this is way out of our remit."

"You're not getting extra," snapped Hilda.

"We make them, you connect them," said the H-Pad 11.

"Thank you, H-Pad 11," said Hilda.

"Connecting, unconnecting . . ." continued the H-Pad 11.

"I'll take it from here," said Hilda.

"It *is* in your contract," said the H-Pad 11, "along with, of course, cleaning . . ."

"That'll be all," said Hilda.

"And, of course, the monitoring of said cleaning robot," said the H-Pad 11.

Hilda, exasperated, turned to the H-Pad 11. "How about I switch you off?"

Cleaner One smirked; Hilda met her smirk with a glare. "Your mission is of high importance."

"Ma'am."

"You'll be making history."

"Which we are doing in out-of-regulation hours," said Cleaner One.

"Saving the planet is its own reward."

"Except in overtime . . . time."

"Overtime is noted," said Hilda.

"Noting doesn't fill the fridge . . ." Cleaner One met Hilda's glare. "With respect, ma'am."

"Well, in this instance perhaps, some careful recording as well . . . maybe then I can arrange"—she coughed—"for some fridge-filling."

"You want us to record?" said Cleaner Two.

Hilda ran her fingers across the screen. "Mere note-taking, nothing more."

"Like those memos of yours?" said Cleaner Two.

"Of course, yes," said Hilda.

"While installing?" said Cleaner Two.

"You catch on," said Hilda.

Cleaner Two blushed.

"This is way above our contract," said Cleaner One, throwing an *I'll do the talking* look at Cleaner Two.

"You'll be held in the highest gratitude," said the H-Pad 11.

"Making this planet a safe place to clean," said Hilda, who, with a curt flick, disconnected the H-Pad 11.

Hilda paused and looked at the two women. "And of course note-taking will take you to a higher grade."

Two footmen grunted underneath the weight of the screen, an instrument way too profound and expensive to be in the hands of a robot.

The cleaners stomped behind in huffed silence and behind them marched a dozen robots, all shapes and sizes, carrying a variety of setting-up equipment.

Since the escape of the 33 robots, the cleaners were allocated all-new robots to break in and, if needed, improve or silence. The robots were all shapes and sizes with a variety of skills. The shapes and sizes made cleaning a breeze and any corner accessible, while the variety of skills extended the cleaning to other more technical things, such as connecting, disconnecting, and wielding hammer-like instruments about.

Sometimes the power of controlling an army of robots went to the cleaner's head, especially Cleaner One.

"Always with the blushing," she said. "You just can't help yourself."

"How am I to control blushing?"

"You weaken our position. We could have bargained for more."

"More what? Tofu in the fridge?"

"It was a metaphor."

"Who eats metaphors?" Cleaner Two sighed. "At least I'm not a crawler. Did you have to salute her?"

"She did offer a higher grade."

"And if the hologram goes belly-up, who's to blame, the robots behind?"

The robots, mid marching, stopped . . .

"Entering tunnel, quiet please," said an elevator voice.

Cleaner One pulled a bucket from Cleaner Two and handed it to a robot. "And how many times have I told you: they do the carrying, we do the ordering."

A jockstrap was not something the Voted In had ever seen, let alone heard of. Lycra, on the other hand, had been the butt of many jokes in the room with a view. Now, as they looked at the jockstrap close-up, it fascinated them.

Baby tried it on and pulled a pose.

"Take it off."

"Why? It feels nice."

"You look ridiculous."

"We always look ridiculous."

The voice from the back tugged at a pair of Lycra shorts. "Apparently it gives," she said.

They heard a crash, thump, and knock; they stopped.

"Who's that?"

"Quick, put it back."

Baby tossed the jockstrap at Voted In Three, while Voted In One and Voted In Two grabbed, fumbled, then stuffed the pile of Lycra back into the box.

"Hide the C-Pad."

"Where?"

"And the jockstrap."

"What?" said Voted In Three.

Senator, thinking on her feet, kicked the C-Pad under a bed. The voice from the back *more imaginative than Senator* stuffed the face reader down her trousers, which, being of the finest silk, allowed the face reader to wriggle into her socks. While Voted In Three stared at the jockstrap like it was a bomb about to go off.

Knock, crash, thump . . . .

"The installation team is here."

Voted In One grabbed the jockstrap from Voted In Three, shoved it under a mattress, surveyed the barracks, then went to open the door. The others followed her into the gym . . .

A footman entered.

"Hear ye, hear ye, make way for the cleaners."

The robots marched into the room.

"Hear ye, hear ye, make way for the cleaners."

The rest of the footmen shuffled in with the seaside screen.

"Hear ye, hear ye . . ." The cleaners, nudging the footman quiet, entered the basement.

"We're here," said Cleaner One, "under the orders of our esteemed leader."

"To sort things out," added Cleaner Two.

"And to check for anything . . . untoward," said Cleaner One.

"Yes," said Cleaner Two, "lots of checking."

She sniffed. *What's that pong?* she mouthed to Cleaner One.

Man smell, mouthed Cleaner One.

Cleaner Two pulled a face as a few of the Voted In began to wave the air with a *where did that smell come from?* look.

The robots continued to march around the room, the cleaner robot's foot rollers working up to a high-pitched squeak.

Left, left, *squeak*, left, left, *squeak* . . . no one had told them to stop.

The footmen, also waiting for orders, teetered under the weight of the seaside screen. One stumbled, another grabbed . . .

"Careful."

"Mind!"

Cleaner Two grabbed a corner and righted the seaside screen.

"Clear designated wall for the seaside!" shouted Cleaner One, who began to survey the screen for *attachment facilities*.

Left, left, *squeak*, left, left, *squeak* . . .

Cleaner One, now looking for any *hidden attachment facilities*, looked up. "What the pickle are you doing?"

"Marching, surveying, getting a feel for the place, important for the installing of a hologram."

"Hologram?" muttered a few of the Voted In.

"Now you've spoiled the surprised," snapped Cleaner Two.

"A hologram, yeah!" muttered the voice from the back with an air-punch and skidded across the seaside screen.

"What you up to?" shouted Cleaner One.

"Balancing at the moment."

Cleaner One stared at the voice from the back. "Step away from the screen."

She appeared with a blank face and a lump in her left trouser above her shoes.

The two cleaners circled her. "What's with the leg?"

"Nothing."

"You haven't been at the Lycra, have you?"

"No."

"Because there'll be no Lycra for you lot, Hilda's orders."

A few of the Voted In shuffled uncomfortably.

Chapter Thirty-Five

THE ROYAL EGG SANDWICHES

"A sandwich tastes better cut in triangles."–The cook

DBO stared at the magnified illustration of Vegas's apparatus up on the screen.

"What is that?" she said, jolting the footman awake. He rubbed his eyes and peered at the illustrations.

"Ma'am, it is but an apparatus for making a woman smile."

"You sure it's not a drill?" she said.

"A drill, ma'am, would not be so colorful."

"I don't understand, how could a drill make a woman smile?"

"As I said, ma'am, it is not a drill."

"Looks like a drill."

The footman shifted uncomfortably on his feet. "Perhaps you could source a film from Earth, there are plenty on the subject."

"What?" said DBO.

"A film, a mere fabrication of events, but best describes said instruments."

The footman rose to his feet and talked of bananas, double meanings, and lonely women. When DBO looked confused, he moved on to *adult films*, which in his youth was a great topic of conversation.

"Back then it was men who used sheds."

"I find that hard to believe."

"We invented them."

DBO tutted. "As if."

"A shed," said the footman, "was a retreat, a solace for men, not the intergalactic spy . . . temple it is now."

DBO looked unimpressed.

"It wasn't easy back then. There was no CTV cameras or mobiles, our planet relied on mirrors to watch Earth."

"Mirrors, as if."

"Yes, ma'am, spying was much harder and stressful; sheds and adult films eased that stress."

The footman sighed with the memory . . .

"Mirror?" tutted DBO. "What could you possibly see from one of them?"

"You'd be surprised," muttered the footman . . .

DBO took the illustration to Verruca, who called it a fine collection of Victorian equipment.

"How do you know about these . . . vibrators?" she said to Verruca.

Verruca looked shamefaced. "Why are you asking?"

"It just that Vegas seems sidetracked. She has been unreachable for hours."

"It'll pass," said Verruca as she eyed DBO's set features. "You should try it."

"Me?"

"Look at you all hunched up."

"I get foot massages."

"Hmmm, not quite the same thing."

The footman watched DBO leave, then settled in front of the dashboard. He slid his feet up, snuggled his head in the right position, and was just heading for a snooze when he heard a rustle at the door followed by a tap.

He opened the door to the silence of the Zen garden and a plate of delicately sliced, crustless sandwiches left on the *wipe your feet* mat.

When he saw the filling he almost drooled; pseudo-egg was just a slice away from delectable hemp bacon, and just as believable.

"Fancy that," he said pulling the note from the top.

For the footman
Sandwiches for saving the planet
From the cook
Thank you

He took the plate inside and prepared himself for peace, quiet, and a mouthful of mayo. DBO would be at least an hour.

He lifted his first sandwich, caught his reflection on the screen, and paused. No one had ever thanked him before—for anything. And now here he was tucking into a four-slices sandwich with garnish! From a grateful cook.

He wondered which one . . . *Hopefully the older one.*

Once the seaside was set up, the cleaners told the Voted In to "use the earphones," which now lay in a heap on the floor, and to "keep hydrated."

The Voted In watched as the footmen left behind the cleaners, carrying the box of Lycra.

"What are we supposed to hydrate with?" muttered Baby, when Alice zoomed into the gym with a beverage machine.

The Voted In groaned.

"What's she doing here?" snapped Voted In One.

Alice stopped mid zoom. *Was anyone grateful these days?* She had just taken the Operators to the Voted In apartment floor. "Pick a room and a suit," she memo-ed. *Did they say thanks, cheers, well done?*

Not even a nod, let alone a smile; instead they raced off like children left loose in a sweetie shop . . .

Alice dumped the beverage machine in the corner.

Alice was what many would call a poor man's messenger. Which, at times, Alice found more than offensive, and no matter how hard she tried to *impress*, nothing worked.

"Where's our messenger?"

"You now have Alice."

"What, why, how can we?"

She hovered above the beverage machine with her arms across her ball figure. "If you're not wanting the beverage maker, I'll take it back."

"Does it make coffee?"

"Well, no."

"Hot chocolate."

"No, just tea."

"Tea," muttered a few of the Voted In.

Alice looked at their downcast faces. "But you have this?" she said, flying across to the seaside screen.

She switched it on with a *ta-da!*

A luxurious picture of glistening white sand with dwarfs lounging in the sun flickered on.

Alice hovered, waiting for the *oohs* and *aahs*.

"What the hell is this?" said Senator, watching a dwarf strip to his shorts and dive into the sea.

"The seaside," said Alice.

"What? Why don't you just suspend a jug of sparky out that slit of a window and tell us to help ourselves?" snapped Voted In Three.

Alice pressed the remote. "You can zoom in if you want."

The Voted In stared at a close-up of a dwarf running his tongue along the top of an ice cream.

"What's the good of that when you're on a bike with only tea to drink?"

"And . . . if you reach your quota, I have access to the holograms," muttered Alice.

The Voted In continued to stare at the screen, now focused on a dwarf massaging oil into his stomach. They looked anything but happy.

Alice slid the remote by the TV and left, realizing any chance of impressing had just flew out the said slit of a window.

❄

Vegas woke up fresh, invigorated, and surprisingly supple. She jumped out of bed and headed back to the library.

She ploughed through plumbing, electricity, and woodwork, finally finding what a real ladle looked like. She discovered the theories of crop rotation, which was just as boring as Hilda's lectures, and the "All you need to know and didn't know who to ask" book.

Which was written by a woman who, once her husband died, took on a new lease of creativity . . .

Men working with women, she wrote. *Didn't work except for the spark plug. An invention that took coordination, understanding, and sitting around talking about said understanding.*

Vegas was getting closer . . .

She flicked through the rest of the book as it branched into sex, being "off the agenda" along with the proper use of a shed, and how reinstallation of bulging groins was a waste of public funds . . .

Vegas closed the book. *Nothing . . .*

Vegas, frustrated, went back into the kitchen. She found a space by the sink and tried to catch the apprentice's attention. The apprentice, however, was arguing with the cook about hard-boiled synthetic eggs while trooping in and out of the walk-in freezer.

"We've just finished the scones for elevenses, and you want me to start on the mayonnaise—do I not get a break?"

The scones looked nothing like the flat, hard variety of the city. These were plump, brown, and filled the kitchen with a scent new to Vegas. She inhaled and for a moment wondered if she would be offered "elevenses."

The cook, who was peeling a synthetic egg, tossed one at the apprentice. "Here, knock yourself out."

"I don't want an egg, I want a break." The apprentice turned to Vegas. "Egg?"

"Actually, I wanted some help with the library?"

"The library doesn't give up her treasure easily," muttered the cook.

"It's a building," said the apprentice.

"Yes, but a building with a soul." The egg broke in the cook's hand; soya yolk spilled over her fingers. "Guess it wasn't as hard-boiled as I thought," she muttered, tossing the remains at a bin.

The apprentice looked at Vegas. "You just need to know the filing system."

A robot sauntered in. "How are we ladies this morning?" he said with a casual twirl and moved towards the scones.

"You can forget about the scones, they're for equal distributing," snapped the cook.

The robot hand stretched to an egg; the apprentice slapped it. "And them."

"Where do I find the filing system?" said Vegas.

The apprentice gestured to the robot sneaking into the freezer.

The cook pulled the robot out and locked the door. "These guys know everything and give it away for a song."

"A scone?" said the robot. "Love a scone."

"They'll tell you, they're rebels, truth is nobody wants them," shouted the cook. "Beryl threatened to reboot them if they ever returned."

"Thought rebooting went out with earphones," muttered Vegas.

"They are too smart for their own good," muttered the cook.

Vegas watched the robot slip a few scones into a side pocket as it backed out and decided to follow.

Chapter Thirty-Six

33 ROBOTS

"You never get the truth from eavesdropping."–Ex–Planet Hy Man man spy

Vegas sat on the veranda with the three 33 robots and watched as they lit a fire. Sitting by a fire made all she'd been through worthwhile. *Well, that and the vibrator.*

"They'd be lost without us," said Pope, the tallest robot. Pot and Prudence nodded.

Pope was the most vocal of the robots, while Prudence talked of things being the *bee's knees.*

"You are the bee's knees."

"She's the bee's knees."

"If only we had some bees," said Pot.

Sometimes they mentioned Pete, which always riled Pope. Vegas got the impression that there was more than a hint of jealousy between Pope and Pete. Especially when Prudence said his yoga was the bee's knees.

"He's not that great," muttered Pope.

"He has carved out a career—what robot has achieved that?"

"Yoga for other robots?" laughed Pope. "Hardly guru status."

Pope pulled a *here we go* face at Vegas.

"Of course, he'll never last on Earth," said Pope. "I mean, a 33 robot in that atmosphere?"

"Seems to be doing OK so far," muttered Pot.

"And his yoga won't help," continued Pope.

"I thought it was all the rage," said Pot.

Pope threw Pot a glare. "In Teflon? That stuff is for fry pans on Earth. Imagine when the sun hits him."

"He is in Scotland," said Pot, "hardly sun city."

"Scotland?" said Prudence. "They fry everything there, even chocolate."

"You know about Earth?" said Vegas.

"We know many things," said Prudence.

"We look after the library," said Pope with a smug stance. "If Pete saw us now he'd be spitting." He turned to Vegas. "Scone?"

Vegas took a scone smothered in jam, cream, and butter. "All from hemp?" she said.

"Either that or the cook's a magician," said Pot.

Prudence took a bite. "Hmmmm, never get tired of 'em."

"We have nothing like this," said Vegas, "ours are flat, chewy, and . . ." She heard a muffled noise in an accent she recognized as foreign. "Is that Woody?"

"No," said Prudence, looking sheepish.

Vegas looked about the veranda. "Where is the voice coming from then?"

"What voice?"

"Here, have another scone."

"That voice. I just heard it, didn't come from the kitchen."

"Try the sauce."

Vegas dipped her scone into another chocolate sauce; for the first time in years she enjoyed eating. "Sounded like Woody," she mumbled with a mouthful of chocolate.

"Woody?"

"Yes," she said.

Vegas heard another voice . . . she turned toward Pope. "I'd know that voice anywhere."

"Don't think so."

"Here, try this," said Prudence. "Lemon butter, excellent after the chocolate."

"That's definitely Mex's voice," said Vegas, shooing away a bird.

"Wouldn't do that with a bird."

"Why?"

"It encourages them."

The birds began to flock.

Vegas went to lick her fingers, but a bird got there first and nipped her. She shooed it away with a robust flick and a mouthful of swearing, only to collect more birds about her.

"See?"

"This is what we have to put up with all day."

Vegas picked up a scone and tossed it at a bird heading towards her. It dodged the scone with a squawk, and the scone rolled onto the field in front of the veranda. The other birds stopped, turned to the scone, and zoomed in. Within seconds it was demolished. The birds looked up and glared at Vegas. The finger-nipper squawked, and the others followed.

"You made 'em angry now."

"How?"

The birds made for Vegas; one plonked itself on her shoulder. It's metal beak began to nuzzle into her hair, which, being metal, was not a pleasant experience.

"What kind of birds are these, for pickle's sake?" she snapped with a shoo; another bird joined in.

"Angry kind. Fault in the chip; first batch," said Pope.

"Always the first batch," muttered Pot.

Vegas stood up and began to wave madly at them, which seemed to attract rather than detract.

"You need the toffee," said Prudence, "sticks to their beaks."

"Toffee, you have toffee?" said Vegas, giving up on the waving. She sat down, allowing the bird to nestle on her shoulder.

"How?"

Pot tapped his nose. *An annoying habit,* noted Vegas.

Vegas watched as the three robots pulled a coffee-colored substance from their pockets and began tossing them at the field in front of the veranda.

Pot like a cricket bowler.

"Must you always be so flamboyant," said Pope.

Pot smiled at Vegas. "Women love a good toss."

The birds flocked to the toffee and began to peck. Soon their beaks were glued together, and their squawking silenced. Their heads hung, and with a silent penguin-like shuffle they disappeared behind the trees.

"That cook is a marvel," muttered Prudence.

Vegas spent the night listening to the robots on the veranda. She heard shuffling, muttering, and when she heard Beryl's voice, she jumped and raced to the veranda.

Pot was sitting cross-legged on a mat with earphones in situ while Prudence was sitting opposite him recording, with a superbly connected face reader and H-Pad.

Pope was snoring in the corner.

"Caught you," said Vegas. snapping the apparatus from his ear. She stopped and studied. It was a super-deluxe, padded earphone. "Where did you get these? I have never seen such a standard."

"We are not just bits of Teflon flung together, you know."

"We are the first batch."

"It makes a difference?" said Vegas.

"Oh yes, the first batch is always of the highest intelligence."

Vegas continued to study the instrument. It was as light as a soya flake.

"It's designed to mold to your ear," said Pope.

"A snug fit for any shape," added Prudence.

Vegas held it to her ear and heard thoughts from Hilda. The color drained from her face, she pulled the headphones off.

"She'd kill me."

"How is she to know?"

Vegas shook her head.

"Try something from Earth, it connects perfectly with a Nokia."

"Nokia?" said Vegas.

"Yes, an implement many laugh at, but it has its qualities," said

Prudence. "Here, try Pete, he's always good for a laugh . . ." Prudence's voice trailed off as she looked at Pope.

"They're heading for a festival," she muttered. "Apparently there is a woman in a box."

"Contortionist," said Pope.

"Contortionist?" said Vegas.

"Yes, bit like yoga but more showy," said Prudence.

"Some would say pornographic," muttered Pot.

"Pornographic?" said Vegas.

"Yes, like using a vibrator with an audience."

Vegas, for the first time ever, blushed.

Chapter Thirty-Seven

MEMOIRS

"Archie, like most first-generations Identities, was suspicious of anyone who chose to forget their heritage."—Don

atsy checked through the memoirs. Eunice, having worked her magic on the broken window, was packing up her tools.

"They are all here," she said to Eunice. "Although it looks like someone has been rifling through them. They're usually stacked like a deck of cards." Patsy sighed. "Anyone would think Madonna had written them."

Eunice picked up a book . . .

Legless
The Blue Period
A story of a rebel
In Lycra that not only gave but breathed.

"Who's Legless?"

"Some client," muttered Patsy, "trying to discover his voice."

Eunice leafed through, curious. "What's a stationary?"

Patsy snatched the book. "She'd have a cardiac if she saw you reading it."

Eunice watched Patsy pack the book away.

"Caught me one day and went mental. Don't know why, must be the most boring writing I had ever looked at."

"That bad?"

"Six hours of my life I'll never get back. He becomes a mime or dance act?" Patsy checked the room. "Or was it something to do with storytelling?" She switched off the light. "Can't remember, it was that boring."

"Doesn't look boring to me," muttered Eunice with a last look at the pile.

After they locked up Bunnie's house, Patsy texted Bunnie the *porn gran* video, followed by a picture of the *wire thingy* (which Eunice made such a song and dance about). Patsy then took Izzie for a walk, while Eunice continued to study the wire thingy; it intrigued her almost as much as Legless's memoirs did.

"Izzie," muttered Beryl. "What did I do to deserve that?"

Beryl was moving through the low emotions of sugar loss accompanied by mutterings of remorse . . .

Archie looked at Beryl's pale face in the revision mirror, making a mental note to skip the tablet from now on. The last thing he needed was a suicidal Beryl, let alone a repeat performance of *Beryl at Bunnie's*. Beryl was his ticket to finding Legless and proving the young Identities wrong—that Legless was more than a legend. He was not only real, but alive and kicking.

"Fancy a McDonald's American?" he said. "Put some pep in your step."

"American? Pep?"

"Black coffee, to put you back on your feet again," muttered H2.

Beryl didn't answer.

"Do you know anything about this?" Bunnie flashed her phone at Mex and Pete. It was playing Beryl's break-in at Bunnie's.

Mex stared at Beryl's bulging eyes and sucked in her breath.

"Yes, no, I mean . . . don't think so."

Pete, catching Beryl mid toss of his precious plugulator, let out a girlish squeal. "Maybe, possibly; well . . ."

Bunnie flicked to the wire-thingies photo.

Pete sucked in his breath, flashing an *oh shit* look at Mex.

"I'll take it that is a yes then," said Bunnie, whipping the phone away.

"Well, yes," muttered Mex and Pete together.

They both knew there was only one thing that looked like what they saw: an H-Pad wire, tossed aside once rebuilt. Not only was Beryl here, but she had Mex's out-of-date H-Pad, and from the looks of things, it was working again.

What did they have?

Bunnie's *feeling in her bones,* Woody's century-old Nokia phone; Don's *who needs a satnav when you're a taxi driver* switched-off satnav?

And, if Beryl was here, who was running the Planet Hy Man —Hilda?

A woman who made Beryl's double-crossing look like an act of love. A woman who knew not only which side her bread was buttered on but how to butter it. And a woman smart enough to not only outsmart Beryl but keep the footmen sweet so as not to rebel.

What the pickled egg were her plans?

Whatever those plans were, there was one thing for definite: there was no place for a Beryl *comeback,* let alone a 33 robot that no one wanted in the first place, or a has-been loyal to Beryl's man spy.

In fact, a rebellion hero was probably the last thing Hilda wanted.

"She has been known to double-cross," muttered Mex.

"Beryl?" DJ shook his head. "Doesn't look the sort."

"Let's face it, she has led us up the potting shed," said Mex.

"Garden path, ma'am."

"For good reason, surely," said DJ.

"Guess we'll soon find out," said Don.

Bunnie tutted. "How long before they find us?"

Silence.

"And then what?"

"A Bunnie-and-Beryl punch-up?" said Don with a hopeful look.

"That is something I would buy tickets for."

DJ stared out of the window. "Me too," he muttered.

Bunnie turned to Mex. "What have you got me mixed up in? The takeover of the world or just a plain ordinary end of the world?"

Mex blushed. Beryl was ruthless, and she could not be trusted. And as for Hilda?

"Because if you have," said Bunnie, "I am not going down without a fight. I haven't faced up to the council, the neighborhood watch and had *get out* written in dog poo on my lawn for nothing."

Mex looked at her questioningly.

"Red light," muttered Woody.

And before Woody could expand on how "no one wants *one of them* in their street," or Pete expand on what *one of them* was, Mex had grasped, understood, then wondered why a woman Bunnie's age would do such a thing.

She had vague ideas about sex, all horrible. Doing it for a living seemed to Mex worse than being a footman. To Mex, crushing a man with her thighs seemed a piece of beetroot, compared to wrapping said thighs around their necks in an effort to not only please but pretend to enjoy.

Bunnie must be a woman of great desperation thought Mex, she tapped on Bunnie's shoulder. "I'm here for you, sister."

Bunnie turned around with a look of fire. "And if you want a fight I'll bleeding well give it to you—in spades."

Chapter Thirty-Eight

DBO

"There is no saving of things, people, or the planet, only double-crossing."–Legless

In the dark, DBO sneaked back to the shed. She was having the time of her life.

She was invisible to all who had teased, laughed at and ignored her and was enjoying every moment of it. She had power over the right honorable Beryl, her so called work colleagues and the not so honorable Hilda.

DBO and H2 had been friends since the day DBO was given a seat beside H2 at the dashboard and told to watch, listen, and keep the questions to a whisper. They secretly shared ideas, discoveries, and note taking, as well as the odd flippant remark. They had the invisibility to get away with it and were in prime positions to soak up unobserved.

DBO was also adaptable. Unlike others who laughed at the *you never know when you might need it* theory, she had embraced it, and the shed was a perfect example of that.

DBO opened the door, mindful of the wind chimes . . . which thanks to the footman had been knocked enough times to dislodge the soya cement. Luckily, wind was a rarity in the Zen garden and its tinkling was kept to a minimum. In fact, the only time it tinkled was when the footman stumbled in half asleep from the *great Hilda move* and the *installation of the seaside.*

DBO silently entered, making another mental note to fix, when she spied the empty sandwich plate, the note, and the footman's feet up on the dashboard, snoring.

"What is this?" she said.

"Sandwiches, ma'am, for saving the planet."

"From the cook? What would she know about saving the planet? She can't even raise a scone."

The footman shifted uncomfortably.

She lifted the plate. "This is Hilda's work."

Woody came from a large family of three rugby-playing brothers *who made his life a misery*, a smothering mother, and a so-called uncle who ran a chain of caravan parks, one near Edinburgh. Woody texted the uncle an "I'm on my way" and without waiting for a reply asked if there were "any of those nice tents we can use for a couple of nights?"

He was sure that his uncle would love to buy Mex a drink or four. And if he and Mex didn't hit it off, he knew he and Bunnie would. Entertaining men like his uncle would be a piece of cake to her.

Woody stared ahead, excited that he had an idea and the means to pull it off.

Don, ignoring Woody's "I know how to get there," set up his satnav, which up till now lay dormant. He, however, was not banking on a connection with another planet.

And not just one connection . . .

The satnav started to make noises unknown. At first it sounded like *it* was answering back.

Hilda was listening with her earphones while footmen were moving her things into Beryl's penthouse. And as she sat on her chair of great comfort drinking in the view of magnificence, the footman shuffled in and out with boxes full of onesies and caped crusader outfits, along, of course, with other *necessary* items. However, footmen moving out of hours were notoriously clumsy on account of their ability to fall asleep mid-manoeuvre. And to be fair, the boxes did weigh a ton.

"Wake up," shouted Hilda.

"What?" said Don.

"That sounded like Hilda," said Mex.

Hilda, hearing Don and Mex, stopped in her tracks . . .

"You take a right here," muttered Woody, "just around the corner, and . . ."

"Was that the satnav?" said Bunnie. She tapped the satnav.

"Just around the corner, nearly there," said Woody.

"Ma'am?" said a footman. "Where do you want this box?"

"Shut it," snapped Hilda.

Don stopped. "Box? Did that just come from the satnav?"

"Just around the corner and . . ." said Woody.

"And what about these capes?" shouted another footman, dumping an armload onto the kitchen bench.

"Not there!" shouted Hilda. "Oh, pickled egg . . . shhh."

"Who the hell is this?" snapped Don.

Pete mouthed a *shhh*, which no one listened to.

"Just take a right and we are there," muttered Woody.

Hilda looked at her earphones, then knocked them against something hard. There was only one person who could help her.

Once they arrived, Woody jumped out of the car, dialed his uncle, and, with his Nokia pressed against his ear, went to find him.

Pete stared out of the window, his thoughts drifting to the lady in the box . . .

DJ stared out of his window, his thoughts drifting to Beryl and her beehive . . .

While Mex stared out the window, listening to muffled shuffling and "just leave it" accompanied by the odd slap filtered through the satnav, and uttered, "I could still slay if needed."

Don made to turn the satnav off, until Bunnie stopped him.

"They don't know we can hear," she said. "Could be a bonus."

"They?"

"Beryl," muttered DJ.

"Hilda," said Mex with a resigned sigh. "And you're probably best to disconnect when it comes to her, she is smart."

"So am I," muttered Bunnie.

Don, unimpressed, turned the satnav off.

Woody's uncle appeared from behind the small reception cabin.

"Five people, at festival prices," he rubbed his hands with anticipation.

"Six," said Woody and immediately regretted it as the uncle clapped his hands with glee.

"Who's he?" said Bunnie, staring at Woody's built-like-an-ox uncle who towered over him.

"A comedian by the looks of his prices," said Don.

"A giant comedian?" said Bunnie.

"Except he's not funny," said Don.

"Nothing is funny with you just now," said Bunnie.

Woody's uncle, with a quick wave at the car, went away to work out the bill as Woody walked back . . .

The car was hot. Don wound down his window and was about to shout about family discounts when another stranger's voice came from the satnav.

"It's OK, they've turned it off."

"I thought I turned that thing off," snapped Don.

"What a joke."

He fiddled with the knobs. "I mean, who's talking now?" he snapped.

"33 robots," said Mex.

"A pain in the proverbial," said Pete.

"Thirty-three robots? How many goddamn robots do you need?" said Don.

"Didn't sound like thirty-three to me," muttered Bunnie.

Pete explained why they were called 33 robots, expanding a little on their history.

"Pete was always a little bit smarter," said Mex. "I mean what other robot would start yoga classes?"

Mex looked at Pete. "They're just jealous."

"Ma'am, it is but a given."

Chapter Thirty-Nine

THE EMPTY PLATE

"Nobody knows what it's like to lead, unless you've led, that is."– Beryl

That night, as DBO was engrossed in note-taking while listening to her earphones, Hilda paid a visit. Mindful of the wind chimes, she stood by the shed door, pushed her portable *reach any shelf* step into position, and peered through her spy slit.

She saw the empty sandwich plate—the bait had been taken—and was about to smile a smile of smug satisfaction when she spied the wireless earphones. She could see they were padded for comfort, molded to DBO's ear.

Hilda, routed to the spot, experienced a sea of emotions never felt before—she who considered herself un-astound-able was astounded by this slip of a girl.

There she was using wireless earphones in a shed transformed into a hub of activity as soundless as her corridor at dawn. The walls were covered with refurbished flat screens; the dashboard was efficiently using little if any energy, purring/cooing information with a soft elevator voice.

Hilda took in the pictures on the screens. There were images from Woody's mobile and Beryl's H-Pad, pictures of the room with a view, the gym. Hilda, dumbstruck, experienced an emotion new to her: admiration.

How did she do it?

Hilda had learnt in the shed, watched Beryl rise to power in the shed, and plotted in the shed. She even worked late in the shed sourcing information.

H2 was like her: better a friend than a foe and separated from the Operators at all costs.

Hilda wondered what to do next. She had to adapt, take stock, adjust her plans. She activated her wristwatch connection to the H-Pad 11. She pressed it on silent and was just about to position it to record when she saw something unthinkable that took her breath away. She gasped; was it true?

She peered closer: pictures of her bedroom with printouts of what looked like thoughts.

"Merely projections of thoughts, ma'am," barked the H-Pad 11's voice.

Hilda jolted.

"You're on silent," she hissed.

"Silence can be overridden, ma'am."

"Then what is the point of . . ." Hilda stopped. She could read the printout . . .

"The whole structure of society is hanging on a knife's edge and you're using us to . . . rearrange things?"-H-Pad 11.

"I will rule better here."-Hilda.

"A ruler is a ruler, a view is inconsequential." -H-Pad 11.

"Big words for an H-Pad 11."-Hilda.

"Beryl liked big words." -robot.

"You should stick to cleaning . . ." -Hilda.

"It's us . . . speaking." Hilda continued to hiss.

"Arguing, ma'am."

"I was being polite."

"Polite doesn't become, ma'am."

H2 looked up.

Hilda, ducked, forgetting about the wind chimes.

Twinkle, twinkle . . .

She skidded, stumbled, and faltered on her step.

Clatter, clang, crash . . .

The wind chimes cluttered to the ground.

The footman jolted awake.

"Footman awake, ma'am," said the H-Pad 11.

"Bugger and beetroot," hissed Hilda. She stepped back onto the step and peered into the shed.

The footman looked towards the door, then decided to investigate. Perhaps there were more sandwiches.

"Footman making his way to the door, ma'am," said the H-Pad 11.

"Shut it," hissed Hilda, fogging up the see-through Teflon of the slit. She wiped it with her sleeve, catching the wristwatch.

"Aw!"

Hilda, with a tut, peered into the slit and caught the rosy red eyeball of a footman staring back at her.

"Bollocking beetroot."

"Shit!" said the footman. He blinked, rubbed his eyes, and looked again.

She was gone.

Did he dream it?

Archie handed Beryl his McDonald's American. Soon she was back, alert, curious, and determined.

"What is a fairy godmother," she said.

"My gran calls it a turn of phrase," said H2.

"Fairy?" said Archie, half listening. He was receiving bits of thoughts: *a dog spewing its ringer?* Archie tried to concentrate . . . hear more thoughts . . . DJ, however, didn't seem to be playing ball. *Was he blocking? Had he fallen under the spell of Mr. I-Am-Man Don?*

Archie muttered something about dishwashing liquid.

"Don't think so," said Beryl. "This one talks."

Chapter Forty

BERYL & CO

"Never underestimate the underestimated."–H2

Beryl, much to the annoyance of H2, sat like royalty in the back of the car silently reading the H-Pad screen. Having worked her way through a selection of McDonald's coffees, Beryl was revived, sitting up and firing on all cylinders—not something either Archie or H2 appreciated.

Beryl was a woman used to ordering. She had been brought up on the right side of the track, a place of white walls and education. Unlike Verruca, Beryl was a baby from the right sort of father. A man who almost had a statue in the courtyard of greatness.

Beryl, like Verruca, was the last generation to come from a man. Her mother, unlike Verruca's, was a woman of privilege and red lipstick who died in bed sipping perfect coffee, her last words being "it's not hot enough."

The only thing Beryl knew of her father was that he was good at making rules and took no nonsense. She knew because she had visited his unfinished statue in the courtyard of greatness. A faceless warrior with the words *"It is no-nonsense ordering that is the making of a ruler"* scribed at the feet. She had one picture of him and a pile of stories.

She lived with the constant "Oh, you're so like him," until all the men were taken away. The last man, dragged to the gym by Mex, glared at Beryl, victoriously standing by the gym entrance.

"You're just like the old man . . . pity," he said.

Beryl, confused, never forgot . . .

In her no-nonsense way, she ordered H2 to the front of the car, then sipped her Americano and let out a long, slow "Arrr . . ."

"Why do you get to sit in the back?" whined H2. "After all I've done."

"It is my role—my place," slurped Beryl.

"Place?" said Archie.

"I could help if I was sat at the back. I could look at the H-Pad and . . ."

"I'll do the reading," said Beryl. "Time you realized who's boss in this outfit."

"Boss?" said Archie. "Outfit?"

"Yes, this . . . saving-of-the-world thing we're doing. I am the leader; the one who knows what to do. I sit at the back and make orders. It's the way of things."

"This is a taxicab, not Parliament House on Planet Whatever," said Archie.

"Parliament? What are you talking about?"

"I can stop driving any time. Just say the word and you're on your own," huffed Archie.

Beryl, with a *that's right* tut, continued to read.

"Did you hear me?"

"I heard."

Beryl knew an empty threat when she heard one. She had seen Archie's face when they had talked of Legless; it was obvious he was an Identity desperate to meet Legless—the endless questions gave it away.

That and his telling of the story to H2 while she was dozing her sugar overload off.

It was the first time H2 had heard the story. She didn't even know there was a story and to be honest wished she hadn't heard. The image of Legless creeping behind a woman at a washing line made her feel a bit sick.

At one point so sick that Archie stopped at a lay-by and H2 jumped out, gagging.

"The story has that effect on some women," muttered Archie.

And they thought she didn't listen.

"To find Legless, we must intercept Mex and this Don," said Beryl.

"Don?" said Archie. "What's Don got to do with things? He's a maniac, a loose cannon, a thorn in the side of the——"

"Don is the least of our worries," said Beryl. "If Hilda finds Legless before we do, I—we are stuck here."

"Is that so bad?" said Archie.

"I am not even going to dignify that with an answer," said Beryl.

"You do seem to age a lot faster here," muttered H2.

"And what do you do on Planet Whatever, return to the womb?" muttered Archie.

"Can I *please* sit in the back?" said H2.

"They are heading to the festival," said Beryl.

"Could have told you that," muttered Archie.

"To camp," said Beryl, "whatever that is."

"Good old-fashioned ESP, can't beat it, better than that . . . H-Pad thing you're so keen on," muttered Archie.

H2 turned to Beryl. "Camping is a form of accommodation involving deckchairs, gas stoves, and . . ."

"I know where to go," said Archie. "DJ is an open book," he lied.

"I think I will stick to technology," Beryl said to Archie. "Thoughts are so . . . imaginary."

She patted her new friend the H-Pad. It was of an inferior quality, but the woman behind it, this *fairy godmother*, made up for that and way more. She, it seemed, had her finger on every pulse going. She knew how many were in the car with Mex, where they were going. She knew about Vegas, the room with a view changes, and even the latest news Deidre was broadcasting. In fact, Beryl was so caught up on what was going on she almost had a plan. She figured at this rate, they could have Legless sussed, sorted with the spark plug in situ, and be back home before Hilda had completely ruined her penthouse.

A piece of beetroot, she told herself.

"This whole fiasco will soon be over," said Beryl. "Then we can all go back to doing what we all do best."

"That's what you think," humphed H2.

"What was that?" said Beryl.

"I said sounds like you have a plan, ma'am."

"That's what leaders are for, plans," said Beryl.

"Absolutely," said Archie, throwing his *best comrades* look at H2.

H2 pulled the plugulator from her backpack. She had never seen one like this before, all burnt out. She turned it in her hands; it fell apart in her lap.

"Bollocks!"

"What was that?" said Beryl.

"Nothing," said H2. She tried to push the pieces together. A corner scratched her skin; she looked at the blood and licked it clean. Saliva dribbled onto the plugulator; it sizzled.

H2 looked at Archie with a *what the beetroot was that?* look.

"Yes, soon we'll be back," muttered Beryl. "According to Deidre, Hilda's making a right mess of things."

"Really," muttered H2.

With one hand on the steering wheel, Archie licked his finger and rubbed the plugulator. It sizzled again, then began to click together like a Rubik's cube.

H2, giving up on the finger altogether, spat silently onto the burnt fabric; it sizzled, and the spit bubbled.

Archie nudged her; she did it again.

DBO, still staring at the empty sandwich plate, jumped to attention. The dashboard lit up; this time she knew what to do.

Archie stopped at the traffic lights. He and H2 watched the plugulator burst alive. Bubbles erupted in between the broken sides of the plugulator; it resized, reconstructed, and rebooted, all by the time the traffic light flashed from red to green.

"Yes," said Beryl, "we just need to find this show—what is it called? Johnny Gets Legless? At the . . . let me see . . ."

Archie, slipping the car into first, pulled a *between you and me* face. "Lizard Lounge?"

H2 slid the plugulator on and covered it with her hair.

"Is that you H2?" said DBO.

"Yes," whispered H2.

Archie smiled with a *between you and me* tap of his nose.

While Beryl issued orders that both Archie and H2 considered as obvious as boiling a kettle for coffee, H2 worked her way through Pete's recordings. And by the time they had passed through Livingstone, H2 was looking at her backstabbing leader with a jaded *I can't believe she did that* look.

Beryl had double-crossed and swindled Legless. Things were going to change—for a start, that cavalier attitude of hers . . .

DBO looked about the shed. She had no idea that Hilda had peeked, spied, and taken notes and no idea that her cover was well and truly blown.

DBO came from the same compound as Hilda. A compound that was full of pictures and quotes from the inspirational Hilda. DBO, like H2, had been told from the day they existed that Hilda, the "woman's woman," had their interest at heart.

Your safety is her concern.

Your complaints her worries.

Your ideas her inspiration.

An easy thing to ponder when you're working your butt off on mindless tasks, invisible, and forgotten, the lowest of the low, while

Beryl and the Voted In ran the place like it was their own personal spar.

Not anymore, she had inside info—pictures; Hilda running around like a madwoman in a onesie, or worse still, a caped crusader.

She sent everything she knew to H2.

They were a team, an incognito force that could nip the heels of the corrupt without them even knowing, or *at least save the planet!*

Chapter Forty-One

THE TAJ

"Women took care of the books until men were overthrown. Then the women did all the things men did and forgot about the books."—The Spark Plug Odyssey

oody, Pete, and Mex sat in the Taj Mahal waiting for the others.

DJ had disappeared, muttering something about contacting his mentor/uncle, while Bunnie and Don were still arguing over the best place to pitch their tent. Don said the only decent spot was the top of the slope, to avoid the rain *damming up*. Bunnie, stating that they weren't otters in a loch, refused to help. She argued that a pitch at the bottom of the slope was way better, along with a "who wants to walk up a slope in the dark after a few" comment.

"Anyone who wants a dry tent," muttered Don.

"Sarcasm is the nether region of wit," said Bunnie.

"I'm trying to whip up a tent and you're talking about nether regions?"

With no witty reply, Bunnie downed tools and sulked.

It took minutes for Woody and Pete to rattle up their tents, once Mex and her *what's this* questions were out of the way.

Woody told her to "go to reception, for pegs." And by the time Mex was requesting the *not-required* pegs, Woody and Pete had two tents flapping in the wind, sleeping mats positioned, and a torch suspended from the middle—Pete's idea.

Mex, who arrived back mid rolling of the sleeping bags, returned with water bottles, two buy-one-get-one-free tokens to the Indian, and an intense desire to know what a *wild goose chase* was.

"Figure of speech, ma'am," said Pete.

"And an Indian?" said Mex.

"You can't beat an Indian," said Woody.

"Beat?" said Mex.

"Another figure of speech, ma'am," said Pete.

Mex looked questionably at her smart-arsed robot as he began to pontificate about "body language" and how it "helps to translate."

"How would a robot know anything about body language?" she said.

No one answered.

Mex, wondering if Earth was full of men talking bollocks, gave up, mutely following Woody and Pete to the *Indian*. Her stomach was making noises again.

The Indian stopped her in her tracks, another new place that had her dumbfounded, confused, and salivating—all at the same time. It was a small room with several empty tables and walls covered in a pattern of pictures which Woody explained was the Taj Mahal. She ran her fingers over the paper tablecloth. *So this is paper,* she thought. She looked at Pete. "For writing?"

"Tablecloth," said Woody.

She picked up the book-like menu. "And this?"

"Menu, ma'am."

Mex sat back in her chair and breathed in the foreign smells; her mouth watering with hunger. She had no idea what a menu was or for that matter how to read said menu, even though some words looked familiar from watching BBC reruns with Pete. On Planet Hy Man, Mex's mind picked up things quicker than a Venus fly trap snapped shut. However, on Earth, along with new feelings of intense hunger, Mex experienced mind fog; her brain, it seemed, was slower and thicker than the trickle of sap from a tree.

Mex shuffled the pages of the menu pretending to understand. *At least the pictures make sense.* She pointed to one. "This looks interesting."

"Kebab," said Woody.

"Yes . . . that's what I thought, a kebab."

"It's meat, ma'am," said Pete.

"Ah yes, thought that," she muttered.

A couple nursing hangovers pulled up at the table next to Mex, and without looking at the menu ordered two pints of tap water, the usual for starters, and then, with complete *oblivious to the world* eye contact, held hands.

The man was about the same age as Don, slim, shiny bald, with a fistful of rings. The woman was Woody's age, blonde, slim, also with a fistful of rings, plus large loop earrings swinging beneath her hair.

"No drinks then?" said the waiter with an unimpressed look. The couple shook their head. The waiter with a curt snatch lifted the drinks menu and left.

"I fancy a bhuna—don't you?" said the blonde.

"Bhuna? Not me, I am for something stronger."

"Must you? You know what it does to your insides."

The waiter returned with two glasses, a plate of poppadums, and a selection of dips. "Your water," he sniffed.

"What's a bhuna?" said Mex.

"The dog's bollocks," said Mr. Bald.

"Heaven," said the blonde, snapping a poppadum in half.

"Sort of like a dry jalfrezi," said DJ.

"Jal . . . what?" said Mex.

"Probably best to start with a dhal," muttered Woody.

"Dhal?"

"Yes, it's wet and dippable."

Mex looked confused.

"Look, just let me order and you can dip . . . in and out."

"Like a pool?" said Mex.

"Figure of speech, ma'am," muttered Pete.

The blonde smiled at Mex. "We always dip," she said, dabbing a corner of her poppadum into a red sauce. She fed the corner to Mr. Bald. "Don't we, hon?"

Mr. Bald, with a chuckle, wiped his chin.

❋

DJ had disappeared to a Wi-Fi hotspot; ESP-ing always worked best in hotspots. Now in range, he began to communicate with Archie. Archie had been giving him a hard time about blocking, not trusting Don, or "Mr. Man" as he called him.

DJ trusted most folk, and despite what the others said about Beryl, DJ knew she would be a great bonus to the whole search-for-Legless mission. He believed in that stiff face even if no one else did.

They would thank him later.

Pete had digested curry on a level unknown by many. His stomach was full of spices, his face flushed with chilli, and his heart (which he was sort of getting used to) pounded like a bass drum. He sat back in his chair and drank in the background music. It reminded him of his yoga poses—he could do with one now. He was beginning to feel all tight and crunchy, like one of those packets of crisps. What he needed was a long, lean stretch followed by a position of great twisting, that would help his digestion. Then he could think again.

His thoughts drifted to the lady in the box. *Now there is someone that can twist.*

Mex and Woody, basking in their full stomachs, seemed energized by the spices and the thought of the mission ahead. They had spent the last hour riffling through the mountains of festival leaflets cluttering up the window sills. There was nothing about Johnny Gets Legless storytelling; only comedy—stand-up, improvs, and parodies, enough comedy according to the blonde to "wallpaper a bleeding synagogue."

"You heard of the Johnny Gets Legless show?" said Mex.

The couple shook their head.

Pete stared at the one solitary mindfulness leaflet . . .

Tired of the hustle and bustle of the Edinburgh fringe?
Then visit the mindfulness centre, sit in our Zen garden.
Why not treat yourself to a buy-one-get-one-free yoga session or a massage?
You don't even need to take your clothes off!

"But we've just been to the most amazing contortionist," said the blonde.

"Cartoonist?" said Mex.

"No, contortionist—street performer," said the blonde. "She folded herself up into a square box . . ."

"Whatever for?" muttered Mex.

"And all you could see was her leotard," continued Mr. Bald.

Pete's face lit up as he reminisced about the lady in the see-through box. "Yoga and so much more."

The blonde showed them a video on her iPhone. "She's like a piece of spaghetti," she said.

Pete ran his golden finger across the screen.

"Every year she's at the festival, this is her tenth anniversary," said Mr. Bald.

"Anniversary?" muttered Pete with a sideways glance at Mex.

Mex ignored him.

"Bet you she gets a few cards."

Pete knew what he had to do. Mex and Woody were still waiting for Bunnie, Don, and DJ. They were talking of coffee and free mints while making plans.

He could sneak off and be back by the time Bunnie had digested her much-talked-about korma.

He looked at Woody, explaining to Mex the intricates of dipping a naan, and took a chance. He headed for the john; it was right by the back door. No one noticed. Bunnie and Don had just entered with a shamefaced DJ.

"Guess who he was talking to," said Bunnie.

"I was ESP-ing and that is private," snapped DJ.

"Not when it's to that goddam Beryl," said Bunnie.

Pete slipped into the toilet. He had seen enough to know that his outfit was a bonus in this city. He slid off his Primark bra and jacket, hung them on the toilet door, wiped the lipstick from his mouth that Bunnie insisted would help with the camouflage, and headed into the crowd like a golden performing statue, asking the first kind face he saw for directions.

Chapter Forty-Two

THE SPARK PLUG ODYSSEY

"Not believing is one of the greatest human weaknesses."– Planet Hy Man National Geographic

"So, you want *The Spark Plug Odyssey*?" said Pope.

"Yes, that is what I am looking for."

"Written by Legless?" said Pot.

"The very one," said Vegas.

"And him alone?" muttered Prudence.

"So I am told," said Vegas.

"Some say it's hidden."

Vegas sighed.

"We can't talk here."

"Why not, everyone is asleep."

"It's too public."

"But no one comes here except you three."

"No, it's not safe."

"Safe? This place is a hippie colony. Everyone is equal—so I am told."

"Well, there is equal and then there is equal," said Pot.

"What?"

"We need to take you to the greenhouse," said Pope. "Via the secret route so no one follows."

"Who is going to follow? One of those pickling birds?"

Pope tapped his nose. "Through the recycling garden, no one goes there."

Vegas looked questioningly from one to the other.

"It stinks," said Pot.

Vegas let out another sigh. *Could they possibly draw this out any longer?*

Pope led them through the recycling garden. He pointed to the James Bond Library. "Avoid it like the plague," he said, "unless you suffer from insomnia."

They walked past brightly colored tanks rumbling like washing machines; about the base were brightly coloured plants, extra-large, that didn't hide the smell.

Vegas, holding her nose while mouth breathing, watched as the robots crept about like they were in a war zone looking for the enemy.

"Is all this absolutely necessary?"

"Definitely."

"Secrecy is what we are about—we're experts," said Pope

"And it's so much more fun," said Prudence. "It reminds us of our legacy."

"Wouldn't call it a legacy," muttered Pot, who was now creeping through a mint patch.

Prudence talked of their great escape from the city and how the grans helped. "That Verruca is a marvel," she said.

"Shhh, someone's coming," said Pope.

"It's a mouse," said Prudence.

Vegas looked about. All she could see was a faint rustle of leaves.

"We were exhausted with the constant massaging," continued Prudence.

"Yes, and those neck-rubbing parties, remember them?" said Pot. "I mean what are we, a pair of hands?"

"Shhh . . ." said Pope. "It's back!"

Pope stuck out his foot. A mouse race by tripped, skidded, looked back, and swore.

"Massage for us Androids is not our best quality," said Prudence. "Especially for banana-fingers over there," she said, gesturing to Pope. "The only thing he was good at was pulverising hemp balls into sausages."

"I heard that."

"Yes, Verruca saved us," said Prudence. She looked at Vegas. "Was it Verruca who helped you?"

"No."

"Told you about the slag heaps?"

"No."

Prudence looked at Vegas questioningly, it was on the tip of Vegas's tongue to say "fairy godmother" when Pope stopped them in their tracks. "It's not a mouse this time."

"What those grans don't know isn't worth knowing," whispered Prudence, "They watch and learn."

"Some say a dangerous habit," whispered Pot.

"Shhh," hissed Pope.

"'Solutions aren't easy,' Verruca used to say. 'They require an adjustment of habit.'" Pot shrugged his shoulders. "Where did she get that from? Not watching sitcom reruns, that's for sure."

"Quiet!"

"And how many of us are prepared to change?" continued Prudence. "As for that Hilda, she based her whole theory of power on 'once a habit always a habit.'"

"Bit more than that," said Pot.

"She watched the downtrodden and saw what kept them that way," said Prudence.

Prudence talked of advertising and how everyone always believed women in white coats.

"Visuals, that's what it's all about," said Pope.

"Flashing pictures at people works wonders," added Prudence.

"Her energy was boundless," muttered Pope to himself.

"Who are we talking about?" whispered Vegas. "Verruca or Hilda?"

"Both . . . I think."

By the time they got to the greenhouse, Vegas was confused, bored, and hungry. And Pope was doing his nut—he had spied foot tracks, heard non-mice rustling, and no one seemed to care.

❄

Hilda had no time for floating platforms, and no humor for capes. She headed back to her room, lifted the H-Pad 11, and marched with a grim determination into the corridor. She knew where to go, and who to blame; enough was enough.

The H-Pad 11 had a questioning quality along the lines of the 33 robots. It had no idea what *no* or *mind your own business* meant due to a faulty *answer back* chip. Hilda had been warned, but did she listen? Now she was looking for someone to blame, and perhaps a miracle worker.

She strode down the corridor parting robots and workers like the Red Sea for Moses. They scurried like rabbits, an impressive feat considering she was still in her onesie.

Hilda barged into the room with a view and tossed the H-Pad 11 across the table.

"These are useless," she snapped, then stopped mid pickle swearing . . . as the H-Pad 11 skidded into two large robotic feet standing on the table.

The room with a view was empty of Operators, and within seconds Hilda knew why.

She looked up to see a tall robot stretching up towards the chandelier, his concertina arms moving from one crystal ball to another as he polished with a hemp shammy. Seeing robots cleaning in action was for Hilda a beautiful thing, and for a moment she stopped to admire . . .

Health and safety insisted on scheduled breaks to allow for cleaning and airing of the room with a view. One of Hilda's *a clean room is a productive room* initiative, which, up till now, she had forgotten about.

The room was full of robots: tall ones running shammies along the top of a mirrors, squat ones beside them rubbing the mirror clean. A hoover robot, sucking up the remaining confetti on the floor (his design inspired by Star Wars R2-D2, although no one would admit it), along with a robot dressed as a maid removing caffeine stains on the floor. She periodically tutted, due to the uniform being designed for admiring rather than movement. A leftover from the *ruling of men* days.

The room was a hive of robotic activity. Lost in their industry, they hardly noticed Hilda.

"Where's the Operators?" she shouted over the hoovering.

"Alice," said the mirror-cleaner without stopping.

"Alice?"

"Yes, ma'am, your orders," said the maid, straightening herself and her hem.

"Alice? Since when do I stoop to using—"

The H-Pad 11 lit up. "Health and safety regulations, ma'am."

"Yes, yes I am aware of said—"

"Alice set to default, ma'am."

"What? Why? How?"

"You," said the H-Pad 11.

"Me? It was a mere thought, a pondering, but the logistics had not been worked out as yet."

"Logistics amended, sorted, and achieved."

"What logistics?"

"Yours," said the H-Pad 11.

"But I hadn't worked it out . . ."

Hilda, exasperated, switched off the hoover robot. It jolted into a perfect incognito mode.

"It's all about timing, which you seem to forget," snapped Hilda.

"Ma'am. My timing is programmed."

"By who, one of those groin-less statues in the garden?"

"You, ma'am."

"Me?"

"Well, someone very like you," said the H-Pad 11.

Hilda picked up pieces of confetti, all that was left of the memo. *Another stupid idea,* she thought, then regretted it as the H-Pad 11 informed her that it was one of her and Beryl's collaborative, data-control initiatives.

Hilda sighed. The Operators were now in the Voted In sleeping apartments, probably arguing over bedrooms, suits, and mugs. She could just see them standing by the caffeine implement. How long before they would discover that two of the Operators were missing, and *then* what?

Hilda looked at the H-Pad 11. The H-Pad 11 flashed its lights along the side.

"Get me Vegas."

"Incognito, ma'am."

"So you keep telling me. Has she fallen off the edge of the planet—down a hole?"

"If I knew, she wouldn't be incognito, ma'am."

Hilda sucked in her breath and glared at the H-Pad 11. *How long does it take to disassemble an H-Pad 11?*

The H-Pad 11 lit up, preparing for an answer. Hilda interrupted with another thought. *As if you'd know the answer to that.*

"We are as indestructible as a mechanical cockroach, ma'am," said the H-Pad 11.

Chapter Forty-Three

THE BARRACKS

"Men always seemed to have fun, but when women took over, they never found out what the joke was."–The Spark Plug Odyssey

ilda headed for the Operators' barracks and was almost there when she heard Vegas's voice on the H-Pad II.

"*Spark Plug Odyssey*—is that a manual or a book?"

Hilda stopped in the middle of the Zen garden. A mouse ran across her feet, followed by two more.

Mice—where did that come from?

"Mechanical, nothing to worry about," said the H-Pad II.

"Verruca has a fondness for mice."

"That's just her fridge; seems to collect them."

"Fridge?"

"Yes, like a drink dispenser but so much more."

Hilda stared at the H-Pad II. As if she didn't know that . . . She thought about Verruca's kitchen, which brought back memories of her childhood. It was rough, dirty, and ancient; was that why she liked going there? Or the fact that Verruca always seemed to act like she was one step ahead?

She looked at the H-Pad II.

How do you know about her fridge?

"I am one step ahead of you too," said the H-Pad II.

"Ahead of me? No one is ahead of me."

"Verruca said you'd say that . . ."

"Verruca? What's Verruca got to do with it?"

"Nothing, forget I said anything."

Hilda stopped. Verruca worked in the shed years ago, when the first of the H-Pads came out . . .

Hilda was about to think, then, flicking the off button on the H-Pad 11, changed direction.

"Perhaps we should pay Verruca a surprise visit," she muttered.

"Not quite shut down yet, ma'am."

As Pete walked closer to the festival, he began to feel excited. The crowd was thickening, the music growing louder, and the roar of applause stronger. By the time Pete reached Princes Street, all thoughts of Legless had vanished. He was lost in a world he had only dreamed of, in a street chock-a-block with color, people, and noise. He could hear cars, buses, and drilling mixed with music, applause, and chattering; people speaking languages he recognized and accents he didn't. The noise vibrated into his being; his head was spinning, as he stared into the kaleidoscope of stalls, and flags.

The people were all shapes, expressions, and ages; children running, laughing, and crying; old folk, some hobbling—getting in the way—others briskly marching, and one in a wheelchair.

Pete had only heard about those . . .

He felt excited, isolated, and curious all at once; he was buzzing off his Teflon tits.

Pete stopped, took in a yoga breath, and inhaled the aroma of sizzling meat. A young boy bumped into him; he didn't even reach Pete's waist.

Pete jumped.

The boy burst into tears.

Pete watched a tear roll down his chubby cheeks and wondered what to do . . .

"Ma'am?" he muttered.

"You what?" said the boy as a woman appeared and, with a cold eye at Pete, dragged the boy away.

Pete thought of Woody; he wished he was there. They would be laughing together, sharing the difference of each world, and he could ask if smiling at little boys and asking directions from men in wheelchairs was appropriate.

Children in the streets were banned on Planet Hy Man along with, wheelchairs, and anyone who coughed too much. Sickness, although rare, was hidden and never spoken about.

Thanks to robot-driven limos and slow-as-snail mopeds accidents rarely happened. And the only place a girl would be seen was either in the compound for the ordinary, or the accelerator for the talented complex.

No one had seen a boy since . . . well, Pete had no idea.

He gazed up at the castle; a piper started up. Pete jumped as the tune blasted into his ears.

"Am I near the Royal Mile?" Pete shouted.

The piper didn't hear.

"Just around the corner," said the teenager, "you're almost there."

Pete continued past a magician with a dog; he skidded on a leaflet, righted himself on a drunk, ignored the insult, and continued.

It was slow work working through the crowds, but finally he made his way onto Mount Pleasant. He passed a seedy-looking man with dreadlocks yelling into the crowd. "You ain't seen nothing like this, me hearties," he yelled, pulling a bunch of flowers from inside his pants.

Some of the crowd pulled faces, other walked on.

If they could see me now, thought Pete, *they'd be spitting lubricant—let's see who's the odd one now!*

The other three 33 robots had run off to the Black Hills and left him for dead—so he heard. One morning, in the middle of preparing Mex's first of many caffeine beverages, he heard a cleaner robot talking of the *great escape.* Claiming they were "too big for their boots."

Unlike him, the other three 33 robots had been moved from one Voted In to another; nobody wanted them. They sniffed at Pete whenever they met, and no matter how much he tried to convince them serving Mex was *no picnic*, they insisted it was.

Finally, in the middle of a *bring and swap* conference, they, fed up with the humiliation of being *un-swappable*, made their escape, without a backwards glance at Pete.

As if he wanted to join anyway! He was in the middle of a festival, no such thing like that on Planet Hy Man.

Pete walked on past two men playing drums. One was sitting on a box and thrashing the daylights out of it while the other played complicated rhythms on a more complicated-looking drum. People were milling about, some clapping to the rhythm.

The complicated drummer stopped. "We travel the world to entertain."

Thrash, thrash, thrash . . .

"So please, give, give, give . . . we can't do it without you."

A few walked away; a little girl skipped up to their hat and threw coins into it.

Pete wished he had a coin to toss.

He moved on past a brown man in a duffel coat sniffing into a bottle in a brown bag.

"Pound for coffee," he said.

No one heard.

Pete, now a body-reading expert, gestured to his empty pockets then, reading the brown man's upright-middle-finger gesture, quickly moved on.

Pete marched up the steep hill of Cockburn Street past more food shops and the smell of waffles, chocolate, and chips.

And then he heard . . .

"You see the lady? The one in the box?"

"Aye, something else."

"Where?" muttered Pete.

The young man whistled through his teeth. "Just keep going, she's worth the walk."

The street was lined with tables and chairs, people sitting, talking, artists drawing, manipulating balloons into weird shapes.

Finally, he recognized the corner. He pushed through the crowd, and there she was. Pete skidded to a stop and stared at the Perspex box. Her limbs folded about her body—all you could see was her leotard.

I want to be like her, thought Pete.

Chapter Forty-Four

THE GREENHOUSE

"An Odyssey is just a fancy word for a journey."—Hilda

The greenhouse was large and filled with smells of hemp, tomatoes and the sound of rustling leaves. Prudence said it was the mice.

Pope, unconvinced, spent a fair amount of time jumping at each rustle—until Pot called him paranoid and told him to cut back on the hemp sugar.

Vegas stared at the miniature eco gardens dotted about the place. Platforms of old shoes filled with plants and long unpronounceable names underneath. Pope pulled a slim book from a shelf of manuals, blew the dust from the cover and handed Vegas the book.

"Here this will help."

Vegas looked at *The Greenhouse Guide*. She flicked through a few pages—*riveting recycling*. "What has this to do with spark plugs?"

"The intro explains how it all began," said Pot.

"It's the only place to start," said Pope.

Prudence overturned an empty plant pot, brushed it clean, and gestured Vegas to sit. "Take your time."

Vegas perched uncomfortably, sighed, and started at the beginning.

The making of a greenhouse . . .

The hippie colony sprung up before the days of Mex's heroic deeds with men. A community established in the windy part of the planet that knew how to collect and store energy.

It wasn't a secret affair, but rather the results of the Liberty of Animal Front, a group of women dismayed at the dwindling numbers of four-legged creatures.

Back then it was the men who were upper class with high penthouse views and clean air, peering down at the ant-like minions below. In fact, that is what they were known as—the ants.

The lower-down level was filled with the smell of animal effluent, air fresheners, and taxis that honked like their life depended on it. Music playing was not chilled elevator music but beating drums and orders chanted like a Muslim's call to prayer. It was a noisy, masculine place.

The upper class shut their windows to the call. They shut their windows to everything, including the loss of animals. They just assumed they would always be there, until it was pointed out that they weren't. The powers that be, not wanting to admit defeat, tossed leaflets from the window—their usual practice of communication.

The leaflets talked of animals needing saving and supporting the non-existent Liberty of Animal Front.

Please help us stand up to the leaders
and
save the animals.

The working class went wild, opening gates and pushing animals into freedom. The only problem was the animals had no idea how to be free, and the fields were empty within days of aimless trampling.

The hippies, in dismay, hijacked the last of the fish and headed across the Black Hills . . . not much was left apart from a few trout, a couple of mullets, and an impressive selection of goldfish. They took all but a couple of goldfish (in order to not raise suspicion). By the time they were missed, a gate had been built and rumours spread of women too old to follow and a desert as dry as their ovaries beyond the Black Hills.

The hippies weren't hippies in the Earth sense but smart women who designed a super hemp seed. They took recycling to another level altogether. Scarecrows stored wind energy, the buildings collected water energy, and the 33 robots were taught the best position to reflect sunlight—hence the veranda sitting—in between, much to their disgust, collecting droppings from the mechanical birds—tiny bullets of compressed solar power, or "gold dust" as some liked to call them.

Leftover anything was for the compost, which was situated near the greenhouse, an in-and-out-don't-hang-about place, as the air-lipo-suction unit was also situated there—a suction so strong it could be felt for miles. A pleasant sensation many enjoyed when bored or after a feast such as the great hemp harvest feast. Which was just as well, as its main function was to suck flatulence.

Everything had a reusable purpose.

All was productive—a hive of recycling activity—until one bright spark, in their quest to make Planet Hy Man a happier place, discovered hemp sugar. The hippie soon, like all good hippies, began to chill, eat too much, and partake of fart parties that lasted way into the next day, leading to exhaustion, an excessive use of air freshener, and an overworked Air-liposuction.

They discover that hemp sugar in coffee or in cake had the effect of mellowing—or worse, not giving a toss about anything, including the size of one's belly, studying in the library, and monitoring the robots.

Vegas turned to the last few pages.

"This is all well and good, but I am no further forward about the spark plug."

She looked up to see the three robots bent over their H-Pad, engrossed.

"Did you hear me?"

"Well, yes," muttered Pope.

"So, what about the spark plug?"

"Don't you get it?" said Pot.

"Get what?"

"The spark plug is obsolete, it's recycling now."

"What about *The Odyssey*?"

"Arrr, well, a funny thing that . . ."

"He took it with him," interrupted Prudence.

"So what am I to take back to the boss, a history book?"

No one answered. Pope, Prudence, and Pot were looking at their H-Pad. Pete had found the lady in the box.

Chapter Forty-Five

LEAKAGE

"He had the patience to listen to a joke longer than a Christmas shopping list."—Bunnie

*V*erruca was a firm believer in controlled leaking, a technique mastered in the compound. Verruca learned and controlled many things using the said *leaking* method and it had got her where she was today: under Hilda's radar and yet *not* . . .

She knew DBO would venture near her fridge, so she plotted, planted, and planned. As she was pondering her next move, Verruca headed into the marsh behind her home; H2's moped had been slumped there for the past week. She began to push it into the shed when Hilda caught her unaware.

Usually Hilda arrived at the end of the week, unannounced, looking large, expansive, and way over the top in her caped crusader outfit. Not today; it was early in the week and she, sporting a onesie, looked pissed, impatient, and like she wanted to hit something.

Hilda watched the lean old woman maneuver the moped into the shed with the ease of tucking a hankie into a pocket. She walked upright with purpose, like a gymnast about to perform, until she spied Hilda and changed her stance to a disinterested mechanic in a garage. She grabbed some lubricant and began to work her way through the components in the engine.

Hilda looked at Verruca. She was looking sure of herself, and it was a little off-putting. Grans in the suburbs, or *the sticks* as some said, made things with hemp, knitted and sewed for the market, not oiled things mechanical.

"Why don't you get the robot to do that for you?" said Hilda.

Verruca looked at her. "We both know that is as possible as a footman doing the splits."

"There was a time when splits were part of their repertoire," muttered Hilda with a wistful look.

"Yes, well, my robot has as much repertoire as an unplugged flat seaside screen."

"You are missing the point of a robot; they are under your guidance, just read the manual," said Hilda.

"And we all know how good a manual is." Verruca slammed the engine shut and began to polish off the seat.

Hilda eyed her. "Your name intrigues me."

"It intrigues most—even robots."

"Sounds like a spy name," said Hilda.

"What sort of spy is named after a fungal infection? Besides, spies are outlawed."

"A decoy name then," said Hilda.

"Decoy—my father couldn't spell the word. He chose the name because he thought it was funny. 'One day you'll thank me for it,' he said. Still waiting for that one."

"Your father?"

"Yes, one of the last; his sense of humor was his only talent."

Verruca eyed her leader. "I heard your father's last *the world's gone mad* speech."

Hilda said nothing.

"If he could see you now. I mean the stationaries will soon be up and running; the energy crisis is, as one would say, no longer a crisis."

"I am here for something else," snapped Hilda.

Verruca motioned Hilda out of the shed, closed it, and headed for the so-called "three-seater" swing chair. Hilda looked at it with disdain. She had seen Mex try to sit on her three-seater.

"Let's go into the kitchen," said Hilda.

"The robot's cleaning."

"Isn't everyone?"

"He is not the easiest to talk in front of."

"Neither is this," said Hilda, producing the H-Pad 11. "Someone has been tinkering with it. And I think you know who."

Hilda motioned Verruca into the kitchen and stopped at the door when she caught sight of the robot with his head in the fridge.

Verruca pulled him out of the fridge and a couple of old Victorian vibrator diagrams fell to the floor, along with the mechanical mouse.

Hilda brushed the mouse to the side and picked a diagram.

She stared at it for ages, turning the paper upside down trying to make sense.

Finally, she looked up. "What is this?"

Verruca smiled.

"Implements for massage," said the robot.

Hilda pulled a face. "Massage with a drill?"

One step ahead, thought Verruca, *and she doesn't even know it.*

Once Hilda left, Verruca rolled up the "drill" instructions with a smug grin and thrust it at her robot.

"You can make one of these, can't you?"

"Piece of piss and pickle, ma'am."

Verruca had the beginnings of a plan, distraction on a grand scale.

Hilda left annoyed at herself. Allowing herself to look uninformed was not something she was proud of, especially in an outback workers' kitchen such as Verruca's.

Why did she think she could help . . .

"Verruca is a mystery to us all, ma'am," said the H-Pad 11.

Why did she keep going back?

"A question many ask, ma'am—you are not alone on that one."

And as for the H-Pad, she was as much help as that useless robot—Hilda looked at the H-Pad 11—*and you.*

The H-Pad 11, for once, was silent.

Chapter Forty-Six

THE BRA

"When women took over, they took over the mess that men left. They knew that solar energy was a hit-and-miss affair. Then some bright spark came up with the stationary."–The Spark Plug Odyssey

It was planned for the Operators to train the Voted In in the riding of a stationary.

Hilda said she had the utmost faith in them, and at first the Operators believed her. But before the Operators had a chance to open a manual, the Voted In were up and peddling like hamsters on a wheel, sports bras firmly in place.

Senator was the first to sit on a stationary. She, with a tentative swing of her legs, landed on the seat with a "well that feels weird" comment.

The Voted In had lost any feeling in their pelvises, and as Senator scrabbled with her feet to find a peddle, feelings tingled in her.

She smiled. "It's not so bad, girls"—she wriggled—"honestly."

The others were dubious.

The stationary was not without its problems. First of all, there was no provision for the ageing of the rider and increased frequency of breaks. Then there were the energy dips during bouts of coughing, getting one's breath back, or brow wiping, followed by the energy surges after beverage breaks; it was not the first time a decent implement exploded during a surge.

Were they to go back to such dark times?

They silently stared at Senator's brave face as she tried to master the peddles, until Baby entered sporting underwear that had them gasping.

Baby had an idea, a rare occurrence for Baby, but since she spied the jockstrap she could not get the idea out of her head. Then when she found a box full of jockstraps she knew she had found her true mission in life.

Inspired by the fifties posters, she quickly rigged two together, forming a pointy bra. It took a bit of fiddling, but once in position, Baby saw a waist she didn't know she had. She held in her stomach looked at her reflection on the seaside screen and there it was . . . the slim bit above the hips.

Everyone wanted one.

The Voted In had never worn bras. They had no memory of what a swing of a breast felt like or, for that matter, to have breasts that got in the way of things. Few did on Planet Hy Man. Who needed an upright breast when men were out of the game?

Some say Fanny's bra-flinging had a lot to do with it. The day she used it as a slingshot. A D cup full of hemp effluent was not a sight to behold but rather a sight to forget, and a bra on Planet Hy Man was never the same again.

Instead, women (apart from the likes of Mex) flatten their breasts with tape, forgetting about them altogether.

Baby made more and tossed them at the girls. Soon they were clamouring around the seaside screen staring at their waists, and with upright breasts and a sense of liberation planted themselves on the stationaries and wriggled. Within minutes they were working up a sweat, moving until puffed and experiencing the joy of a breast in full swing.

An experience which they didn't even have a word for.

They spent all day riding, and soon had a sense of their pelvis again. By the end of the day they had found a sexual energy which, in the end, led to joshing, a form of joking that didn't require bitching. The cleaners didn't know what hit them when they arrived. They walked in flanked by robots intent on "notching up the speed of the stationaries," and there was Baby, flinging her bra across the gym shouting, "Here's hemp in your eye."

There were no instructions for that sort of carry-on . . .

No one had warned them that the Voted In could be so playful. They, like many, had heard that the Voted In were wet, ineffective, and miserable.

Cleaner One began to shout at the robots, "Quickly, two notches on each bike, and make her"—she looked at Baby—"three. Bra tossing," she sniffed. "Should be outlawed."

Cleaner Two, with an unconvincing nod, muttered, "Dangerous."

"Bra tossing was all the rage years ago," said the voice from the back, another ex-shed worker. She gleefully began to talk of the at-the-end-of-a-shift bra toss . . . "To the shed and beyond." She laughed.

The others stared. They knew she was making it all up, but no one had seen the voice from the back laugh before. The most you could expect from her was a mild tilting of a lip when the caffeine was of the perfect temperature.

"We could even have a bra slinging competition," she laughed . . . again.

"Dangerous," muttered Cleaner Two, "pickling dangerous."

Bras were the last thing on the Operators' minds. They were arguing over whose suit fitted who and which mug was whose, when Operator One noticed two of the bedrooms were empty. Which, being the same number as the Operators, meant two were missing.

"Is there someone missing?" she said.

They looked about.

"Not sure?"

Operator One counted the faces.

After the attack of the underwire, as Cleaner Two put it, they headed for the kitchen to elaborate, discuss, and spread the word. Spreading the word, along with cleaning, was part of their job.

"I mean underwire from a jockstrap?" said Cleaner Two.

The younger cook jolted. "Jockstrap?"

"At their age," said Cleaner One, "what're they playing at?"

The cook, being of a similar vintage, choked on her tea. "What do you mean their age?"

"What's a jockstrap?" said the young cook.

"A smelly piece of equipment," said the older cook with a sniff.

Cleaner Two, picking at a leftover scone, continued, "Yes, the Voted In are more spritely than first imagined. Didn't even need the Operators to show them what to do, they have taken to it like a robot to yoga."

The younger cook laughed. "Well, all I know is they are tucking into scones like there is no tomorrow. Today's elevenses had me running ragged."

"No one else would eat the pickling things," snapped the older cook.

"We've put the stationaries up a few notches, increased the speed," said Cleaner One.

The cook stopped mid stirring. "You what?"

"Increased their speed, those Voted In are obsessed having speeding games."

"That will bugger things up—the energy levels," said the cook.

"No wonder my fondues sunk," muttered the younger cook.

The cook glared at her apprentice, and it was on the tip of her tongue to say they always sunk when the light died.

"See," she said. "This is what happens when you muck about with the speed."

"How were we to know—were we given any training? Any manuals?"

"Manuals," spat the cook. "They're as much use as this yin here and her scones."

The lights flashed on, the instruments began to whirl, the cook as quick as a flash turned off her mixer as other instruments began to blow.

"Just like the pickling old days," she muttered. "This afternoon's sponge is never going to happen."

Hilda planned her next move with an entrance to shock, surprise and dominate. And she did it all with a blank mind and a glare at the H-Pad II.

Hilda, flanked by two footmen, appeared at the entrance of the Voted In barracks. She slammed the door shut. The Operators standing by the beverage equipment at the other end looked up. There was Hilda in her favourite caped crusader outfit balancing on her floating platform.

"*This* H-Pad is a load of hemp effluent," she shouted.

"We did say the tweaking was unfinished," muttered Operator One.

"What?" yelled Hilda.

"Tweaking, ma'am, there is only so much it can achieve."

"Tweaking? This equipment needs more than tweaking. It is beyond functional, I mean if we had one of those good old-fashioned skips then that is where I would toss this pile of . . . pickle."

"I am still here," said the H-Pad II, "and for the most part find that rather offensive."

"I told you to . . ." muttered Hilda.

The H-Pad II began to control the floating pad . . . Hilda grabbed onto the wall for balance.

"It is more than useless, it is a hindrance . . ."

"It? I am more than an it!"

"*She*," said Hilda with a scowl at the H-Pad II, "needs a complete overhaul."

"That was pointed out to you," yelled Operator Two.

"A reassessment, a breakdown and total reconstruction, followed by—"

Operator One took charge. "Ma'am, we are in the Voted In's bedroom quarters; there is only so much you can do with a beverage machine."

The floating platform zoomed forward, Hilda jumped off.

"If you are not willing to help, we could always go back to the good old-fashioned method of spying."

There was a sharp intake of breath as the platform headed for the wall.

"Perhaps if we could go back to the shed for a few instruments?"

Hilda smiled. "What a good idea." She turned to DBO's footman, who had up till now convinced himself that last night's apparition was a dream. "Why don't you escort them—and here, take the manual with you."

Operator One looked at her girls and for the first time realized who were missing.

Chapter Forty-Seven

COFFEE CUPS

"Dictatorship suits you."–The H-Pad 11

As they drove on, H2 listened to DBO, who told her about the old lady with the walking stick *who wasn't an old lady*, robots on verandas *which to H2 sounded like fun*, and arguments in Bunnie and Co's car. DBO then explained where the Johnny Gets Legless *shindig* as Archie put it was to be performed, what Bunnie would like to do to Beryl, and how the others thought this was totally illegal.

Archie pulled out one of his notebooks and passed it to H2, a woman whose tidy habits—as opposed to Beryl's *someone else will pick it up* attitude—impressed him.

Thanks to Beryl, his neat-as-a-pin car was now littered with her coffee cups and napkins.

"Can you not just use the plastic bag like everyone else?" he snapped.

Beryl didn't hear; she was being bombarded with information and tutting like a smoke alarm needing a battery.

"I mean look at my car," said Archie. "How many napkins does a woman need for a coffee, for Christ's sake? It's like the ground at the end of a football match."

Beryl continued to tut.

Archie watched Beryl wipe her lips with yet another napkin and toss without a glance. He had as much chance getting her to use a bin as he did seducing her—*not that he would, given the chance.*

Beryl, against the advice of the "fairy godmother," was working her way through Deidre's articles. The latest being about the closure of the shed, the restructuring of management—replacing the old with the young, and how getting exercise was what the Voted In really needed—despite them being *incognito.*

"The room with a view is run by the Operators," said Beryl, "and the shed it seems is full of tools? Imagine that, a shed full of tools."

"Imagine," said Archie.

"How can that be possible? I mean who's running things?"

"Bet they use bins in the shed, not much room for tossing."

"You haven't seen the shed," muttered H2.

Deidre was a reporter happy to bend the truth. She had worked on the lower levels of the Building of Opulence, taken orders from any above, and knew the higher she went the easier life would become. She was an expert crawler, who creeped into Beryl's favors, writing what pleased the leader until the leader looked like she was going to topple.

Then she switched sides.

Beryl continued to read, and when she got to the amazing ways of our esteemed leader, her tutting turned to pickle swearing.

"I made her who she is, so much for gratitude."

H2 told Beryl to focus.

"That's what the fairy godmother says. Apparently Planet Hy Man is no longer my concern."

Beryl tossed her empty cup on the floor.

"Bin!" snapped Archie.

"How the pickle can I focus when I read this beetrooting rubbish? She should remember where she came from."

H2 picked up the cup. "Legless is your answer. That's what my gran would say."

"Verruca, what would she know?"

Beryl paused to listen. "The fairy godmother says I'm to listen to both of you."

"Could have told you that," muttered Archie.

"Apparently he's an expert." Beryl gestured to Archie.

"Well, I wouldn't say that, but I do know my way around," said Archie.

"On Legless," muttered Beryl.

"I see," muttered Archie. "Well, that Identity is the legend of all legends."

"Legend?" said H2. "From what you just told me, he's a sexaholic."

"Legless would never touch that stuff," said Beryl.

"That's an alcoholic," muttered Archie.

"I mean, all those women," said H2.

"A legend, the greatest rebel of all time," said Archie.

He started on about the story, took one look at H2, and stopped.

Beryl didn't listen. She looked out at the pink skyline. A sadness rose from deep inside; she almost felt a tear.

She remembered walking past the stationaries and seeing Legless in Lycra. He was the perfect height for a stationary, and when he rose to a standing position, she felt things she never dreamed of.

Beryl wondered what he was thinking.

"He was special," she muttered with a wistful look. *Not a legend or a rebel, just a man who wanted to make me happy. I saw it in his eyes, read it in his notes, and still I pickled it up.*

She sighed. "The decisions a leader must make."

Chapter Forty-Eight

THE BOX

"There are many uses for a box, opening it is just one."–Pete

It was Woody who noticed that Pete was taking way too long in the toilet.

They had ordered and finished their coffee, almost found the whereabouts of the Lizard Lounge, and still . . . no Pete.

What could a robot do for so long in a toilet?

"Gone, sweetie," shouted the chef, "out the door as quick as a vindaloo clears the pipes."

The blonde pulled a face.

"Bet you he left to find the girl in a box," said Woody. "Did you see the look on his face when he saw her?"

DJ, still in Bunnie and Don's bad books, muttered, "I wasn't there." Which thanks to a cold flash of the eye from Bunnie he immediately regretted.

They agreed to split up. Bunnie and Mex were to go to the Lizard Lounge, which no one seemed to have heard of, while Don offered to act as a diversion for the said Beryl and Co.

Neither offered to take DJ along.

"Come with me," said Woody, who was going to find the lady in the box and, hopefully, Pete.

They discussed their plans at length (apart from DJ) while the couple on the next table poked at their jalfrezi and bhuna. Their new resolution to stay off the booze was all but gone thanks to the *carry-on* at the next table. They strained to hear more, feigning interest in their curry . . .

Don jumped as voices began to blare from his satnav.

He pulled it out, fumbling with the off switch, as female voices continued to shout.

Robots heading for the greenhouse with someone called Vegas and *a footman massaging in a shed?*

"Bloody thing," said Don, giving it a good thump on the table.

"Robots," mouthed the blonde.

"Massages in a treehouse?" Mr. Bald whispered back.

Confused, they ordered a beer.

There was trouble in the shed. Trouble that DBO couldn't handle. Thanks to the Voted In's enthusiastic cycling, the dashboard was experiencing floods of energy followed by lulls (during the "I'm puffed" breaks) and it was playing havoc with her connections . . .

She frantically searched through her manuals for a solution.

Don remained at the table as the others left. After several abortive attempts to adjust the volume on his satnav, he stared out of the window and thought about sex. How much he enjoyed it, way better than that storytelling/dancing malarkey that Archie preached . . .

Until the *prostate issue* kicked in, then he had to be inventive or, as Bunnie suggested, dress up. The last thing Don wanted to do was dress up. The only thing he wanted was Bunnie. He could not get enough of that woman and her nagging, annoying ways. Winding her up was better than any one-night stand any day.

He wanted to grow old with her, make it through to that back bedroom—and not for decorating.

Bunnie, however, had no idea about Don's feelings and continually paired him up with ladies looking for *playful companionship*.

Maybe once this was all over, he thought, *she'll look at me different—play a few games.*

Don skulled his coffee. He could feel a tugging at his thoughts; he knew it was Archie. This time he didn't block, instead he listened to his Identity intuition, which for years he had ignored. Like it or not, Bunnie was part of something, and the only way for that something to go away was to sort it.

He sighed. Archie was part of that sorting.

Voices started again on his satnav . . .

"H-Pad 11 . . . *Spark Plug Odyssey* . . . takeover . . ."

Mr. Bald and the blonde downed their beer and listened.

"Imploding . . . exploding . . . self-destruct."

"Gives us a vodka," said Mr. Bald to the waiter. "In fact, make it a double."

DJ, like many Scots, had never been to the festival and, like most Identities, had avoided it; reading minds in such an atmosphere could make an Identity sick. Festivals and the like were flooded with emotional women seesawing the highs and lows of having fun while looking for fulfilment. The evenings were worse when many had been drinking and met the worse sort of men.

DJ, however, with thoughts full of Beryl, had forgotten all of that until they headed onto the Royal Mile and stared into the crowd. Immediately his head was buzzing with thoughts from women coming from all directions. The street was busy with people jostling and lonely women pretending to be happy. His brain felt like a roulette wheel, with foreign balls of thought whizzing around.

They passed a female statue performer in the corner . . .

Wanker!

Tosser!

He sighed.

The street was lined with performers competing for the attention of the crowd; it was hard to keep moving. DJ was soon sandwiched between a young girl lamenting her one-night stand and an elderly woman wishing for one.

Wanker.

Arsehole.

Nice bum . . . sigh.

DJ started to feel sick. It was like being back at school.

He caught sight of an escapologist wriggling in a locked straitjacket.

"Let me tell you a story," grunted the performer, "of Alcatraz and my escape."

The crowd muttered and jolted forward. DJ and Woody were about to move on when they heard a chainsaw start up. They turned to see a large, hairy, masked juggler pose with a chainsaw.

The sound drowned out everything. DJ basked in the noise.

"Alcatraz the unescapable," shouted the escapologist.

The juggler tossed the chainsaw into the air. The crowd gasped as his thick muscular arms caught the saw.

The escapologist watching his audience dwindle nodded to his sidekick, who wheeled on a unicycle . . .

Woody motioned to DJ.

DJ ignored him.

"Alcatraz, oh Alcatraz, the place where no bird sings."

The crowd was silent as he leveraged onto the unicycle, his arms still twisted in the straitjacket. He was a thin man with a thin ponytail and birdlike features, which at the moment were pinched with discomfort as he balanced on the unicycle.

An older woman stood beside Woody. Woody smiled.

"What's that you said?"

"This is way better than the lady in the box," she said with a confused look. "I mean how long can you stare at a box?"

"Is she still there?" said Woody.

"Oh yes, she's got a sidekick as well; a bit of comedy, he got into the box like a robot."

"How do you do that?" whispered DJ.

"What?" said Woody.

"Read her mind, then make it look like she had said it."

Woody looked confused, unaware of what he had just done. "Being a dwarf? No one is rude to us these days," he muttered.

DJ eyed his small friend. He had never met a dwarf before, and at first that was all he saw, until he got to know Woody. Woody was an expert at rising above intimidation, and when DJ met Woody's uncle, he understood how.

Woody's uncle, like his brothers, was a large ex–rugby player. DJ knew because the uncle who could *talk for Britain* invited him, along with Bunnie and Don, into the reception. Which was just as well, as Don had just caught DJ pretending to use a phone with more animation than Marcel Marceau.

Don knew that look anywhere.

"Who you ESP-ing?" he said.

"No one," said DJ.

"Funny kind of no one," muttered Bunnie, who couldn't leave Don alone for more than five minutes. "It's that bloody Beryl, she who did my Izzie in."

DJ blushed and was just about to make up some sort of lie when Woody's uncle spied them and dragged them in for a "blether."

The reception was full of photos of Woody's family, all large like his uncle. Funny enough, there were no pictures of Woody. Woody didn't seem to mind when DJ asked him.

"They think I'm an idiot," said Woody, "laughed at my sci-fi stories, but then the only thing they read is the sport page in the *Record*."

"Sci-fi?" said DJ.

"And now I have met you and Pete, I can make them eat their words."

Don was just on his final sip and wondering how much to tip a sour-faced waiter when he saw her . . . the old lady with the stick.

She threw him a muscular arm wave, and for the first time he wondered: was she really a lady?

Finally, Woody and DJ arrived at the top of the street. A large crowd had gathered, full of men.

Unbelievable.

Like spaghetti . . .

First her, then him.

I feel sick!

Woody stared between the legs; he could almost make out a clear box on the ground with a pink leotard–covered hip squashed against it.

DJ looked at the multitudes of backs. A piper walking by spied the ever-expanding crowd, pulled out his pipes, and took a chance.

Then DJ saw it—a golden finger.

"Woody!" shouted Pete.

They tried to push through.

"Pete?" said Woody.

Pete looked up and in a muffled voice said, "Hey, Woody, look at me." And then to the crowd: "He's my best pal. He got me where I am today."

Chapter Forty-Nine

IMPLODING AND FOLDING UP

"For most of the Voted In, how it worked was not important—as long as it worked."—Operator Unknown

H2's footman gulped. The Operators were going to the shed, and not alone but with Hilda. He fingered his earphone. He thought about the egg sandwiches, Vegas, and the foot massages.

What should he do?

Archie parked the car near Princes Street. Beryl, clutching her H-Pad, jumped out of the car and looked about. She had a plan . . .

Find the Lizard Lounge, grab this so-called Johnny, and, with her father's no-nonsense approach, demand the whereabouts of Legless.

It was a simple plan, but sometimes they were the best. Besides, she told herself, *she had her fairy godmother—what could go wrong?*

As they headed towards Princes Street, she told H2 to wait with Archie. Inside her she had a deep urge to explain to Legless why she double-crossed him, and the last thing she needed was a *know it all* getting in the way.

For the first time, H2 didn't argue. The last person she wanted to be with was her swindling so-called leader Beryl. Besides, she also had a plan—remarkably similar to Beryl's. And, to quote Her Leadership, the last thing she needed was *ol' bossy boots* interfering.

Archie and H2 watched as Beryl marched towards the crowd. For a moment Beryl wondered why she—H2—was so keen to split. H2 argued over everything; a minute ago she wanted to sit in the back seat. Beryl stopped and looked back. *Why didn't they argue? Did they know something she didn't?*

H2 gave her a tentative *on you go* wave.

Beryl, with a sense of reluctance, walked on and wondered where the pickle the fairy godmother was when you needed her.

"We should go after her," said Archie. "She is not safe on her own."

"You go if you want," said H2.

Archie looked at H2. "We should stick together."

"Easy for you to say, you don't have to put up with her," said H2.

Archie thought about his messy car.

They watched Beryl's beehive disappeared into the crowd. No one looked twice at the high-heeled gran, as there was more than one beehive strutting down the street. In fact, there was a whole group of beehived drag queens, singing at the top of their lungs, dressed in outfits that made Beryl's look like a tracksuit, with mile-high beehives that made Beryl's look like a small purple pimple.

"We are family; you must come along and see . . ."

They were a performing troupe, with a show on at the festival, and they spent most of the morning (like most acts) handing out leaflets—in costumes and in character.

It was their opening night tomorrow night and they were full of energy.

Beryl stopped as they swanned by, stunned at the beauty of their costumes.

"We are family; you must come along and see . . ."

She looked at the bright pink leaflet, "Cinderella for Men." She opened it and stared at the outrageous costumes. What should she do with it? Read it? Hand it on? Say something?

A dark drag queen caught sight of Beryl and skidded to a stop on her six-inch stilettos. Beryl looked up; it was the same dark face as on the leaflet. Impressed, she gave her best regal nod and smiled.

The drag queen was dressed in a gold fairy godmother dress, showing off muscular, tattoo-covered arms fit for weightlifting. Beryl had never seen a fairy godmother outfit before, let alone a tattoo, and she had no idea what *bitch* meant. However, her sixth sense told her *bitch* scrawled across an arm was there for a reason, and it was best not to ask about said reason.

The tattooed lady thrust another leaflet at Beryl, setting her bangles into a spasm of jangling.

"Here, honey," she said in a deep voice, "bring your friends."

"Honey?"

"Any beehive-wearing sister is a honey in my book."

Beryl adjusted her beehive and smiled. She had spent enough time on Earth to recognise a friendly opening. "Do you know where the Lizard Lounge is?"

The drag queen linked arms with Beryl. She had a grip like a python, which Beryl found more than reassuring.

"I'm Eddie the fairy godmother, what I don't know ain't worth knowing."

Archie watched as Beryl and the drag queen linked arms.

"She's a swindler," muttered H2.

"A broken-hearted swindler," said Archie. He had read her thoughts of Legless, her sadness. "She's desperate to find him. What if she gets to Legless before you?"

"That's hardly going to happen, is it," said H2. "She couldn't find a footman in the room with a view unless he coughed, passed out and *she* tripped over him. She's hardly going to find a man she hasn't seen in years, in a world she has no idea of . . . not unless you tell her."

Woody could see Pete's face mashed against the side wall, along with a tattooed *up yours* foot down the side of his head, the big toe danger-ously close to his Teflon nostrils.

Pete sneezed, a new experience; he smiled.

"That was fun."

He sneezed again, followed by a small squeak of wind.

Pete sighed in perfect peace.

The box lady coughed and pulled a face.

Woody knocked on the box; his dreadlocks crashed against the Perspex. Pete looked up and saw a magnified Woody face peering back at him. He looked more handsome than ever.

Pete sighed again.

"We have to go," said Woody.

"What?"

"Meet the others at the Lizard Lounge."

"Oh?" said Pete and sneezed.

The Operators headed back to the shed. Hilda, clutching her H-Pad 11, was in the lead.

They weren't hopeful of a positive outcome; they were missing two, and it was only a matter of time before Hilda would bring it up.

The footman lagged behind. He thought about H2's perfect feet and knew what to do. A woman with that sort of feet deserved a running chance.

DBO sipped her coffee and stared at the empty egg sandwich plate. Where was her footman?

A message flashed on her headphone receptor, followed by the loud noise of a chainsaw on the festival viewing screen. DBO switched the festival screen to silent, read the footman's message, swore, then began to implement emergency plan A (although she didn't have any other plan).

Then she connected with H2.

She began to talk with great drama of Legless, Vegas, and a very decent footman.

"Don't believe all they say about footmen; despite the egg sand-wiches, he did not waver."

Then she, in panic mode, talked of "downloading files," "closing all lines of communication until she could track the antivirus implement" (not to mention installation issues), followed by a flamboyant shout "self-destruction, five minutes—you three stick together; you're on your own."

H2 and Archie watched Beryl fade into the crowd while the files downloaded, nodding like they understood.

DBO's idea of self-destruction was not what happened. She had planned a gentle imploding . . . a folding-up of the dashboard and all its instruments into a box. The sort of box she could carry to the Black Hills and beyond. However, she did not figure on the energy of the Voted In and their cycling.

No one did.

The Operators headed into the garden by the kitchen.

"Wait, your elevenses," shouted the cook, who had a thing for routine. "I didn't bake 'em for nothing you know."

The cook had spent a whole morning trying to adjust to an oven that rose and fell in temperature—and she wasn't going to let all that work go to waste.

"Feed them to the fish," ordered Hilda with a dismissive wave as a whining filled the garden.

They stopped.

"What is that sound?" said Operator One.

"I think I know what that sound is," said the cook, who had lived through the great-liberation-of-animal times. She pointed to smoke from the shed. "It's a warning siren."

Hilda strode on. "Ridiculous, alls we need is water," she snapped.

"Water is the last thing you need," said the H-Pad 11.

The cook handed around the scones as they watched a charging Hilda in her cape run like Batman to his cave with a bucket of water.

Hilda wasn't old enough to remember sirens.

DBO's footman also saw the smoke, and for the first time in a long time thought of someone else—his DBO. He followed Hilda and within seconds was panting like an asthmatic.

Download complete, H2, still with headphones on, slid her jacket on, lifted the latest batch of egg sandwich left at the door, and slammed it shut.

Hilda, catching a glimpse of H2, tossed the water at the door; it hissed, sizzled, then slammed shut.

The footman, now wheezing, stopped to catch his breath.

H2 looked about her beautiful shed one more time, pressed the *in one minute* button, climbed up onto the dashboard, pushed open the hatch, and pulled herself onto the roof.

It was a jump and a half, she could do it . . .

Archie looked at H2. "When she says on your own, does she mean . . ."

"I mean," said DBO, who sounded like she was running, "all communication with Planet Hy Man are pickled, buggered, you'll not hear from me for a . . . *beep* . . ."

Silence . . .

H2 and Archie, now with no connection, looked at each other.

"Never expected that to happen," said Archie.

"I hope she's alright," said H2.

"Maybe Beryl's H-Pad is still connected," muttered Archie. He looked into the crowd. "We could still catch her."

Hilda grabbed the door handle.

It burnt her hand.
5 seconds to imploding.
"Oh, pickle!"
4 seconds to imploding.
Hilda began to run the other way.
2 seconds . . .
1 . . .

Chapter Fifty

THE EXPLOSION

"A fairy godmother does not always need a wand."–The ugly sister

Eddie was a drag queen who loved to talk; once he opened his mouth he could not stop, and today was no different. He had a story to tell and no one was going to interrupt—not even a dominating Beryl. In fact, that was why Beryl was lumbered with him. The other members of the show were fed up and wanted rid of him.

Eddie in his strong mid Atlantic accent explained about his costumes, his role in the new Cinderella For Men show, which had come all the way from an unknown town in America. Then, ignoring Beryl's blank look, he explained the various meanings of "I'm your fairy godmother."

Beryl after several attempts of "are we near the Lizard Lounge yet?" finally gave up.

She fingered her H-Pad; it was making weird un–fairy godmother noises. She pulled it out of her pocket and turned it in her hand. She could hear panic in her fairy godmother's voice, mumblings of *imploding, folding into a box*, and lots of *pickling* words.

"Who's your drama queen friend?" said Eddie.

Beryl stopped as the H-Pad made a prolonged beep . . . followed by silence.

The lights flickered out. Beryl shook the H-Pad, pressed each button, then in an *I don't know what else to do* panic pressed and shook some more, finally shouting "Not again!"

Eddie took the H-Pad from her, turned it about in his hands, and talked about charging.

Beryl now silent, stared.

"It's dead . . ." she muttered.

"Bit dramatic, aren't we? All's you need is one of those mobile shops and a nice man who will—"

"My fairy godmother." Beryl's face crumbled. "I think she's gone."

"What are you talking about, honey?" said Eddie. "I'm *the* fairy godmother."

"You go, girl!" shouted a voice from behind.

"My plans . . ." muttered Beryl.

"Plans?" said Eddie. "Who has plans at the festival?"

He gestured to H2 and Archie heading towards them. "Looks like your buddies are coming for you."

Beryl, still stunned, looked at them.

"Ma'am," said H2.

Eddie stopped in his tracks. "Ma'am?"

Beryl looked at H2. "She's gone, the fairy godmother."

"What am I, Kentucky fried?" said Eddie.

"She's gone for the moment, but hopefully . . ." said H2.

"The fairy godmother's coming back?" said Beryl with a hopeful look.

Eddie gestured an *I'm here* with his wand.

H2 explained about DBO.

Beryl's face dropped. "I was taking orders from an Operator."

"A dashboard Operator, if you want to nitpick."

"Dashboard? I didn't even know there was one."

"Well there is/was . . . now she's gone."

"So, there wasn't a fairy godmother in the first place?" muttered Beryl.

"What am I, pumpernickel bread?" snapped Eddie.

Beryl stopped, "Wait a minute, how do you know all this? I am the one with the H-Pad."

H2 and Archie, looking uncomfortable, said nothing.

Then Beryl spied the plugulator.

"That's why you didn't argue—you have your own connection."

"Well I did," muttered H2.

DBO landed with a silent thud on the ground and moved to a decent distance. Clutching her super-deluxe headphones, she waited for the imploding/folding. It never happened . . .

Outside the kitchen as far from the shed as possible stood the cook, her assistant, and the Operators. They watched their leader run to the shed, uselessly toss water at the door, scream at the splashback, and then backtrack like a chased rabbit.

"Watch out for the rock," muttered the voice from the back.

"Watch out for the stick . . ."

". . . and the mouse."

The blast filled the garden as Hilda flew into the air. One minute she was flying like Superman into the sky; the next the view was a blanket of fog puffed from the shed like a silent pufferfish. For a moment the deluxe headphones appeared then disappeared into the cloud followed by a curse of pickles . . .

They waited . . .

"Hilda?"

"Sirness?"

"You still . . . there?"

Hilda emerged clutching the H-Pad 11. She staggered towards her subjects in a dazed fashion, her ripped cape now as black as her face.

Her rage took a while to surface.

At first, she was surprised she was in one piece, which was followed by a momentary feeling of relief.

She tripped.

"Mind," said the H-Pad 11.

"Shut up," snapped Hilda as a mechanical mouse ran across her path, tripping her again.

Her blackened cape billowed across her face. She pushed it aside.

"Did you not teach them anything?" she shouted at the cleaners.

"Them?" uttered Cleaner One.

"The Voted In?"

The cleaners blankly stared at Hilda.

"The stopping and pickling starting of a stationary," shouted Hilda.

"We are but cleaners," muttered Cleaner One.

Hilda, now struggling to remove her blackened cape, pulled a fragment from her lips.

"You did put up the notches," said the younger cook with an accusing look.

"You what?" spat Hilda.

"They had made bras, ma'am . . ." said Cleaner Two. "Pointy, upright . . ." She gestured with her hands.

"With underwire," added Cleaner One.

"What's bras got to do with it?" Hilda shouted at the top of her lungs then stopped. The fog had cleared, to show DBO's footman, blackened, wig-less, and unconscious, with his limbs spread out like a starfish.

The first thing Hilda spied was his deluxe headphones by his side . . .

Prudence, Pope, and Pot had never seen a lady in a box before. To them, a box was something you stood on—after filling it.

"It's a bit too much, don't you think, taking the whole flexible thing too far."

"Typical," snapped Pope, "he always was a show-off."

"Makes me feel a bit sick," muttered Prudence.

Vegas, whose impatience had really developed since leaving her home, said, "Who cares about a box, we need to focus on Hilda and the spark plug."

It was then she heard a whining, a clutter, and a panic-stricken DBO shouting, "Folding-up procedure commencing."

"Folding-up," said Vegas, "what is that?"

"It's a procedure," said Prudence, "which leads to . . ."

Bang, crash!

"Oh, pickle and beyond."

"A lot of swearing," muttered Prudence.

Woody pulled out his Nokia and shouted "I found him!" into it.

The lid of the Perspex box flopped open and two slim arms appeared, followed by a young woman's beaming face. The crowd cheered.

"You want a photo," she laughed, then spied Woody's phone. "Perhaps not."

"We are going to the Lizard Lounge," came Pete's voice muffled through the box.

The lady elevated her pelvis onto the side of the box. Pete's head appeared; she pushed him back into the box.

"Wait, let me milk 'em a bit," she whispered.

She posed several times while standing in the box as the crowd continued to cheer, clap, and wolf-whistle.

"The Lizard Lounge," said the lady mid pose. "I wouldn't go there, it's rubbish, great if you're an insomniac."

She jumped out, bowed, then grabbed an empty hat and moved through the crowd collecting money. She looked like a bright pink Barbie doll's mum.

"Insomniac?" said Pete, mid unfolding.

He jumped out of the box with an expectant look; when no one noticed, he slumped.

"Well done, mate," muttered a homeless man in the corner.

Pete nodded a half-hearted thank-you.

DBO, earphones on, stood at the Black Hill gates.

Verruca took one look at DBO heading for her kitchen and with a sense of drama decided to head her off at the pass.

"Stop," she shouted, "head for the Black Hills," and handed her a plan.

DBO pushed the gates open.

"I'm going in," she said to Vegas.

"Does the footman know?" said Vegas.

"Not yet."

"This is a good thing," said Vegas. "Listen to me, I will tell you only once."

"They're fixable," said Hilda, thrusting a dead pair of earphones at Operator One's face.

"With all that smoke it's a long shot," said the voice from the back.

Hilda threw her a glare.

"Technically yes," said Operator One. "But as she said, a long shot."

"Long shot, what are you talking about?"

"The fixing equipment went up with the shed," said the H-Pad 11.

Chapter Fifty-One

THE PUNTER

"Wearing a white coat does not mean you know everything."—H2

Mex followed Bunnie down Princes Street feeling lost and useless, like a geriatric footman waiting for his final-destination limo. Even Pete didn't seem to need her anymore. Her mission was not hers anymore; Bunnie, a woman plump enough to fill a double bed, had seen to that. She had taken over, talking to Mex like she knew nothing . . .

Bunnie was jealous of Mex's porn star–like figure; even the clothes that Beryl gave her didn't hide it. What made it worse was that Mex had no idea that her body could cause a stir.

Mex felt anything but strong and without her man spy outfit almost invisible; in fact, she was starting to feel a panic coming on. The cobbled lane was heaving with people: men dressed as women, women dressed as what, Mex had no idea, some even performing. She wasn't used to crowds or performers; the closest she got to a performance was Pete's salutations in the morning, and even then, it was behind the patio curtain. The last thing Mex wanted to see was arty-farty men singing arty-farty songs; culture brought her out in a sweat.

Mex stumbled behind Bunnie in a way-too-large track suit and trainers which she couldn't walk in. Bunnie, oblivious to Mex's tumblings, skirted down a cobble lane like a posh prostitute advertising her wares. Her heels clicked like a tap dancer, while her flamboyant beads bounced on her large breasts as she occasionally joshed with the so-called punters—all waving leaflets.

"There are more leaflets in this street than I've had punters," said Bunnie.

Mex glanced at Bunnie's pink jacket, wondering what a punter was —which seemed to be everyone but her.

She huffed as they carried on, Bunnie steadfast in the knowing of where to go and Mex losing faith.

"You sure it's this way?" Mex whined.

Bunnie, brushing aside a leaflet, snapped, "Of course."

"So why so fast?" she said, snatching the leaflet Bunnie brushed off. "Do we have to go at the speed of a cat? I mean it's not like we have to be there for ages."

"Honey, this isn't fast, this is parading."

They moved past a passageway dimly lit with fairy lights and full of young animated drunks. Bunnie stopped and with a smug grin pointed to the seedy-looking bar with "Lizard Lounge" written across the top.

The ol' fella knew enough to know that Beryl would end up where he had planned. Dressed as the ol' lady, he headed to the back of the Lizard Lounge and into the changing room—if you could call it that. It was more a wardrobe with a leaking heater and also doubled up as the "unisex" toilet, but he was used to dives like this . . .

He thought back to the days with Beryl, the days when he was known as Beryl's Legless and couldn't read minds. How simple it was back then—*but who wanted simple?*

Legless's life had not been easy; swanning about planet Earth making women happy was not the picnic many thought.

Women always wanted him to stay, linger—Beryl sneered at lingering, she was more an in-and-out sort of woman. It took him time to catch on, that women wanted more—perhaps friendship, often laughter; sometimes affection, sometimes not. In fact, it seemed to him women were as different as the curries in a takeaway and as hard to understand as the said curries were to pronounce.

Legless, however, was nothing if not determined, a man who wanted to succeed. He developed an act for every occasion. To make women laugh if needed, the ability to listen if required and act concerned when called for . . . it worked for a while—for years—but the world had changed since his sowing-his-wild-oats days.

Back then, TV was a piece of furniture, not the large soul-sucking screen of today.

On Planet Hy Man, such screens had been used in the past but were discarded as they caused too much discontentment, the brainwashing effect being outweighed by the inability to control what was on the screen. When the great picture screen was first developed, it like most innovations was tested on robots. Soon robots became aware of what they didn't have and spent their days sprawled on a sofa moaning about back pain and how the other half lived.

The development of a "screen for all" was quashed. Instead, the screen was used for the filtering of information. Played in large spaces to the masses, usually with presenters in white coats looking like scientists who knew what they were talking about.

TV on Earth was something else altogether.

Legless—or as Archie and Co. knew him, "the ol' fella"—hung his rucksack behind the door. All these years, he thought, was she still an in-and-out woman?

He pulled out a flask, took a swig of cider, then, still in his ol' lady disguise, went out to wait.

Chapter Fifty-Two

THE LIZARD LOUNGE

"A mirror is only as good as the light above it."–Beryl

When Mex and Bunnie headed into the Lizard Lounge, Mex had no idea what a lounge was, never mind a lizard. And neither had any idea that Beryl, along with half a dozen drag queens, would soon be there.

The room was dark and smoky with a few empty tables and a couple of pinball machines in the corner repeating annoying chimes.

Bunnie pulled her Johnny Gets Legless leaflet from her bag.

You work hard, you play hard
Now you're looking for something spicy, sensual, spellbindingly different?
Something to tickle your senses—your fancy—your nether regions?
Come down under to the erotic event of the century:
The Johnny Gets Legless show.

Bunnie looked around at the barman whooping over a pinball machine. "This place is about as erotic as a banana split."

Mex, knowing what a banana was but unsure of the split bit, muttered a "pardon?"

"And as spellbinding as watching your bins being emptied," Bunnie, enjoying her wit, continued. "It is as much like a lounge as my porch is, well . . . a porch. It's a dive."

"Dive?" said Mex.

"Yes, a dump, a dead end, a hole."

The barman thumped the pinball machine, swore, and turned to Mex and Bunnie.

"Ladies," he shouted, "what is your pleasure?"

"We are here," said Mex, "to see . . ."

"Johnny Gets Legless," interrupted Bunnie.

He gestured to the door with *enter only with estrogen* scrawled on it. "But you're early, it doesn't open for an hour." He looked at his watch. "Make that two."

Mex looked at Bunnie. "What'll we do until then?"

"The only thing you can do in a place like this—drink," she said and ordered a couple of vodkas.

Legless, in ol' lady mode, shuffled into the bar, pulled up a chair in the corner, and stared at the man spy—looking nothing like a man spy. She looked older, thicker in the middle and tentative, not her usual self. He knew why, he was an expert mind reader. Which is why he stopped reading his writings. Most were bored at the "funny thing happened on the way to . . ." his favorite beginning.

Mex and Bunnie didn't even notice the thin ol' lady sipping cider, until she hovered about the pinball machine, won three games, and was told by the barman to "cut it out or leave."

She looks familiar, thought Mex, downing her first vodka. After the second, she didn't care.

After three double vodkas, Mex was feeling fuzzy, and when her leader came in she didn't even notice. She was too busy watching the TV; "*Three Men and a Baby* was halfway through. It had her transfixed.

"Dippers?" said Mex.

"We call them nappies," muttered Bunnie.

"But isn't it dipper sauces?"

"No, that is dippers . . . I mean dips."

"And doodles." Mex started to laugh. "I mean doodles—isn't that a dog?"

"No that is a poodle, a doodle is a drawing sort of thing," said Bunnie, who was beginning to wonder about another vodka.

Beryl entered. The ol' lady, counting his winnings, didn't notice.

Bunnie looked across the room and nudged Mex. "Is that her who nearly did my Izzie in?"

Mex busy working on her first doodle on a beer mat looked up. "so it is." She waved. "Yoo-hoo, Beryl, over here."

The ol' lady peered at the door, his view blocked by the pinball machine; his heart skipped a beat as he heard her . . .

"What the pickle are you wearing?" snapped Beryl.

The ol' lady saw Beryl's beehive before he saw anything else. It was purpler, and stiffer than it looked on a mobile screen. His heart skipped another beat.

Beryl entered the dark pub to see her best man spy now sporting a lopsided grin and dressed like something out of daytime TV. She rubbed her eyes, then caught sight of the infamous Bunnie—the weird face on the H-Pad.

She drew herself up to full height and motioned H2 to follow.

H2 humphed; she was fed up. They had spent the last hour trudging the streets with a group of men singing "We Are Family" while looking for the Lizard Lounge, which no one seemed to have heard of. Finally, after losing most of the cast apart from the fairy godmother and an ugly sister, they found the only pub in Edinburgh no one would venture near, only to have ol' bossy-boots Beryl claiming she knew where it was all the time.

"We're not on your planet now," muttered H2. "I can choose my own seat."

Beryl ignored her and marched to the toilets.

The ol' lady watched, admiring the swing of Beryl's hips until he told himself to stop.

He followed her instead . . .

❋

Beryl stood in front of the mirror in the toilets and looked her face. Puffy from sugar and powdery from Earth makeup, she hardly recognized herself. She tried a smile; it didn't make any difference. She stood back, held in her breath, and looked at the side; it didn't make any difference. She adjusted her beehive, pulled some spray from her pocket, and stopped mid pout as the ol' lady entered.

Beryl caught the ol' lady's eye in the mirror and for a brief moment their eyes locked.

"It's free"—Beryl gestured to the only toilet—"but make sure you've got a tissue . . ." She eyed her. "Or two."

"Thank you," said the ol' lady, tugging a few paper towels from the holder.

Beryl after a flourish of spray offered some to the ol' lady. "Don't mind if I do," he croaked, slid the spray can into his bag, headed into the toilet, and locked it.

Beryl knocked on the door. "Excuse me, that's mine."

"Kind of you, dear."

"No, I mean that spray, I want it back."

Silence . . .

Beryl knocked. "It's not good near heat."

Beryl heard a muffled "Thank you, dear," followed by a rustle of paper, nose blowing, and a robust trumpet of wind. With a confused look, she headed into the bar.

H2 was sitting on a bench seat away from everyone, staring at her plugulator and wondering what had happened to her pal.

"Budge up," said Eddie the fairy godmother to H2 as he pushed his way in.

"Cheer up," said the ugly sister, plonking herself on the other side of H2. "It may never happen."

"It already has," muttered H2. "My best pal."

"Plenty more fish, honey," said the ugly sister.

"Not for me," said H2.

Eddie spied Beryl. "Get us a couple," he shouted, then gestured to H2. "And this one here a cocktail."

Beryl pretended not to hear.

"Mine's a vodka," shouted the ugly sister.

Beryl threw her a *me?* look.

"Me too," shouted Eddie the fairy godmother.

"Don't you have a play to perform?" said Beryl, posed in her best *I am leader* stance.

"Not till tomorrow," said the fairy godmother. He gestured to H2. "And make her a cocktail while you're at it."

Legless leaned against the toilet door and caught his breath. Up close she looked so much smoother. He gulped; not a wrinkle—not a droop. He tried to slow his breath down, this was not going to plan, he was supposed to be in control, he was supposed to be relishing this . . . showdown.

Instead, feelings from the past came up like an out-of-date vindaloo. He felt sick!

He began to rummage with his disguise, fumble with the buttons.

He tore his bra off, socks cluttered to the ground—in a puddle of what, he hated to think.

He tugged at his grey hair, pins clattered to the ground.

Someone knocked on the door.

"You all right in there?" said the owner after a complaint from Beryl.

"Yes," he grunted, "almost ready."

"Yes, well, don't be scaring punters off. At least not until they've a few more rounds in."

"Aye, right you are."

The barman left as Legless scraped his hair into a ponytail, flashed Beryl's spray across it, coughed, and pulled his storytelling outfit from his rucksack.

Not an easy undertaking in the tiny boxlike toilet. A kilt, long socks, and a large sporran fell to the floor.

"Bugger," he grunted as he picked them up, slid his kilt on, and secured it around his slim waist.

Beryl had no clue who he was or what was going to happen—for that matter, neither did he. He had a rough idea, a plan, but now as he saw his "ex" *as they liked to call them on Earth*, his feelings had mulled. Legless thought about the potting shed, and the formula for the spark plug. How was he going to tell Beryl?

Timing, he told himself, *it was all about timing and laughter—would a bit of laughter work on her?*

He listened . . . slid his head from the door, slid out, and sighed with relief. He caught a glance of himself in the mirror. *Shit.* The light was not kind, his face was like a road map of wrinkles, would she recognize him?

His heart raced, thumped against his chest. *Is this wise?* He was about to open the door, walk into the pub, when he heard it: Bunnie's *just joshing* cackle.

Shit, forgot about her—bugger.

Chapter Fifty-Three

VODKA

"A crossdresser's bra should never be seen, especially by a lover of lingerie, and the undoing of such things."–Don

Archie waited outside the Lizard Lounge for Don. He had a feeling in his bunion—Don was allowing him to read his thoughts and Archie wanted to know why.

Don followed the ol' lady through the streets of Edinburgh—not an easy thing to do as she had a talent for slipping through the crowds and was by no means slow. He almost lost her a few times, but then just as he gave up hope, there she was annoying some passer-by with irritating questions.

They arrived at the Lizard Lounge and he watched her disappear into the back. Don didn't see Archie, but he felt his presence, heard a whisper.

Don wanted to follow, jump right in, grab the ol' lady, find out who she really was, and, of course, get his money for the car damage, but his intuition told him otherwise. He stood by the back door and listened. Finally he saw Beryl enter, the ol' lady head in, Beryl leave, and finally the ol' lady—now an ol' fella dressed in a kilt—heading to the Performers Only door.

I knew it, thought Don, *knew there was something dodgy about that ol' lady*.

For a moment he basked in the glory of being roughly right, then he entered the toilet for a snoop. It was not a pretty sight. A broken door, a constantly flushing toilet, and an unbearable smell. Behind the door hung the familiar ol' lady's bag. He opened it. It too was not a pretty sight.

Don paused at the padded implement, a smelly sock stuffed in a bra. This was a man who rushed things, who did not enjoy dressing as a woman. He tossed it aside. This is Johnny? Our link to Legless? How could such a man know anything about the so-called Legless?

Never judge a man by his sock, Don heard a thought from Archie.

And why not? thought Don. *A man who cares little for his socks—what does he care of other things?*

Typical, came a thought from Archie.

Don, with not much hope, rummaged. He had no idea what he was looking for.

Something to do with Legless and a spark plug, came another thought from Archie.

Don, now seriously irritated by Archie and his annoying interruptions, pulled open the rucksack and began to feel Archie's voice—like he was next door.

Easy, remember, you have to put it back like it's not been touched.

Aye, like I hadn't worked that one out, thought Don.

He felt a tap on his shoulder and turned to face Archie, a man he hadn't wanted to see in years.

Bollocks.

Right back at yer . . . thought Archie.

DJ and Woody consoled Pete as he unfolded to a mere trickle of an applause, and a couple of coins. He stared at the lady, who was in the box basking in the glory of a generous applause and a hat full of money. "What's she got?" he muttered.

DJ and Woody steered him through the crowd with an *isn't it obvious?* look.

"Don't worry. Even the chainsaw juggler would compete with a flexible woman looking like her."

Pete stared at his couple of coins in his Teflon palm. "Not even enough for a Kit Kat."

Archie looked around the toilet. His face could not hide his disappointment; was this mess to do with his hero?

Don for a moment felt a small spark of empathy for Archie, then saw a book in the pocket of the rucksack: Legless's *Odyssey*. Archie pulled it out. *Well looky here!*

Legless entered the room behind the *enter only with estrogen* area and, through a one-way window in the door, watched his *used to be* Beryl. Her face was pinched with disapproval.

He knew everything about Beryl. He had followed, plotted, and planned from the moment Planet Hy Man stopped using mirrors to spy. His Nokia had transformed his retirement, giving him unlimited access to the Operators in the shed without anyone knowing. How long should he wait? He watched her as she sipped her vodka with a screwed-up face. She wasn't faring well.

Beryl was struggling to hold her own with a fairy godmother and an ugly sister who, realizing it was happy hour, decided to make the most of the half-price cocktails (cocktails being vodka along with anything fizzy, a straw, one cube of ice, and, if you were lucky, a cocktail umbrella thrown in).

They took over the table, the bar, and the TV with their American accents, larger-than-life bodies, and demands.

Flicking the TV on to an eighties best-hits channel, the two drag queens gyrated to Wham's "I'm Your Man." Even Bunnie and her *I will not be ignored* shelf-like chest seemed to fade into the background.

Bunnie had decided if you can't beat 'em, join 'em. Dancing to Wham! was not her favourite pastime, but if it annoyed Beryl, it was worth it. Her bright beads bounced across her chest . . .

"Those beads dance like beans on a hot plate," laughed the ugly sister.

Mex nearly fell off her chair laughing; in fact she probably would have if she wasn't leaning against the wall.

Mex, behaving nothing like a man spy, was well oiled; she laughed at everything while trying to draw, or, as she slurred, *doodle*. Each time she chuckled she looked surprised, like she had never experienced such emotions before . . .

Eddie, the fairy godmother, slid a vodka and Iron-Bru to H2. H2 turned the glass in her hand, then sniffed it. She smelt sugar, sickly orange and . . . something foreign. H2 placed the straw on her tongue and took a tentative sip. It tingled her tongue and slid down her throat like warm treacle—nothing like she had tasted before.

"And by the way," Eddie the fairy godmother shouted to Mex, "a doodle in my country is a number two."

"Isn't that a doo-doo?" said the ugly sister.

Which confused Mex even more.

Don tossed the book at Archie. "There is bugger-all in this."

Archie flicked through the pages; the book talked about the perfect bike seat, Lycra that breathed, and the best caffeine for cycling.

Archie scratched his head. "I don't understand."

"Well let's go and ask shall we, and while we're at it, I'll get the payment for the damage to my car."

As they entered the pub, the ol' fella nodded to the barman who, with a sigh, nodded back.

Beryl had her "I've had enough" look on her face. It was now or never, he thought.

Chapter Fifty-Four

GEORGE MICHAEL

"I'm not planning on going solo."–George Michael

Pete, swallowing the last of a Kit Kat with an unimpressed look, followed Woody and DJ into the so-called dive.

They arrived to hear Wham! on full volume and the girls a few vodkas down. Pete's heart skipped a beat as he heard the music. It was the same song he performed to in Dunoon—*a lifetime ago.*

Pete was already tapping his foot before he entered. Soon he was joining in with the ladies doing a pretty good George Michael impression (for someone who'd never heard of him). Pete's supple hips had the girls oohing and aahing, and it felt so great he just had to do his famous down-into-the-splits and up again . . .

Eddie took in the gold supple form and, under the influence of several vodkas, assumed he could jitterbug. He grabbed Pete and pulled him close, crushing Pete's chest against his padded bra. Pete looked into the dark eyes hooded with extra-large falsies and let out a small squeak. Then, without a chance for a second squeak let alone an escape, Pete was twirling around the sticky floor with a muscular arm controlling his every move.

Lynx aftershave wafted behind the couple as they took the dark pub by storm. Woody and DJ started to clap. Mex, open-mouthed, tried to take in a Pete she had never seen before. H2, fuzzy from vodka, looked up and for a moment forgot her DBO, while the ugly sister cheered, and Bunnie chuckled; even the jaded barman, posed at the play button, stopped and smiled.

Eddie began to jive. Pete tried to keep up, and after several stiletto stamps on his toes he quickly moved into an avoid-the-stiletto shuffle. Eddie, now spurred on by the ugly sister's "you go girl," lifted Pete onto one side of his hip and then the other . . . Pete's feet flopped against one side of Eddie's body, crashing into a mountain of nylon—a little too close to the bar.

Glasses crashed to the floor.

The barman stopped clapping.

Legless, waiting for his queue in the performance room, jumped.

Ignoring the crash of glass, Eddie swirled Pete around his waist as Pete's digested Kit Kat made its presence felt.

Pete was starting to feel sick . . .

Legless was getting restless; nerves were getting the better of him. He had splashed out on a smoke machine and had a whole story about the spark plug planned, a sort of witty repertoire which he hoped would put Beryl in her place after lulling her into a false sense of meditative peace. He had no idea if it would work, or if it was possible to lull Beryl into anything, let alone shame her, and the waiting was killing him. The crash of glass startled him. He looked into the bar; the barman was miles from the play button picking up glass . . .

Bugger.

He had to do something. He dived into the bar and the smoke followed. Bunnie, who was not a big George Michael fan, moved to the bar for a drink; she looked up to see a sea of smoke flow from the *enter only with estrogen door.*

What next?

Eddie swung Pete onto his feet. Pete tried to catch his breath and caught sight of his master, with a lopsided grin, frisbee-ing a beer mat.

He ducked.

The chorus started, Eddie pulled Pete close to his chest and went for another spin around the room. Pete's stomach swirled, his head whooshed. He sailed past Woody imprisoned against the chest of Eddie with a beseeching *help me* look. But in the smoky darkness

Woody misread the look for a *look how much fun I am having* and cheered him on.

Legless appeared from the smoke, a thin kilted old man.

"Johnny?" said Bunnie.

The song was coming to an end. Eddie manoeuvred Pete into his favourite move: the slide through the legs and back.

Eddie pushed Pete though his legs; Pete's back skidded across the sticky floor swooshing through a sea of nylon, a flash of muscular legs, and a peek of fluffy underpants.

It was so fast and yet so unforgettable . . .

Pete shook his head, and before he had a chance for breath, he was heading back again . . .

Swoosh . . . tear . . . stop.

His Teflon back caught on something. And before he had a chance to close his eyes or have Eddie pull him up, Pete saw not only the fluffy underpants but what was underneath.

Silence . . .

Legless flicked the TV off and with an *I'll do it myself* look pressed the play button as Eddie helped a stunned Pete to his feet.

Bunnie watched. "Johnny?"

The barman, with a dismissive sniff, dumped the glass into a bin. Beryl looked up and caught Legless looking at her—she caught his eye —he looked away—she stopped. *It can't be . . .*

Legless's soundtrack began to play soft meditative music from behind the *enter only with estrogen door.*

The women looked about, confused, as the barman pulled the bin bag from the bin, thumped it on the floor with a crash, and closed it with a knot at the top.

A smooth elevator voice interrupted the hum of music.

Are you sick of the festival?

Pete with a shaky hand took a sip of H2's drink.

Have you had enough of the hustle and bustle of the city, of leaflets, comedians, political jokes; performers grabbing you for your attention—the drag queens . . .

"Here, just a cotton-picking minute . . ." erupted the ugly sister.

"Legless," shouted Beryl, "I don't believe it . . ."

"I don't believe it either," muttered Pete. "All that under a petticoat."

Archie and Don, hearing the noise, made their way to where the ol' fella had gone. They snuck in and watched as the ol' fella spied through the one-way window and prepared himself for his performance. They watched as his impatience grew, listened to George Michael, and then heard Beryl.

"Legless," whispered Archie to Don. "He's Legless?"

"What did you expect?" said Don.

"Something more . . . heroic, rebellious, maybe not so old."

"Can't help getting old," said Don.

"But he doesn't look strong enough to lift a pillow, let alone mount a woman."

"And yet," said Don. "It all makes sense."

Chapter Fifty-Five

LEGLESS

"All my stories did was make people yawn. I blame it on technology: mobiles apps, games—how could a man in a kilt compete?" —The Spark Plug Odyssey

Legless never got to see if Beryl could be lulled or shamed, George Michael saw to that. Instead, what he saw was the Beryl of old: aggressive, defiant, and in total denial. But then there were more people putting their words' worth in than he or even the barman thought possible. And it didn't take long for the barman to close the bar.

Don suggested he join him and Archie in their tent. Legless jumped at the chance; spending the night with Beryl was as palatable to him as one of the barman's cocktails. He had spent enough time with her disappointment.

Don, a man's man as he liked to call himself, ushered Legless into his "sanctuary" and with a curt "not now Bunnie" zipped the tent closed.

For a moment Bunnie stared at the closed tent, then rattled it. "I have a right to stay in my own tent, you know."

She was told to go away.

Bunnie wondered what she had done wrong, why her so-called pal Don was giving her the cold shoulder. She slumped into Mex's tent to find a grumpy Beryl and a comatose Mex taking up most of the floor space.

"I don't know what's wrong with Don," she muttered, "and as for Johnny, you'd think I punched him in the face."

"It's Legless, not Johnny, and it's me he wants to punch in the face."

"You? What's my Johnny to do with you?"

"It's Legless," shouted Don from the next tent. "There is no Johnny."

H2 poked her nose into Mex's tent to see a tight-lipped Beryl and retreated. She'd rather sleep in a bus shelter than with her; spying a light at the reception, she headed there.

Pete was in the reception with Woody, who was looking for a plaster for Pete's back. Pete, still traumatized by the giant hairy apparition dangling an inch from his nose, muttered about size and sausages.

Finding a plaster, Woody placed it on Pete's back, setting off a Teflon-in reaction. Woody, without a word to Pete, quickly pulled it off again.

"Never in my wildest dreams," said DJ, "did I ever think Legless would be so . . ."

"Small?" said H2.

"What's wrong with small?" muttered Pete.

Woody patted his back. "You'll soon forget, mate."

"Disappointing," said DJ. "I mean, alimony from a rebel?"

H2, still a bit woozy, poured tea. "Beryl's to blame," she muttered, "should be ashamed of herself—all that double-crossing. Poor guy, I feel sorry for him."

"All those women," muttered Woody.

"One of them was my mum," said DJ.

Beryl had pushed Legless's nerves to the brink with only a few words about his ageing. In front of a full bar and a barman who treated Legless like he was a cold sore rather than a customer, Beryl had belittled him.

"You used to look so good in Lycra," she said. "Now look at you."

"Lycra, him? As if," said the barman.

"You sent me here," snapped Legless, "what did you expect? It's not easy keeping a million and one women happy . . . it would age even Superman . . ."

"No one said anything about procreation."

". . . understanding their nuances; knowing when to play rough, when not. Reading a woman's mind is like trying to walk blindfolded through treacle—sweet, slow, and sticky. Even now I have no idea what women want despite reading their minds."

"You read minds?" blushed the barman. "Shit, sorry mate!"

"I thought a visit now and then, keep the fires burning, was enough. After all, that was all you wanted," said Legless.

Beryl moved to speak.

"How wrong was I?" continued Legless. "Nothing prepares you for Earth, nothing. I mean celibacy down here is as out of date as your getup."

"My getup?" said a flustered Beryl. "Eddie says it's the height of sex."

She looked about for Eddie to back her up, but he had gone, along with the ugly sister. Once Pete had seen his tackle, Eddie, a sensitive man, knew it was time to leave. Besides, the happy hour and George Michael were well and truly over.

"A man in nylons, what would he know about sex?" tutted Legless.

Beryl glared at the long features of the man she had thought about for years. She wanted to say so much, and yet every time she opened her mouth she made it worse.

"How was I to know I was so . . . so . . . fertile?" continued Legless.

"You, fertile?" said the barman. "As if."

"And you have no idea what motherhood could do to a woman."

"That's why we have the eggplant thingies . . ." muttered Beryl.

"Eggplant?" said the barman. "What's that got to do with motherhood?"

"I played just about every pinball machine in the country for those offsprings, not to mention the scratch cards, the lottery, and the horse racing. The birthday cards alone cost a bomb."

"Thanks, Dad," said DJ.

Legless didn't say much more.

❄

That night, for the first time in her life, Beryl slept in a tent alongside other women. She stared out into the sky from the clear plastic window in the roof and wriggled with discomfort.

The stars looked different from Earth, the ground felt different, hard, lumpy, and cold. And as for the sleeping bag? She wriggled; anything but sleep was possible in the pickling thing, getting into it was bad enough.

Bunnie laughed her head off; she laughed so much she cried. "You just pull," giggled Bunnie.

Beryl told her there were no zips on Planet Hy Man . . . just sticky pads.

"You mean Velcro," chuckled Bunnie.

Beryl wriggled some more, huffed, then pushed Mex onto her side. They had no way home, and whose pickling fault was that? H2 was right . . . it was all because of her.

Mex let out another snore.

Beryl rolled onto her side until her shoulder hurt, then rolled onto her back.

No way home . . . this is what Legless must have felt like . . .

"Just doodling," mumbled Mex in her sleep.

And he was alone . . .

Several times that night Beryl thought about jumping out of her sleeping bag, explaining to Legless why she did what she did, a leader's choice, the best for the planet; but in the end, she didn't. She couldn't work out how to get out of the sleeping bag and Bunnie was fast asleep. Legless's monotonous speech saw to that, putting Bunnie in a trance of boredom, muttered something about slitting wrists—then she was out, almost purring like a cozy cat.

Legless, sitting in Don's tent cross-legged like a yogi in a kilt, talked for hours. With a blanket around him and his long grey hair loose about his lined face, he talked of the mice and hens—Dunoon and his safe place—dead of emotion. He hadn't had much company for years.

And Beryl in the tent next door listened . . .

"I hid it, *The Spark Plug Odyssey*," said Legless, "at the back of the cottage."

"Your shed," said Archie.

"I know you'd think it would be safe there," he said. "Didn't count on mice. Hens always bring mice with 'em, no matter how many bleeding cats you have. Apparently, paper from Planet Hy Man is to die for when it comes to rodents." Legless sighed. "Thought it was safe. In fact, I forgot it was there until she"—he gestured to Bunnie's tent—"upset things; that's when I realized it was a pile of shreds."

"A shed?" said Archie. "Who hides things in a shed?"

"Tried to write down from memory but it was so long ago. I got as far as . . .

> *Oh, to a spark plug . . .*
> *Spark plug, ye of little faith . . .*

Beryl looked up into the stars again. *Is that what I'll end up like, all lined and forgetful, living with hens?* And within seconds she was snoring.

EPILOGUE

Woody looked at Pete's back and applied cream. When the Teflon began to bubble, he panicked and tried a wet wipe.

Pete winced.

"You get used to it," muttered Woody.

Pete sneezed; he wasn't sure if he wanted to get used to it.

"Let me," said H2. She rummaged in her bag and pulled out Verruca's all-purpose lubricant. Pete's back bounced back into shape.

Woody's Nokia beeped. He pulled it out. "DBO? Who is DBO?"

H2 couldn't get to the phone quick enough. "DBO, you sure?" she said with a snatch.

H2 read DBO's message. "'I have made contact with the other 33 robots.'"

Pete pulled a face. "Those show-offs?"

"'Working on connections. Soon we can talk,'" read H2. She looked up. "They said the lady in the box is worth keeping an eye on."

"What would they know?" said Pete.

"They said anyone that flexible has to be more than human," said H2.

"Don't think so," said Pete. "My nostrils were this close to her toes, I'd know if there was something fishy."

"They made contact with my Nokia," said Woody.

Pete tutted. "Nokia, piece of piss."

The cleaners took care of Hilda. They took her back to the kitchen and wrapped up her burns in hemp mesh. Hilda, stretching out her one good hand and with great drama, said

"Here, take this pickle-forsaken H-Pad 11—do what you have to."

Operator One dusted clean the H-Pad 11 and switched it off.

"It will take more than that to turn me off," said the H-Pad 11.

The Operator disengaged the front from the back.

"Here, here, no need to do . . . to do . . . to do . . . shutting down . . . shutting down . . . all is black . . ."

Sipping tea, Verruca watched her robot enter the kitchen.

"Vibrator, ma'am, or as some would have it—a drill. Ha ha ha."

Verruca looked at the implement made from the designs. *The craftsrobotship was spectacular—what woman could resist?*

"Genius," muttered Verruca. "Now you must deliver it—wrapped of course."

"Rapture, vibrator, ha ha, very funny."

"No, wrap it in paper," said Verruca.

"Paper, writing, need pen."

"No, I'll write the card, you wrap," said Verruca.

"Rapture, pleasure, need lubricant."

Verruca wrote the card, wrapped the vibrator up, and delivered it herself. When the robot tried to follow, she told him to clean the fridge.

"I have a diversion for Hilda," messaged Verruca to DBO, "should buy you some time."

Eunice pulled out a small box from the linen cupboard.

Patsy, busy in the kitchen making soup, shouted, "What you up to?"

"Nothing."

"Are you looking at that box again?"

"No."

"Told you to throw it away."

Eunice looked up to see the love of her life staring at her with not much love and a lot of impatience.

"It's just that I have never seen anything like it before," said Eunice.

She picked the wiry thing up with her hot hands. Sweat dribbled onto the wire; it buzzed, then lit up like a fairy light.

"Look what you've done," snapped Patsy.

Eunice gulped. "I didn't do anything."

The deluxe earphones sitting by the H-Pad 11 in the room with a view lit up. But no one noticed, except for the cleaning robot. She picked it up, polished it, and put it back on the table.

The Operators would be back in the morning.

****

Would you like to read more? Does Bunny and Don get it on? Does Legless forgive Beryl. And does Eunice work out what that wiry thing is?

Book 3 **Rebel Without a Crew** is out now at your favourite store....
Turn the page for a taster

REBEL WITHOUT A CREW

Chapter One-DBO

"A good footman always knows who to spread a secret to."
—Beryl

DBO stood at the same "no need to shut" gate Vegas had stood at.

She inhaled the damp air. She knew the moment the shed exploded that there was no turning back. And did she care?

Not one jot.

She felt excited, liberated, a new woman. All her life she had been waiting for something *big* to happen, something better than, well, anything so far, and here she was—out into the unknown, advising Vegas, the biggest Voted In since Hilda herself.

She stopped for a moment to take it all in . . .

This was her chance to make her mark, change things, and the thought thrilled her.

"I am going in," she said to Verruca. "When there is saving to be done, you can't hang around."

"And Vegas," said Verruca. "She knows you're coming?"

"Vegas is in panic mode—I think Hilda may have made contact," said DBO.

Verruca chuckled. "Don't you worry about Hilda, I have her in hand."

Vegas waited for the so-called fairy godmother on the veranda. Squinting into the distance, she wondered how she was making it through the fields. She hadn't heard a pickling word for ages.

What was taking her so long?

Unlike Vegas, DBO's curiosity gave her no time for fear. She was making her way through the fields like a scientist, taking notes. To her, the fields were a thing of fascination. She had, like many, heard little of what was outside the city and, like a few, often wondered what it was like. She had asked many times, but no one seemed to know apart from Verruca, whose only comment was "All in good time."

She moved across the stony footpath like an expert walker, her tough shoes impervious to the dry stones and odd mud patch. Her clothes, hard and scratchy, were similar to the workers' and gave her protection against the rain and wind. In fact, the fieldworkers assumed she was one of them, lost from another field. She had the walk of a worker, she took notes like a worker, and she didn't wave, even when the odd head appeared from the high hemp crops. Workers never waved; they had been brought up to be invisible.

DBO carried on, her imagination in full flow as her face was pelted by the rain, followed by a biting wind, then a scorching sun. It was a continual cycle of hot and cold that had her pondering how anyone could work in such conditions—conditions that made the shed seem like a palace.

"Which field are you heading?" shouted one of the workers.

DBO looked up. She saw three weather-beaten faces peering from the high hemp grass.

"Or are you lost?" said another.

DBO stopped. "You talking to me?"

"Don't see anyone else on the road," said a worker.

DBO stopped and smiled. "Well, that is true."

Vegas looked at the sun making its way down toward the horizon. *How long did it take to walk through the fields?*

"She'll be there a while," muttered Prudence. "Those workers are a curious lot; seeing nothing but hemp can do that to a woman."

"Women? Those workers are women?" said Vegas.

"Of course, what did you think they were?"

"Well, workers . . . never really thought about them being all feeling, all moaning women . . . like, well, *me*." Vegas eyed Prudence. "You sure? I mean aren't they another more, you know, robotic sort of thing?"

"No, just women," muttered Prudence.

Vegas squinted into the horizon. "I couldn't even last an hour in that field. How do they stand it?"

"They don't," said Prudence. "They usually squat."

DBO stood at the edge of the field as three workers made their way onto the road. They eyed each other as the wind died down.

Up close, DBO looked nothing like a fieldworker. Her skin was white and smooth, a sight new to the fieldworkers. Worker One reached out to touch her pale cheek; the rough skin of her forefinger scratched against DBO's cheek, but DBO didn't flinch. Instead, she touched the face of the worker and felt the leathery face.

DBO had seen brown wrinkled skin on women at the market stalls, but these women were blacker, muscular, and much taller. Worker One's gnarled finger moved to DBO's hair as Worker Two blurted out questions.

Soon, DBO was explaining like an animated storyteller the life of a shed Operator as the sun came out (yet again) and began to burn her skin.

"You work inside?" said Worker One.

"Yes." DBO squinted at her.

"In a shed?"

"She said that already," said Worker Two. "The shed is for communicating?"

"We put tools in ours," said Worker One.

"We did have tools, but not anymore," said DBO.

"Yeah, that'll be right," said Worker Two. "A worker with no tools." She pulled a face. "A worker ain't a worker without tools." She turned to Worker Three. "Ain't that right?"

Worker Three didn't answer. She, pondering such curious ways of using a shed, was scribbling notes.

"Too right," said Worker One.

DBO talked of her footman (leaving out the massages) and how she recycled old equipment to intercept the enemy (bragging just a little) and finally ended with, as she called it, "the phantasmagorical explosion of the shed" with an illustrative *capow!*

The fieldworkers looked unimpressed.

"Our tools are incombustible."

"Really?" said DBO, breaking out in a sweat.

"Need to be, you should try working with hemp effluent under this sun."

DBO, who had never heard of hemp effluent, was about to ask what it was when Worker One began a barrage of questions on why she was here and where she was going.

DBO, trying to keep Verruca's plan *hush-hush*, talked of Earth, Beryl's landing, and a dwarf named Woody, who "once seen could never be forgotten."

The fieldworkers' eyes widened. Even Worker Three stopped writing, pencil hovering. "A dwarf?" she said. "That's the stuff of legends."

"And Beryl is our leader?" said Worker One. She turned to Worker Two. "We have a leader, is that the stuff of legends?"

"You have more than one," said DBO.

"More than one? That's taking it too far," said Worker One.

"Ridiculous," muttered Worker Three.

"Hilda," said DBO.

"Beryl *and* Hilda," scribbled Worker Three.

DBO began to describe the Voted In and the much-talked-about *room with a view*.

The three fieldworkers looked from one to the other and started to laugh.

"And this woman with those stupid gloves for shoes, she is one of those?" said Worker Three.

"Well, yes?" said DBO. "Apparently the room with a view is so high that we women below look like ants."

Worker Three began to scribble. ". . . look like ants . . ."

"Well, they know nothing about walking, I can tell you. Her shoes were as ridiculous as two leaders."

The three workers chuckled.

"Those shoes were as good at being shoes as I am a man," said Worker One.

Worker Two let forth a roar of laughter, startling Worker Three from her writing.

DBO didn't see the joke.

"You don't like puns?" said Worker Two.

"Puns?" muttered DBO.

Worker Two let out a louder roar which echoed across the field. A sea of heads popped up. DBO started to count and stopped at twenty.

***

Book 3 ***Rebel Without a Crew*** is out now at your favourite store.

I hope you enjoyed the adventures of Mex and her friends inspired by my time performing at the Edinburgh Fringe.
Over several years I performed my brand of comedy just because I didn't want to "die wondering".
The buzz at the Edinburgh fringe is something I will never forget, despite often performing to audiences of five *or less,* once just a kid I was babysitting.

You can find me and my groovy blogs at
www.kerrienoor.com
Like me at

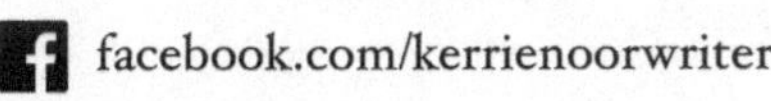

facebook.com/kerrienoorwriter
x.com/kezzamac
instagram.com/kerrienoor

This is a work of fiction.
Similarities to real people, places, or events are entirely coincidental.

Rebel without a BRA

First edition. February 02 2019.
Copyright © 2019 Kerrie Noor.
Written by Kerrie Noor.

❀ Formatted with Vellum